The Mirror and the Mask

The Mirror
and
the Mask

ELLEN HART

MINOTAUR BOOKS ❧ NEW YORK

This is a work of fiction. All of the characters, organizations, and events portrayed in this novel are either products of the author's imagination or are used fictitiously.

www.minotaurbooks.com

Library of Congress Cataloging-in-Publication Data

Hart, Ellen.
　　The mirror and the mask / Ellen Hart. — 1st ed.
　　　　p.　cm.
　　ISBN 978-0-312-37527-0
　1. Lawless, Jane (Fictitious character)—Fiction.　2. Women detectives—Minnesota—Minneapolis—Fiction.　3. Missing persons—Fiction.
4. Minneapolis (Minn.)—Fiction.　5. Lesbians—Fiction.　6. Psychological fiction.　I. Title.
　　PS3558.A6775M57　2009
　　813'.54—dc22

2009028479

First Edition: November 2009

10　9　8　7　6　5　4　3　2　1

For Diane Ferreira,
with much love

Cast of Characters

Jane Lawless:	Owner of the Lyme House Restaurant and the Xanadu Club in Minneapolis.
Cordelia Thorn:	Creative director of the Allen Grimby Repertory Theater in St. Paul. Hattie's aunt.
Annie Archer:	Bartender at a resort in Steamboat Springs, Colorado. Mandy Archer's daughter.
Jack Bowman:	Owner of DreamScape Builders in the Twin Cities. Susan's husband.
Susan Bowman:	Branch VP of Northland Realty. Curt and Sunny's mother. Jack's wife.
Kristjan Robbe:	Real estate agent. Barbara's husband.
Barbara Robbe:	LPN. Kristjan's wife.
Curt Llewelyn:	Medical student at the U of M. Sunny's brother. Susan's son.
Sunny Llewelyn:	Senior in high school. Curt's sister. Susan's daughter.
Octavia Thorn Lester:	Stage and screen actress. Hattie's mother. Radley Cunningham's wife.
Hattie Thorn Lester:	Octavia's five-year-old daughter. Cordelia's niece.

Maggie: "Truth, truth! Everybody keeps hollerin' about the truth. Well, the truth is as dirty as lies."

—**Cat on a Hot Tin Roof,**
Tennessee Williams

We are what we pretend to be.

—**Mother Night,**
Kurt Vonnegut

The Mirror and the Mask

Traverse City, Michigan

Summer 1990

For the third time in less than ten minutes, Annie's mom rushed into the bathroom to redo her makeup. It was definitely weird behavior. Her mom had a routine that never varied. She was the assistant manager of one of the big resorts near Traverse City and always looked perfect when she left for work late in the afternoons. Today was her day off, so Annie figured something was up. On days like this, her mom usually dressed pretty grungy. Sweats. Tank tops. Old T-shirts. But this afternoon, she was so incredibly wired, rocketing back and forth between the bathroom and the bedroom, that Annie wasn't even sure her mom knew she'd come back from the mall.

Annie Andrews was thirteen. She and her mom lived in an apartment complex not too far from the Miller Creek Nature Preserve, which was a way cool place with lots of great walking paths. This was the best place they'd ever lived. There was a workout room, a playground, and even a putting green. Annie had taken up putting after her mom bought her a used putter for her birthday. If she did say so herself, she was getting pretty good at it.

But best of all, the apartment was close to the Grand Traverse Mall, where Annie met her friends almost every day during the summer. Her mom had always worked resorts, starting with her first job as a housekeeper at the Boardwalk Plaza in Rehoboth Beach, the town where Annie was born. Over time, she'd moved up the ladder all the way to management. After Annie's dad died of cancer—when she was five—they'd lived in a whole bunch of places. One time, Annie attended three different schools in a single year. But that was a while ago. Annie's mom promised that they wouldn't have to move again for a long time, which was good because Annie adored her current school. She was working on her first boyfriend and couldn't bear the thought of ever leaving.

Making strangling noises, Annie's mom wiggled into a tight pair of white jeans, examined herself in the full-length mirror in her bedroom, pressed a hand to her stomach, and let her shoulders droop. "Ugh."

"What's up?" asked Annie from the doorway.

Her mom jumped. "Honey, you scared me. I didn't know you were back."

"Figured."

Pulling on a pink lace camisole, she stood with one hand on her hip, nervously turning one side, then the other, to the mirror. "I got a call while you were gone."

"Yeah?"

"There's someone—a man—coming over in a few minutes. He's . . ." She hesitated, easing down on her bed.

"He's what?"

"Well, actually, he's somebody I met a long time ago. We've been writing each other for years."

"You have? How come you never said anything about it?"

"This is kind of hard to explain, honey. He's . . . been . . . in prison."

Annie arched her eyebrows.

"Nothing violent. He just made some bad decisions and ended up in jail."

Annie didn't respond, mainly because she had no idea what to say.

"I . . . care about him a lot," continued her mother, gnawing at a fingernail. "His name is John. Johnny Archer."

"Uh-huh." It was a dumb response, but it was all Annie could manage.

"See, I knew he was getting out of prison this month, but he never told me the exact date. And now he's here. In town. He wants to see me. And you, too."

"You said you care about him. Does that mean you, like, love him?"

Her mom gazed down at her hands. She'd taken off her wedding band years ago and replaced it with a red garnet set in silver. Annie thought her mom had bought it, but now she wondered if this Archer guy had given it to her. "Yes, honey, I do."

"Does that mean you want to marry him?"

"Honestly, I haven't thought that far ahead."

"If you do marry him, do I have to change my last name?"

"Oh, honey, I'd never make you do something like that, not against your will. We'll have a lot of time to talk. Nothing's going to happen right away."

The phone rang.

"That must be him," said Annie's mom, leaping up and dashing past her into the kitchen. "Yes?" she said, snatching the receiver off the wall, sounding breathless, excited. "You're here. I'll buzz you in. We're on the east end of the complex. Third floor. Turn right when you get off the elevator." She listened for a few seconds. "Yeah, she's here." Turning her back away from the door, she whispered, "Me, too. Fingers crossed."

Annie walked into the kitchen. She had big ears and had picked up

3

everything her mother had said, but she wasn't quite sure what it all meant.

Her mom hung up the phone. Slowly, she turned, her face flushed, her eyes darting nervously. "You're gonna love him, I know you will."

"Where does he live now?"

"Well, ah, when he was a kid, his family lived all over."

"But what about now?"

"Like I said, he just got out of prison."

"Is he gonna stay with us?"

"Would that be such a bad thing?"

Annie truly didn't know. But she had a suspicious feeling that it would. She and her mom were a team. They didn't need anyone else to make them happy. Her mom had never dated after Annie's dad died. Annie asked her about it once. Her mom said she was too busy earning a living to worry about romance.

Annie was still deciding what to say when the doorbell rang.

"How do I look?" asked her mom, searching Annie's face for reassurance.

"Okay, I guess."

She rushed to the door.

Out in the hall stood a dark-haired guy wearing a red-and-blue plaid shirt and jeans. He held a beat-up suitcase and a paper sack.

"Mandy?" he said, letting the suitcase drop. He whipped off his sunglasses. "God, you haven't changed a bit." He grabbed her and squeezed her tight, his eyes closed. He opened them while they were still hugging and looked at Annie. And then he winked.

Annie frowned. The wink made her feel weird.

Tugging at Johnny's arm, her mom led him into the living room, where they all sat down, Johnny and her mom on the couch, and Annie in a chair across the room.

"Johnny, I'd like you to meet my daughter, Annie."

4

Johnny nodded, grinned. That's when Annie decided he was sort of good-looking. His skin was really pale, and he wasn't much taller than her mom, but he was built. And he had twinkly eyes and a smile that promised something fun.

"Hey," said Johnny, reaching around behind him for the brown paper sack. "I brought you both a present."

"You didn't need to do that," said Annie's mother, although she looked pretty darn happy about it.

"Here," he said, handing her a small box.

Her mom acted a lot like a dog they'd once had. When you said "treat," he wagged his tail so hard that his entire body shook. That's what Annie's mom looked like. She was vibrating. Annie wasn't into obvious emotion and thought the reaction was pathetic. Old people could be *so* uncool.

When her mom opened the gift, her eyes lit up. She held up a tiny bottle of perfume so Annie could see it. Unscrewing the cap, she sniffed. "It's wonderful. I love it."

"So do I," said Johnny, one eyebrow raised at her, another grin spreading across his face. "And for you, Annie." He pulled a paperback out of the sack and tossed it across to her. "Do you like novels?"

"Sometimes," she said nonchalantly, one leg draped over the other. He wasn't about to get some stupid overreaction out of her.

"What's the title?" asked her mom.

"*Catcher in the Rye,*" said Johnny.

Her mom's smile dimmed. "You think that's an okay story for a thirteen-year-old girl?"

Johnny shrugged. "I read it when I was thirteen. It was my favorite book for years."

Sensing that there might be something off-limits about the novel, Annie got up. "Think I'll go down and sit by the putting green."

"Honey, I'm not sure—"

"Oh, let her have some fun," said Johnny.

Annie had just opened the front door when Johnny added, "Take your time. Your mom and me, we'll just be up here getting reacquainted. And hey, I thought I'd take you both out for pizza later. That sound good to you?"

"Johnny?" said her mother. "Can you afford that? I could make us something here."

"Hell, woman, if I can't afford to take my two favorite ladies out to dinner, they might as well shoot me right now."

Favorite ladies, thought Annie. *Pathetic beyond belief.* But she glanced back at him because the defiance in his voice connected with something inside her. For the first time since his name had been brought up, she found herself smiling.

Present Day

As Jane saw it, there were several possibilities. For one, she would turn forty-five in the fall. Her mind froze as she mentally tiptoed around the numbers. It wasn't all that long ago that she thought thirty-five was the departure lounge. Now sixty was only fifteen years away. Not much time. But time, as she'd learned, was a malleable concept. It often depended on where you were standing.

At the moment, she was standing in the dry-storage room at the Xanadu Club, a restaurant she owned in the Uptown area of south Minneapolis. A pipe had burst, flooding the room with several inches of water. Jane had planned to spend the day at her other restaurant, the Lyme House, but just as the lunch rush began, she got a call from Henry Ingram, her maintenance man, with the bad news. She arrived shortly after one and found him in the basement hallway, dragging a wet/dry vac toward the storage room door.

"It stinks," she said, waving the foul air away from her face.

The old guy flipped on the light to reveal the disaster.

Crouching down, Jane touched the flooring. "This will all have to come out." She looked up at the metal storage racks filled with canned and dry goods. "I'll call Jimmy Mason and get someone out here as fast as possible to rip it out. Think we'll have problems with the sub-floor?"

"Not sure there is one."

"What about the pipe?"

"I been at 'er since eleven. We had some leakage last week. I called our usual plumbing guy, but he made a mess of it. This time I did it myself."

"We need to empty the shelves right away."

"I've already made a few calls. George and Terrance should be here shortly."

George Anderson and Terrance Keegen were two of Jane's waiters. "That's all you could find?"

"On such short notice."

Jane was glad she'd worn jeans and an old sweatshirt because she was probably going to be part of the work crew. As usual, disasters never picked a good time. She had two meetings this afternoon that might have to be canceled.

She took the measure of the loss one more time. "What a freakin' mess."

"That about covers it."

There were other possibilities, of course, that added to her current malaise. It might not be her looming birthday that had pushed her toward the edge; it might be a full-blown midlife crisis. Whatever the cause, what used to get her up in the mornings and fuel the rest of her days simply didn't work anymore.

Jane had spent the last few months examining her life and finding it wanting. Part of her current predicament was a kind of disharmonic convergence. She owned two popular restaurants in Minneapolis and had recently begun to develop a third. Due to some financial problems caused by the tanking economy, those plans had been put on hold. Instead of pushing harder, trying to work through the problems, she'd simply stopped and taken some time to look around. What she saw was a deep crack in what had always been her limitless career ambition.

The other half of the disharmonic convergence was a messy romantic breakup last November that had left her feeling uncharacteristically confused, sluggish, and depressed. Jane and her partner of two years, Kenzie Mulroy, had parted ways. Jane wanted to work things out, but Kenzie had thrown in the towel with such force that no amount of apologies or promises to change made a dent in Kenzie's resolve. And yet Jane didn't want to let go. There had to be a way to make this long-distance relationship work. One of Kenzie's major objections was that Jane was too busy, that she never made enough time in her life for Kenzie. It was an arrow that hit the mark. Jane couldn't argue the facts away. And so, because the breakup had been mostly her fault, she'd been fighting with a sense of personal failure that she couldn't seem to shake. Even more troubling was the brutal suspicion that, in all her efforts to live the good life, she had somehow taken a wrong turn.

"Have you had lunch?" asked Jane.

"I'm full up," said Henry.

Jane had skipped breakfast. If she was going to haul things around all afternoon, she had to put some fuel in her tank. "I need to grab something to eat and then I'll be back."

"Nothin' in this room is goin' anywhere without help," said Henry, switching on the wet/dry vac.

Jane spent the next few minutes talking to her executive chef in the kitchen, all the while eyeing the daily specials. Before she left, she dished herself up a bowl of the minestrone she loved so much, along with a couple of slices of bread. By the time she reached the Speakeasy at the front of the house, her stomach was growling. She helped herself to a cup of coffee and was about to sit down at the far end of the bar, when one of the bartenders got her attention.

"There's a woman here who wants to talk to the manager about a job."

"Fine," she said, easing onto a stool. "Have her talk to Len."

"He wasn't feeling well, so he ran over to Snyders to buy some ibuprofen."

"Don't we have any here?"

"Guess not."

"Okay, then have her fill out an application and give it to Len when he gets back."

"Where would I find the applications?"

She should have stayed in bed and hidden under the covers. "Where is she?"

He nodded toward the other end of the room.

Standing by the cash register was a woman wearing an army green wool sweater, brown cargo pants, and hiking boots, with a sheepskin jacket slung over one shoulder. She was tall, blond, and fashion model pretty.

"I'll take care of it," said Jane, hiding her groan. Leaving her stool with a longing backward glance, she introduced herself to the woman. "I'm the owner."

"Oh, great. I'm Annie Archer."

"You're looking for a job?"

"Just something temporary. I need to make some money, but I won't be in town long."

Jane invited her back to end of the counter, where her soup was rapidly cooling. "Something to eat?"

"No, I'm fine. I'd be willing to do just about anything. Wash dishes. Prep food. I'm a trained bartender, although you probably don't need one of those."

As they talked, Jane learned that Annie lived in Steamboat Springs, Colorado, and that she was in town looking for her father.

"It's kind of a long story. He disappeared after my mother died. I was twenty the last time I saw him. That was twelve years ago."

Jane did the math. Annie was thirty-two. "You think he's living in the Twin Cities?"

"A friend of mine who was passing through town on a business trip a couple of weeks ago said she was positive she saw him in a bar."

Jane ate her soup while they talked. "No luck?"

"Not yet. And money is getting tight. I took a leave of absence from my job back in Steamboat Springs. Like I said, I'm a bartender at a ski resort."

"I suppose you do a lot of skiing. I used to ski all the time when I was in college."

"Not anymore?"

"It always seems like I'm too busy."

"You should make the time. I can't imagine my life without riding those hills." For the first time, she smiled. She had a small space between her two front teeth, and a couple of her bottom teeth were crooked. It probably meant that Annie's family hadn't had the money for orthodontia when she was a child—and that in adult life, Annie hadn't either. Not that the teeth detracted from her looks. If anything, the flaw seemed the exception that proved the rule.

"Look," said Jane, finishing her soup. "You've actually come at a good time. I have a job, but it's not pretty." She explained about the flooded dry-storage room. "I'm headed down there myself. I could use an extra pair of hands."

"Sure," said Annie.

"There'll be some heavy lifting."

"Not a problem."

"I'll pay you what I pay the other two guys who agreed to help. Twelve seventy-five an hour. It might take the rest of the day."

"Count me in." She hopped off the stool, ready to get to work.

Terrance and George paired off, as did Annie and Jane. Henry acted as straw boss, moving the tall racks, as they were emptied, out into the hallway and helping the flooring crew pull up the old vinyl flooring.

As they worked, Jane and Annie talked. Jane learned that Annie had received a degree in folklore and mythology from the University of Colorado, Boulder.

"My major interest was in Greek and Roman mythology," said Annie, hoisting a sack of rice over her shoulder. "I did my senior thesis on the mirror and the mask as they're used in the myth of Medusa."

"The woman with the snakes in her hair."

"It's a fascinating story with lots of variations. She was a beauty. Either she was raped by Poseidon in Athena's temple or she had consensual sex with him. Either way, Athena saw it as sacrilege and punished her by turning her golden hair into serpents."

"Why didn't she punish Poseidon?"

"He was immortal. Medusa wasn't."

"Figures." Jane hefted a fifty-pound sack of flour out into the hall.

Annie followed with the rice. "Athena also turned Medusa's face into something so horrible, so ugly, that when men looked at it, it turned them to stone. Apparently, Athena didn't want any handsome young men to sleep with her."

"Sex as rape, or sex as sin."

"Yes, but it's more than just a story about sex. It's about the destruction of innocence."

"A theme that interests you?"

"Very much."

Jane wondered why, but it seemed too intrusive to ask for details. Instead she said, "What about the mirror and the mask?"

"You really want to hear this? Most people change the subject after the 'destruction of innocence' part."

Jane laughed as she walked back into the storage room. "No, I'm interested."

"Okay. Stop me when your eyes start to glaze over. It's all about paradox and duality. The hero as victim and the victim as hero. A mirror is something that reveals; a mask is something that conceals. But when you think about it, mirrors and masks are dualities as well as paradoxes. You see your reflection in a mirror—but it isn't you. You're separate. Sometimes a mirror is an illusion—it shows you only what you want to see. And with a mask, you can hide behind it, but the real you is still there. I think that's the way life works. Nothing is ever simple, just what you see on the surface—the mirror's reflection or the mask."

"Do you think we all wear masks?"

"Pretty much."

"All the time?"

"Not every minute. Not with everyone."

Jane didn't disagree. "What did you intend to do with a degree in folklore and mythology?"

"At the time, I wasn't thinking that far ahead. I was fascinated that Greek and Roman gods and goddesses could be both good and bad, heroic and flawed. I guess I was hoping that if I studied them, I'd learn something about myself."

"Did you?"

"The jury's still out."

The more they talked, the more Jane found herself wanting to know Annie's story. "How long are you going to stick around looking for your dad?" she asked, standing with her hands on her hips, gazing at the shelf they'd just emptied.

"As long as the money holds out. I was thinking about hiring a PI, but it would cost too much. I did an Internet search. Everyone who looked halfway decent was priced way out of my range."

Jane picked up a case of lychee nuts. "What's the name of the bar your friend saw your dad at?"

"That's just it. She can't remember, except that it was on West Seventh in St. Paul."

"That narrows it down some," said Jane, feeling a sudden stabbing pain in her right leg. She set the case down and leaned one hand against the wall.

"You okay?" asked Annie, touching Jane's shoulder.

"I just need a minute." The last thing she wanted was for Annie to get the impression she was old and out of shape. Forty-four wasn't *that* ancient.

"The thing is," continued Annie, picking up a sack of sugar, "I can't leave. Not yet. Not when I feel so close."

"What's your dad's name?"

"John Archer. I left home right after I graduated from high school. The only time I went back was the year I turned twenty, for my mom's funeral. I only stayed a couple of days."

"Where's home?"

"Traverse City, Michigan."

"What'd your dad do for a living?"

Annie set the sack on an empty rack. As she turned around, she tucked a shock of blond hair behind her ear. "He flipped houses. Bought them cheap, fixed them up, and resold them at a profit."

"And you have no idea why he disappeared?"

"None."

If Annie thought Jane was asking too many questions, she didn't let on. Jane had a reason for asking them. "Your father's never tried to contact you?"

"I assumed he was dead. But then my friend said she saw him, so

I had to come see for myself. Tracy, my girlfriend, and I went to the same high school. She knows what he looks like because she was over at our place all the time. He's probably changed some, but she seemed positive."

"Was your mother ill before she died?" asked Jane. The pain in her leg felt a little better. She put some weight on it, just to make sure it was steady, and then picked up the case of lychee nuts and continued on out into the hall.

Annie followed with another case of lychee nuts. "No, it was a heart attack. Completely unexpected."

"She must have been awfully young."

"Forty-one. She didn't like doctors. My dad said she'd been unusually tired before it happened, and had some bad indigestion, but they both thought it would pass. It was a real shock when she died. Dad took her to the hospital, but it was too late. Her heart was too damaged. I was so angry at her at the time that I didn't really deal with her loss. I see the world very differently now. I wish I'd had the chance to put things right."

Jane had been thirteen when her own mother died. Deaths always left unfinished business behind.

They talked for a while about Jane's past—how she'd grown up in England, returning to the United States with her family when she was nine. She explained that her father was a criminal defense lawyer and her brother a photographer and videographer. Their conversation ranged widely, and yet, over the course of the next few hours, they kept coming back to the loss of their mothers.

"How come you left home right after high school?" asked Jane, pulling the last bag of sugar off one of the racks.

"I wanted to be on my own. Make my own decisions, my own mistakes. You know what it's like when you're that age. You think you know everything."

"It takes a bit more living to grow some healthy humility."

"Tell me about it."

They worked in the storage room for the better part of four hours.

When they finished, Jane invited Annie up to her second-floor office. As Annie sat at the desk filling out a W-4 form, Jane sat down in the love seat behind her.

"I might be able to help you find your dad."

Annie turned around. "Are you serious? How?"

"I have a friend who's a PI. I've worked with him on a couple of his cases."

"You worked with him?"

"Another one of those long stories. For now, let's just say that I'll talk to him, see what he can do to help. I promise, he won't charge you." She saw a faint glow of hope rise in Annie's eyes, which in turn gave Jane a sense of satisfaction. It made her feel as if she was doing something real, something tangible for another human being. Maybe that's what was missing in her life.

"I'd be so grateful."

"Write down where you're staying and be sure to include your cell number. Oh, do you have a picture of your dad?"

"I made a bunch of copies before I left home," she said, digging a small stack out of a pocket in her cargo pants. "Here." She handed them over.

Jane glanced at the snapshot. John Archer, wearing nothing but swim trunks, was sitting at the edge of a pool holding a beach towel and mugging for the camera. He was nice enough looking. A square face and prominent chin. Shaggy brown hair.

Annie turned back and finished filling out the form. "If you can help me, I'll owe you forever."

"Let's not get ahead of ourselves. I'll talk to my friend, get his thoughts on the subject, and then I'll see what we can do."

"Would it be pushing too hard to ask if you needed any more help around here?" She handed Jane the form.

16

Jane checked the phone number at the top of the page to make sure she could read it. "Count on it. I'll give you a call tomorrow, okay?"

Speaking slowly but with evident emotion, Annie said, "You know, I've never considered myself lucky before, but thanks to you, maybe that's about to change."

2

Susan Bowman stood at the window in her office, eyes closed, hands clenched, waiting for the fear to go away. Her best friend, Kristjan Robbe, the man she'd counted on for years to listen to her troubles and offer not only a compassionate ear but also sage advice, had somehow morphed into a risky, even dangerous association.

Susan had known Kristjan longer than she'd known her second husband, Jack. They'd first met in a real estate class twelve years ago, when they were hoping to become licensed agents. Susan's first husband, Yale Llewelyn, had died the year before, leaving behind a massive debt. Everyone told Susan to get into real estate, that if she worked hard, she could make a good life for herself and her two kids. It was the midnineties, when the real estate market was still booming.

A year later, Susan and Kristjan joined the same company, and the same branch office. Kristjan had just married, and for a time, Susan, Kristjan, and his wife, Barbara, got together in the evenings for dinner and drinks. All their easy camaraderie ended when Barbara gave birth to a daughter. Twin sons came along eighteen months later.

By then, Susan's career had taken off and she'd met the man of her dreams—Jack Bowman. Her friendship with Kristjan cooled, although she did see him occasionally at this or that corporate function. But no matter how much time had elapsed, it always seemed they could pick right up, as if their separation had been only momentary.

In early 2005, when Susan was made the branch vice president of the Northland Realty office in Hastings, she invited Kristjan to move from the Woodbury office. He'd been having problems with his branch VP, so she offered him the chance to work with her. She thought it would be win/win. He was a solid agent with a good sales history but hadn't been progressing in his career the way he'd hoped. Hastings, a small town about thirty-five miles southeast of the Twin Cities, was a bedroom community for the metro area and a growing town in its own right, with real estate selling at a fast clip.

Kristjan had come on board in the fall of 2005. They both commuted from their homes in St. Paul. In 2006, Susan and Jack moved into a new home just outside the city limits of Stillwater. Jack was a successful contractor and this was his dream house, built by his own company and designed down to the last detail by him. It was a wood, glass, and steel structure set into a steep bluff above the St. Croix River. It wasn't only Jack's dream house, but hers, too. With few exceptions, this was the life she'd dreamed of since she was a child. And that was the essence of the problem.

A knock on her office door brought her crashing back to the moment. She turned and said, "Come in."

Her administrative assistant, Amy Lahto, stuck her head inside.

Amy was divorced, in her late fifties, a chain-smoker who took well over a dozen breaks each day to step outside and light up. Susan put up with it because she liked Amy's gutsy personality. She got her work done and that was all Susan cared about.

"I'm leaving," said Amy. "It's getting nasty out there."

Ice crystals hitting the outside glass registered. "Oh, you're right. Have you heard a forecast?"

"Rain, sleet, and snow—in that order. I was hoping to make it home before the roads turned into a skating rink."

"You go," said Susan, checking her watch. It was still early, not even six. She often stayed late these days. "Everybody else gone?"

"Bob's still here. His commute's pretty short. Oh, and Kristjan just came back from a showing. I think he wants to talk to you."

"Sure," said Susan. "Leave the door open. And drive safely. I'll see you in the morning."

Amy backed out of the doorway, pulling the hood of her coat up over her head. "If I don't end up in a ditch," she called over her shoulder.

Susan stood behind her desk chair for a few seconds, thinking about the weather—if she should try to make a run for it. She sat down and opened her laptop, checking to see if the daily sales board was up. Finding that it was, she went through the motions, scanning the stats. In the mood she was in, it was impossible to concentrate. She was waiting, marking time.

"Susan?" Kristjan stood just a few feet away, smiling at her in his double-breasted tan cashmere sport coat, tight where it hugged his hips.

Susan cleared her throat. "I hear you just got back from showing a house."

"Amy tell you that?"

She nodded, forcing her attention to his face.

He stepped inside, casually unbuttoned his jacket, and folded his tall frame into one of the two chairs in front of her desk.

"You think they're going to buy?"

"Way over their budget."

"Maybe the seller will come down."

"Not fifty thousand."

"Stranger things have happened." Her gaze strayed to the door. She wondered how long Bob, the last remaining agent, intended to stick around.

"If it's still on the market next spring and my clients haven't already bought something, we'll revisit it." He nodded toward the window. "Noticed the weather? I was listening to the radio in the car on the way back. We've got a full-out winter storm brewing. They're telling people not to travel."

She tapped a key on her laptop. "That right?"

"Hey, you two," called Bob as he sailed past her door. His fur hat was pressed firmly on top of his head. "You better get out while the gettin's good."

"We'll do that," called Susan. "You be safe."

"That's the plan."

Neither of them moved until they heard the door close.

Kristjan waited a moment, then said, "It's not safe to drive back to Stillwater on a night like this."

"No, you're probably right."

"I called Barbara, told her I was planning to stay at a motel here in town." He waited until she looked up at him. "I booked myself a room at the Country Inn. I also took the liberty of booking you one, not a room, but a suite. Space to stretch out. All the comforts of home."

"Hardly."

"All right, but they've got clean beds and hot showers. What else do you need?"

They gazed at each other, letting the delicious tension build.

"I guess I better call and make sure the kids stay put," said Susan, picking up the phone. Her son, Curt, was twenty-six, in med school at the U of M. He lived in a condo near the university. Curt was sensible when it came to bad weather. Sunny, her daughter, was just about to turn eighteen, a senior in high school, and not the least bit sensible about anything. "I'll call Jack. He can track the kids down."

"You know, Susan, he'll tell you the same thing I'd tell you given the same set of circumstances. You should stay in Hastings over-night."

"You'd tell me that if you were married to me?"

He grinned. "As I think about it, it's never good to get too hypo-thetical. Let's just stick with the facts. The weather sucks and we're both stranded. Make the call."

3

Cordelia's chin sank into the bubbles. "Stop that infernal knocking. I'm not talking to you." She was beyond pissed, and when she was in one of her moods, only a bubble bath helped. That and an icy cold can of black cherry soda. And tonight, not even *that* was working.

"Come on," came Jane's voice through the closed door. "Don't be mad at me."

"I'm not mad. I am deeply, *deeply* wounded. We are a *team,* Janey. Did you come to me, ask me to help you find that woman's father? No. You went to Nolan. Every time I turn around these days, you're talking to him, taking your cues from *him.*"

"He's a professional. An ex-cop."

"I'm a professional."

"A professional *director.*"

"What's your point?" She roared up out of the water and began to towel herself off.

"What are you doing in there? Why all the sloshing?"

Pulling on her bright red robe with the dragon embroidered on

25

the back, Cordelia picked up her can of pop and yanked the door open. She leveled her gaze on Jane. "I do not *slosh*. I occasionally splash around with childlike abandon, especially when I'm playing with my toy boats. Only boors with no manners *slosh*."

Jane backed up and let her pass.

Barreling into the kitchen of her loft, Cordelia saw that Jane had brought along her laptop. She'd set it up on the kitchen table between two chairs. "What's that for?" She crushed the empty pop can in her fist. Silly, perhaps, but satisfying.

"Look, just calm down. Nolan showed me how to do an Internet skip trace tonight. I know it's late, but I came by to show you what I learned."

Cordelia fluffed her short auburn curls. "Are you working the case with him?"

"It's not a 'case,' and I'm doing this on my own. But I asked for his help, just like I've done dozens of times."

"He wants you to cease being a restaurateur and work with him full-time."

"It's not going to happen."

"Never say never."

"Cordelia, listen to me. You're the creative director of the most prestigious repertory theater in the Midwest. You're up to your ass in work. You're in demand for speaking engagements all across the country. You have a girlfriend who demands time."

"She left for Kansas City this morning."

"She did?"

"Everyone in her family was born in February. Except her. They call it Birthday Month. She'll be gone for ten days."

"Okay, so Melanie's off your to-do list for the moment. But you're mounting that new show."

Cordelia turned to glare. "If you paid even the smallest amount of attention to your supposedly *best* friend's life, you'd know that the play is up and running, to rave reviews."

"Great. Good for you. But my point is, you're busy. And you don't know anything about finding a missing person. Nolan does."

"Nolan, Nolan, *Nolan*." Scooping Melville, her smallest cat, up off the floor, she stood erect and attempted to look menacing. "He doesn't understand the creative temperament. He sees me as some kind of artistic flake. A dabbler. A ditz. What he doesn't understand is how much of your private investigative successes over the years has been due to my brilliant intuition—your brawn and general plodding nature, and my preternatural insights."

She carried Melville into the living room and dropped him on one of the many IKEA chairs. She'd grown to loathe Scandinavian modern but refused to change a thing in the loft until her niece, Hattie Thorn Lester, came home. Cordelia steadfastly refused to entertain the notion that Hattie might never come home. And frankly, at this moment, it was all too much. Jane's betrayal. Hattie's loss. Melanie leaving her.

Jane came into the room, carrying the laptop. "Let me show you what I learned. It's fascinating." She set the laptop on the coffee table in front of one of the couches and switched it on.

Reluctantly, Cordelia lowered her majestically plus-sized frame down next to her, batting at the tears streaming from her eyes.

"Oh, Lord," said Jane, turning to look at her. "Are you actually crying? I didn't mean for any of this to hurt your feelings."

"I am . . . overwhelmed."

"Because I spent a few hours with Nolan?"

She sniffed, flopped back against the couch cushions. "That. And Hattie. I was so sure she'd be back by Christmas."

Cordelia's wicked stepsister—actually, she was Cordelia's real sister, but "wicked stepsister" was more emotionally accurate—had stolen

Hattie away eighteen months ago. Hattie was Octavia's natural child, but Cordelia had been the one who'd raised her during the two most important years of her life. She expected that Hattie would live with her until she went off to Juilliard. But now, here she was, five years and two months old and living with Octavia and her umpteenth husband in England, of all the cold, dreary, Oliver Twistian places, being raised by dour nannies and exposed to Octavia's temper, her self-centeredness, and her general disdain for anything that stood in the way of her film career. She might be younger than Cordelia, but she was aging every second of the day, and for that, Cordelia silently cheered. "May her magic mirror crack," she said out loud.

"What?" said Jane. "Oh, you mean Octavia?"

"Who else?"

Cordelia had tried everything to get Octavia to listen to reason. Lawyers. Private investigators. Friendly intermediaries. Not-so-friendly intermediaries. She'd even flown to England to have it out with her in person. When Octavia slammed the front door in her face, Cordelia had been forced to climb a trellis on the outside of the house in a last-ditch effort to get to Hattie's room. It was thoroughly disgusting how insubstantial they made trellises these days. Nothing like the ones in old movies. She'd ended up in the bushes, sustaining many excruciating cuts and bruises. And still, Octavia would not budge.

For the last few months, Cordelia had been reduced to letter writing. She composed missive after missive, night after night, employing gripping, utterly captivating logic, explaining with great care and detail how Octavia simply wasn't mother material. Sure, perhaps Cordelia had never thought of herself that way either. Maybe she had been a tad negative on occasion about children, sometimes even leaving restaurants in a huff if one happened to be seated next to her. But then, kids could be so loud and sticky, with no sense of proportion. Hattie had changed Cordelia's opinions.

The real reason Octavia had swooped in like a vulture and whisked

Hattie off to England was that her new husband, an English film producer named Radley Cunningham, liked kids. Couldn't Octavia see that Hattie was the one who was suffering? Standing in the early morning light of a drafty, dreary kitchen, asking politely, in a tiny frightened voice, for another cup of gruel? Locked daily in the cellar with rats and spiders?

"I thought you told me that Octavia and Radley were having marital problems," said Jane, screwing the cap off a bottle of Moose Drool beer she'd taken from Cordelia's refrigerator. "That it was only a matter of time before they split."

Cordelia sucked in a deep, cleansing breath. When she started thinking about Hattie and Octavia—the entire outrageous situation—she'd get so worked up she'd start to hyperventilate. "That's what one of the English PIs I hired told me. But I haven't heard from her in ages. Who knows? Maybe Octavia had her whacked."

Jane took a sip of beer. "Your opinion of your sister has sunk to a new low."

"For good reason."

"I know, I don't disagree." She took another swallow. "Look, maybe this isn't the best time to show you what I learned."

"No, no. I need diversion."

Stoically, girding her loins, putting on the face of a tragic survivor, a true heroine—in other words, doing her best impersonation of Joan Crawford in *Mildred Pierce*—she leaned forward. But before she could focus on the screen, a soft pinging noise caused her to look over at the wall of factory windows in the living room. "It's sleeting."

"Yeah, we're supposed to get a major storm tonight," said Jane. "Up to half a foot of snow. We're actually having a winter this winter. Not like last year."

Cordelia groaned. "Take me away, Janey. If I can't be on a beach with white sands and blue water, then drop me into a mystery, something that can be *solved*."

"I wouldn't go quite that far, but I'll bring you up to speed."

For the next few minutes, Jane explained everything she knew about Annie.

"I had to call her to get more info," said Jane. "I now have her father's date of birth and place of birth. John William Archer, born August 23, 1954, in Savannah, Georgia. He had two older brothers, both of whom died in Vietnam. His father was a teacher. Don't know about his mother. His parents moved a lot. What I ended up trying to focus on was his time in Traverse City. Annie said he had a business partner, although she couldn't remember his name. Archer was apparently a loner. He never talked much about his past, so Annie didn't know a lot of specifics."

"She didn't find that strange?"

"Not when she was a kid. She simply took it as a given. But she does wonder about it now."

Jane ended by saying that a friend of Annie's had sworn she'd seen Archer in a bar on West Seventh in St. Paul in late January. "Annie arrived in town a week later. That was six days ago. The first thing she did was to check every bar on West Seventh, but nobody recognized her father from the photo she'd brought with her."

"Did she give you the picture?" asked Cordelia.

Jane pulled one out of the back pocket of her jeans.

Cordelia studied it for a few seconds. "He looks really familiar. This is weird. I know this guy."

"One of the bartenders at the club said he looks like some actor."

"Yeah, Bruce Campbell."

"Never heard of him."

Cordelia was aghast. "You've never seen the Evil Dead trilogy? Or *Man with the Screaming Brain*?"

"Alas, no."

"He does look like Campbell. Same prominent chin. Same purposeful, squinty eyes. Same amused smirk. But I don't think that's why he's familiar. Can I keep it?"

"Why?"

"Because . . . because I collect pictures of people who remind me of Bruce Campbell."

Jane gave her a pained look but let her have it.

Pulling the laptop closer to them, Jane said, "Nolan thought there was a chance we might be able to locate him. The main problem is, he's probably changed his name and his social security number. That really limits our options. Without his alias we can't do a local police check, a court check, a neighborhood check, a credit check, or an employment check. What I did end up searching was a Social Security Death Master File. That's for the entire country. There are a few sites that let you search the database for free, but most cost. And most aren't updated all that frequently. Nolan likes one called RootsWeb.com." She typed an address into her browser and the website appeared.

"So is John Archer dead?" asked Cordelia, trying to stifle a yawn. She didn't want to put a damper on Jane's enthusiasm, but if this was how PI work was done these days, she thought it was deadly dull.

"None of the John Archers who were deceased fit our profile or his social security number."

"What next?"

"We did a cross-country search for the name John William Archer. Found hundreds."

"Yippee skippy."

"Yeah, I know. It could take forever to get through them. Or at least longer than I want to spend. Annie said her dad had never been in prison, but Nolan suggested I check federal and state prison records anyway. Only problem is, that will take more time. No wonder private investigators cost so much. I can pop up the sites if you want to see them."

31

"Thank you, no. I've already had my daily dose of frustration."

Jane rested her elbows on her knees. "My feeling is that John Archer has been slippery from day one. Annie may realize that about him, or she may be completely in the dark."

"Tell me again why she wants to find him?"

"Because he's her dad—and he disappeared. She said on the phone that she wants to put things right."

"That could mean anything."

"True. But as Nolan pointed out, when you're a working PI, it's not really any of your business."

"You're not a working PI, so that doesn't apply to you. Besides, you can't be a good investigator if you aren't nosy."

"You come from the Miss Marple School of Investigation. He's more—"

"Hard-boiled. Mean streets."

"Well, yes. I guess you could put it that way."

"And never the twain shall meet."

"Actually," said Jane, "I think they meet in me."

"How very diplomatic."

"None of the stuff I've got looks very promising. I need to catch a break, but so far I haven't found one."

"Have you called Annie to give her the bad news?"

Jane shut down the computer. She contemplated the question as she sat back and took the last few swallows of her Moose Drool. "I thought I'd get up early in the morning, check out the rest of the leads I found in Traverse City. I'll talk to Annie later in the day if I haven't made any progress. She'll be at the Lyme House tomorrow, doing prep work in the kitchen."

"How come you're going to all this trouble for somebody you don't even know?"

Jane looked at the bottle in her hand. "I'm not really sure. Partly, I guess I liked the feeling I got when I said I'd help her. I need that in

32

my life right now. Am I being too utterly earnest for your urbane tastes?"

"No, I get it. You need a problem to solve to get your mind off Kenzie."

Jane gave her a sideways glance. "Maybe. But I like Annie. I'm curious about her. And quite honestly, I think there's more here than just a simple case of a daughter trying to find her long-lost daddy."

"Is that a Miss Marple pronouncement or a Sam Spade observation?"

"It's a Jane Lawless stab in the dark. But I'd bet money I'm right."

4

Annie waited while the woman with the pale, ferretlike face behind the counter called the Thrifty Comfort Motel's owner. The woman was always perfectly cordial, but at the same time sort of not there, like she was off somewhere in another part of the solar system. Annie didn't think it was drugs, just her personality, which, unlike the occasional illicit pharmaceutical, she was stuck with.

"He's not answering," said the woman, holding the phone away from her ear.

"Could you give him my message?" asked Annie. She didn't want to show it, but she felt a little desperate. The owner had promised he'd leave an envelope for her with the night manager.

The woman waited a beat, then said, "Mr. Samuelson, it's Karen. There's a woman here—Annie Archer—who says you owe her for a bunch of housekeeping work. She's staying in eleven. Give me a call when you get a chance. Oh, and by the way, she's hasn't paid for tonight. She said the room rate was supposed to come out of her housekeeping money, but I don't see a note about it anywhere and I'm supposed to charge her before I let her stay. Could you let me know what I'm supposed to do? Thanks." She looked over at Annie. "When I hear from him, I'll let you know."

"Does he usually call back pretty fast?"

"Depends. Just go on back to your room and I'll call when I know something."

Feeling discouraged, Annie dashed back through the sleet, down the narrow, cracked sidewalk, past rusted screens, chipped paint, and heavy brown-curtained picture windows. Once inside her room, she brushed off her clothes. The last few days had been so mild that she hadn't expected winter to kick back in with such a vengeance.

Dooley, her dog, was lying in a tangle of blankets on the bed. When he saw her, he sat up and wagged his tail. She'd taken him with her when she left Steamboat Springs because she didn't know anyone who would agree to care for him indefinitely. She hadn't planned on being gone more than a week, but she couldn't be sure. And now it was going on seven days, with no end in sight.

"Hey, Dools," she said, lying down next to him. She turned on her side and wrapped herself around him. "I guess we'll have to wait on dinner. After gassing up the car, we've got exactly twenty-two dollars in cash. I think we need to save it, just in case."

Dooley was a small black poodle-cocker mix, all curly hair and sweetness. He was just over ten pounds. Whatever it was that had gone into making the sum and total of Dooley, he was her dog and she loved him. She was glad she'd brought him now because without such a gentle presence, she would have felt completely alone. Not that the feeling was new. Still, for the past six years, Dooley had worked his magic on her, taking the edge off some of her worst times.

They both dozed for a few minutes, Dooley no doubt dreaming of meat bones and green summer fields while Annie conjured up the woman she'd met at the Xanadu Club earlier today. Maybe lightning would strike and Jane would locate Johnny. Whatever happened, this was probably Annie's last chance.

Sliding a hand into her pocket, she removed her cell phone and punched in her friend Tracy's number. It rang a few times before Tracy's boyfriend answered.

"Hey, Matt. Is Trace around?"

"This Annie?"

"Yeah." She flipped onto her back.

"Wait a sec. I'll go get her."

Tracy came on the line. "Hey, where are you?"

"St. Paul."

"You actually went."

"I had to. Listen, you're sure—absolutely positive—it was Johnny you saw in that bar last month?"

"As sure as I can be. I mean, I didn't talk to him. But I know what he looks like. It was him, Annie. I swear to god. Same smile. Same teasing look in his eyes. It was like déjà vu from when we were kids. Except he'd put on weight. Mostly around his middle. I'm not saying he looked terrible, but not like he used to."

"And you said he wasn't alone?"

"He had some girl hanging on him. She looked young. How old would he be now?"

"Fifty-five. You can't remember anything more about the bar?"

"Look, between you and me, I was getting pretty wrecked that night. I'd been on the road for over a week and I was tired, sick of working and missing Matt. It was the third or fourth bar me and my girlfriend—Jenny—were at, so it was late, and I wasn't the one driving. Jenny was pretty wrecked, too. Remember I told you she was from Rochester? She didn't know where we were any more than I did. I wish I could remember more details about the place. There was lots of neon, I think. And a TV over the bar. For sure it was somewhere around West Seventh."

Dooley crawled up on Annie's stomach and plopped down. Absently, she stroked his back. "Think hard, Trace. This is my last shot."

Tracy was silent for a few seconds. "I was sitting in a booth, not ten feet from him. It was his laugh, Annie, that's what made me look over. You know what I mean. Part giggle, part howl. And he still had that sly, easy grin, the one that makes you think he's up to something. He looked . . . prosperous. Nice clothes. Leather, I think. I swear, the bartender seemed to know him. You didn't find anyone who could ID him from a photo?"

"Not a soul. You think the woman with him was his wife?"

"The way he was manhandling at her? Not likely."

"Doesn't say much about marriage, does it."

"Yeah, well, Matt and me, we're going to be different."

Annie hoped she was right. Somewhere in this chaotic, godforsaken world, there had to be real love. Just because Annie hadn't found it didn't mean other people weren't happy.

"Hey, Annie? What are you planning to do when you find him?"

"I'm still exploring my options."

"It was me, I'd buy a gun."

Annie had given it some thought.

The landline in the room gave a jarring ring.

"I'm getting another call. I better take it."

"Keep me updated, okay?"

"Will do. Love to Matt." She switched off the cell and grabbed the phone on the nightstand. "Hello?"

"Archer?"

She recognized the motel owner's voice. "Mr. Samuelson. Thanks for calling back so quickly. You said you were going to leave me cash for cleaning those rooms, minus the price for staying the next couple of nights."

"About that," came Samuelson's high voice. "The guy in number nineteen came to the office around three this afternoon, said his watch was missing."

"Yeah? And?"

"An expensive watch. He said he noticed it was gone after the room was cleaned."

"You think I took it? I never touched his watch."

"He was pretty upset. So was I. Here's the deal. You listening? I'm not only not paying you, I want you out of that room immediately."

Dooley tumbled off her stomach as she sat up. "This is total bullshit. You're just looking for an excuse not to pay me."

"If you're not out of that room in ten minutes, I'll have Karen call the cops. Save us both some time and trouble and just get the hell out."

Before Annie could respond, the line disconnected.

"Screw him," she yelled.

Dooley growled, hopped off the bed.

Annie went into the bathroom and tossed all her toiletries into her duffel. Rushing around the bedroom, she picked up her clothes. She took Dooley's water bowl and dumped the water into the toilet. After stowing all her stuff in the trunk of her rusted white Corolla, she got Dooley settled inside the alpine sleeping bag in the backseat. And then she stomped down the row of motel rooms to number 19.

She banged on the door.

It took a few seconds, but a man finally appeared. He was un-shaven, in a dirty T-shirt and sweats. "Yeah? What?"

"Did you tell the motel owner that your watch was stolen?"

His eyes were lit. She could smell the booze on his breath right through the screen. "What'd you say?"

"Your watch. I cleaned your room this morning. Did you tell the guy who owns the place that I took it?"

"My watch?" He held up his wrist, pointed to a crappy Timex. "Hard to steal it when I never take it off. The guy's messing with you."

"Figured. He just tossed me out without paying me what he owes me."

"Huh. Too bad." He leaned his hairy arm against the door frame. "Hey, pretty lady, you're welcome to stay with me if you got no place to go. Hell, even if you do——"

"No thanks," said Annie.

"You change your mind," called the guy to her retreating back, "my door's always open."

5

When Susan awoke the next morning, Kristjan was in the shower. She could hear him singing a country-western song, all "crying in my beer, but I still love you darlin'" stuff. He was off in his own world, a happy world, while she was stuck in bed in a state of anxious hyper-clarity. After a night of passion and whispered promises, the morning light had dawned in dread.

The genesis of that dread had less to do with Kristjan than it did with Susan's husband, Jack. The onetime love of her life would never give her an easy divorce. She'd never be happy as long as she was married to him. It was an impossible situation. And if Jack ever found out she was cheating on him, that she and Kristjan had been meeting in motels for months, digging whatever time they could out of their busy schedules to be together, he'd make her pay. At this early morning hour, she wasn't sure of much, but she was sure of that.

Susan's record was far from spotless when it came to other men, although she'd done a good job of keeping Jack in the dark about her affairs. On the other hand, Jack had all the real power in the relationship and thus could be far more blatant about his.

When Viagra came on the market, he was at his doctor's office the next day demanding a prescription. He'd been popping them daily for years, which made his once waning but now energetic sex life possible. Susan found Viagra deeply creepy even though Jack swore by the little pills. He said he felt like a kid again. He refused to call his sexual encounters with other women affairs because he never got emotionally involved, and that was the trump card he always played. He loved one woman—her. Till death do they part. Although his brand of love came with little extras Susan didn't consider loving, it was a package deal. She'd made a bargain with the devil on Viagra and had been forced to cope, mainly by her obsessive need to live the kind of life Jack could provide.

Since the beginning of their relationship, Jack had put her down for the way she raised her kids. And lately, whenever she shared a job frustration, he would twist it around to make her feel like an incompetent businesswoman. The fact that she let him get away with it—in *this* economy—said a lot about how much frustration and downright hate she'd had to stuff in order to stay married. He belittled her political opinions, criticized her clothes, her hair, but never said a word about her body. She pretty much lived on three snacks a day and spent enough time at the gym to ensure she was in top shape. Even so, when he eyed younger women in her presence, his blatant sense of entitlement infuriated her.

The worst part of the bargain was that, every now and then, Jack would use a night of brutal sex to keep her in line. It happened rarely, although the threat was always on the table. She hated herself for allowing the situation to continue. She'd been justifying it for years by telling herself that no relationship was perfect. Every human being had rough edges. When you got close to someone, those edges seemed that much sharper. It was simply the price she had to pay to keep the things she wanted. But now that she had Kristjan with her, that price was beginning to feel too high.

Jack liked his home life peaceful and orderly, and since it was good for the kids, Susan rarely challenged him. In fact, he'd been such a great father to her children that she sometimes wondered if they loved him more than they did her. He was careful with them, never let them see his bitterness. He wasn't a deep thinker, but instinctively he must have known that what was inside him had the power to destroy relationships.

Jack put on a face for the kids, for his business clients, and for his all-consuming charity work. He was positive, confident, generous. But over time, perhaps because he'd grown to trust her, he'd allowed Susan to see who he really was. And sad as it might be to admit, his intuition had been right about the corrosive nature of his inner self.

Jack Bowman was a deeply angry man, full of hostility toward the world in general and, specifically, at people from his past. He didn't talk much about his personal history—his childhood, his early life— but when they were alone, especially at night in the privacy of their bedroom, certain things leaked out.

For instance, his father enjoyed humiliating both him and his mom. Jack had once let it slip that his dad liked to make him watch while he had sex with various babysitters. Jack's mother was an alcoholic, loving one minute, pushing him away or screaming obscenities at him the next. The worst, he said, was when she got sloppy affectionate, made him come sit with her while she cried and slobbered about how much she loved him. He said it was the first time he understood what people meant when they said something made their skin crawl.

Susan wasn't positive, but she thought Jack might have spent time in prison. She knew enough not to press him for details. As frightened as she could be of him, and as surely as his relentless criticism and bitterness had dissolved any feelings she'd once had for him, she also found this slow process of discovery fascinating. She'd never know the full story now. As soon as he sniffed out any disloyalty, all intimate communication would cease. Maybe if she'd known the full story she might have been able to find some compassion for his short-comings. But Jack would never have accepted compassion. It would be easier for him to handle outright loathing. At the very least, loathing was something he understood.

Hearing the shower snap off in the bathroom, Susan drew back the bedcovers and swung her legs out of bed. She'd just put on her satin robe when Kristjan breezed into the room, still singing, a towel wrapped around his waist, his blond hair wet and slicked back from his high forehead. They both traveled with a small overnight bag, so they had clean clothes to wear when they had to spend a night away from home. Weather in Minnesota could be treacherous, and that provided an easy excuse for equally treacherous husbands and wives.

"I'm famished," said Kristjan, pawing through his bag for a fresh shirt. He slipped it on, let the towel drop to the floor, then stepped into a clean pair of boxers. Sitting on the rumpled bed, he drew her down next to him. "I love you more than I thought I could ever love another human being."

"What are we going to do?"

"I don't know," he said softly. All of his happy energy faded. "But we can't go on like this. I want a life with you, not all this ridiculous sneaking around."

A few weeks before Susan had married Jack, he'd come to her with a prenup to sign. She'd been expecting it, so it wasn't a surprise. Once upon a time, before the housing market tanked, she'd made a good living, but even then, Jack was the one with the big earning potential. Even combining their earnings, she and Kristjan didn't make a tenth of what Jack made a year. And that was a huge issue for Susan. She was infatuated by Kristjan—she'd come to the sad conclusion that she might not be capable of love—but that didn't alter her practical side. Perhaps that was why, in the middle of the night, she'd found the courage to whisper in Kristjan's ear: "We'll never have what we both want as long as Jack's around."

It was a simple enough statement. It could be taken any number of ways. And yet, in her heart, she was sure he knew what she meant. The comment had wedged itself between them in the night, like a restless third person in the bed, an unpredictable, possibly even desperate presence. She realized as soon as she woke that it wasn't some ghost in bed with them; it was a possibility. A next step that stank of madness.

"I can't stand the idea that you're going back to his bed tonight," said Kristjan, smoothing the tangles in her hair.

"How . . . how will Barbara take it . . . when you ask her for a divorce?"

He expelled a deep breath. "Not well."

"And your kids?"

"That's the worst part for me. What's a divorce going to do to them? They're all so young, so happy and well-adjusted. But other people split and it isn't the end of the world. The children survive."

"Do you want joint custody?"

"Hell, yes. We've never talked about that. You up for raising three more kids?"

"Of course I am," said Susan. She could feel her heart rate speed up. Kristjan was eight years younger. Not a big deal to either of them. But did she really want to plunge back into child rearing just when she was about to get off the mommy track? The truth was, she doubted it. But that was something they could deal with . . . after. Right now, she needed his help.

"So what's our next move?" asked Kristjan, buttoning his shirt, not looking at her.

"I'm not sure."

"The longer we continue sneaking around, the better the chance that Jack will find out about us. If he does before we've made some serious decisions, it will be the end. We'll lose the only chance we have to . . ." He couldn't seem to finish the sentence.

"To what?" she prodded. She wanted him to say it first.

"To take care of business. To do what we talked about last night."

"But we never talked about anything. Not really. Not . . . specifically."

"We'll never have the kind of life we've both been dreaming about unless Jack . . . dies."

She felt a sudden panic, as if she'd reached the edge of the earth and was about to fall off.

"But for the life of me," he said, his eyes searching hers, "I don't know how to make that happen."

"I do," she said, trying to keep the coldness out of her voice. She didn't want to scare him. Intuitively she knew that Kristjan had to be handled carefully—kept at a sexual pitch. She'd been working toward this moment for weeks. "You and me," she said. Her confidence permeated every word. "We'd make it happen because it's what we want. It's what we deserve. Jack's treated me like dirt for years. I've put up with it far too long. Are you with me, Kristjan? Because if you're not, tell me now and it stops right here. This is the last time we'll ever be together."

After a long, agonized moment, he looked over and whispered, "I'm in."

6

Two rings. Three. A voice said hello.

"Is this Steve Glennoris?" asked Jane. She'd been in her office at the Lyme House all morning trying to locate a man in Traverse City who'd worked with John Archer back in the nineties. She'd found Archer's name on a number of property sales, along with the name of Steven Glennoris. She was pretty sure she'd hit pay dirt.

"Yeah, this is Steve."

"My name's Jane Lawless. I work for a lawyer in Minneapolis. We're trying to locate a guy named John Archer. I understand you worked with him?"

"What's this about?"

"His uncle, Calvin Archer, recently died and left him some property. I was hoping you might know where he is."

Jane had been working her way through various options, trying to determine how best to get the information she needed without tipping off Glennoris that Archer was under investigation. If they were still friends, he might refuse to talk to her if he knew the real story.

"Property, huh?" said Steve, sounding amused. "Something big?"

"Forty acres in northern Minnesota."

"Lakes and trees?"

"Lots of trees."

"Really." He laughed. "This is crap, right?"

"Why do you think that?"

"Because, for one thing, I don't remember Johnny ever talking about an uncle Calvin. But mainly, nobody would leave that sack of shit anything worth spit. You're a PI, right? Or a cop? What'd he do now?"

"Are you still in touch with him?"

"Hell, no. But if you find him, let me know. I'd like to have a little chat with him myself. He swindled me out of a couple hundred thousand dollars back in ninety-six. We were business partners back then in a house rehab company."

"How'd he steal the money?"

"We set it up so we could both sign for our business account. One day he up and splits. But before he does, he cleans it out. I was left holding the bag on three properties without a dime to do the work. I looked for that asshole for years. Never found him."

"You know anything about his family?"

"First tell me who you are. Don't lie this time."

"I'm private. Working for his daughter."

"Like I said, lady, don't lie. He don't have a daughter."

For a moment, Jane was thrown. "Her name is Annie Archer."

"Oh, you mean the stepdaughter. The cute one. But she's not his."

"You're sure of that?"

"Hell, yes. Johnny couldn't have kids. Bad plumbing."

"He told you that?"

"He loved it. Said he could sleep around and nobody could ever nail him with a paternity suit. If your client thinks he's her father, she's not giving you the real story. She knows better."

48

Jane remembered something Nolan once told her. Basic rule of investigating: Everyone lies. Nolan warned her to keep that in mind. If she did, she'd never be blindsided.

"Tell me," said Jane, pulling her writing pad closer, "did you ever meet Archer's wife?"

"Mandy? Yeah, she was another looker. Nice, too. Too good for Johnny."

"Why do you say that?"

"Hell, first off, he was an ex-con."

"He'd been in prison?"

"Don't ask me for what, but yeah. You saying his stepdaughter didn't tell you?"

"She never mentioned it."

"Well, shit, lady, you better sit her down and get the real story. She's playing with you. Actually, I'm kinda surprised they aren't still in touch. The two of them were pretty tight. But then, after the mom died, he took off. I think the girl had already moved away by then. I was told, secondhand a'course, that he got this big insurance settlement when his wife kicked."

"Are you saying—"

"That he had something to do with it? No idea. Johnny was a thief, but he didn't strike me as the wife-murdering type. Then again, who the hell knows? He was money hungry, that's for sure. But he also had this weird, generous streak. He'd steal from you and never give it a second thought, but if he thought you were having a hard time, he'd empty his wallet, give you all the cash he had. I'd like to have a quarter for every woman who bent his ear with a sob story. I mean, the guy got a reputation for being a soft touch. My opinion, that's the kiss of financial death."

Jane wrote quickly. "Is there anyone you can think of who might still be in touch with him?"

"He might be an easy mark, but he didn't make friends."

"Do you remember any of his wife's friends?"

"Nah. She worked at one of those resorts around here. If you can figure out which one, maybe you'll find someone who knew her." He coughed, then added, "Anything else?"

"You've been a big help."

"Yeah, right. Hey, tell me something. Your last name really Lawless?"

"It is."

He made a sound that was half laugh, half wheez. "Kind of strange, wouldn't you say? A PI with the name Lawless. You must get razzed about it all the time."

Not as much as her dad, the criminal defense attorney, did. "Thanks, Steve. If you think of anything else, let me give you my number." She waited while he found something to write on. He took down the number, then kidded her one more time about her name and finally hung up.

After leaving the motel in Hastings, Susan drove home. Frosted ice crystals clung to the trees along the side of the road, weighing down the branches, even snapping a few, but the effect was nothing short of breathtaking. By the time she reached Stillwater, the rising temperature had melted away the winter wonderland.

Feeling dispirited, she found Jack finishing his breakfast in the kitchen while reading the local paper. She set her overnight bag next to the island. The pitiful pantomime she'd once thought of as a marriage was about to begin again.

Jack asked her how the roads were. He didn't really care. She told him they were fine. They hadn't been. He rumpled the newspaper, turned a page, nodded to the coffee, said it was fresh. She poured herself a cup. Sat down across from him. The mail was on the counter. She sipped her coffee. He sipped his. Neither looked at the other.

It was surreal, acting as if nothing had changed when in a matter of days he would no longer . . . be. The whole idea seemed so utterly impossible that she wondered if she'd dreamed it. But looking at him, at his garish Hawaiian shirt, at a face she'd once found so handsome but now caused nothing but revulsion, she saw more clearly than ever before that she had no other way out.

Susan had never understood killing, not even in war. Taking a life seemed incomprehensible. When she heard about murders on the nightly news, it was always at a distance. She might think for a moment about the strange mind that wielded the knife or pulled the trigger, but it had nothing to do with her. She lived a normal, orderly existence. As soon as the subject on the TV changed, the violence was all but forgotten. And yet here she was, about to become the person those anchorpeople talked about in disgusted, semidetached tones. Sitting across from Jack, watching him shovel breakfast cereal into that yawning void of a mouth, the mystery revealed itself.

Murder was an act of profound ego. It was the voice inside the soul screaming, *I want. I deserve. I take because I can.*

While finishing his breakfast, Jack asked where she'd stayed the night. She answered easily. Conversation proceeded in the usual way. He had a noon meeting. Sunny had already left for school. Susan's sister had called last night from Fort Worth, said she'd try to reach Susan after church on Sunday. Nothing urgent, she just wanted to check in. But in all the normality, Susan could feel something slip from her grasp. One minute everything was fine and the next the room had turned airless and blurry. A powerful tension heated up inside her. Was it then that Jack began looking at her in that critical way of his? She'd always thought of it as X-ray vision, afraid that he could see inside her. Her words grew stilted. The gaps between comments seemed to grow longer.

Susan couldn't stand it another second. "Is something wrong?" she asked.

"Wrong? With me? No."

"It's probably me. I thought we'd seen the bottom of the housing market, but it's still dropping. I guess I'm a little preoccupied."

"Join the club." He got up, set his dishes in the sink. "We need to relax, chill out. Why don't you join me in the hot tub?"

She hesitated. It was the last thing she wanted. "Sure. Good idea."

He turned back to her before he left the room, stared at her for a couple of extra seconds, then said he had to run back up to his study and make a quick call. She smiled at him, told him to take his time, that she planned to work from home for the rest of the day. There was no hurry.

And so it went, Susan scrutinizing each new shift in topic, taking Jack's emotional temperature every few minutes, weighing each word on the slippery scale of normality. She learned one important truth over the course of the morning. Spending time with a man you're about to kill was agonizing.

Ever on the tip of readiness, Cordelia had formulated a plan. No noodling around on the Internet for her. She believed in direct assault.

Cordelia Thorn was a supersized woman, six feet tall and well—*well*—over two hundred pounds. She was also drop-dead gorgeous in a curvaceous, Queen Latifah sort of way. More to the point, she knew how to use her zaftig, larger-than-life persona to get what she wanted.

Every morning—as late in the morning as possible—she crafted and costumed herself for maximum effect, depending on what she had planned for the day. There was one rule, and only one: No fading wallflower clothes were allowed, unless dictated by a necessary role. Not that Cordelia ever performed on the legitimate stage. She was a director, not a performer. She understood the difference between real life and acting, although in her opinion, the line was often a tad fuzzy. The world was Cordelia's stage, and she commanded it like a diva.

Today, for a little round of sleuthing, she'd chosen the Wagnerian cone-breasted look, the one seen on nurses in the fifties and in modern bondage flicks. She wanted to project sexual power and menace. Toss a low-cut red blazer over a tight skirt and sell it with black fishnet stockings and stripper spikes, and it was an image made in heaven for a jaded bartender sick to death of the long parade of excess derma and nightly ass grabbing.

Cordelia was smokin' and loaded for bear when she left her loft. Nobody knew the bars along West Seventh better than she did. Theater people were creatures of the night, and the night, after a show, was made for bars. A few of the best bars in that neighborhood were just off Seventh, and some were attached to restaurants. This Annie Archer person might have missed one of them. Cordelia intended to be thorough. She intended to find the father dude.

By one thirty, the huge head of steam she'd worked up had dwindled to a puny puff. She was fed up with all the twelve-year-old, second-string bartenders, their eyes falling out of their sockets as they gaped at her alpine cleavage. Sure, her breasts might be exclamation points honed for maximum effect, but *pullease.*

The Promised Land, half a block off Seventh, was the last place she intended to visit. She had a meeting at the theater at two—with a pastrami sandwich, extra mustard, no pickle.

Sauntering into the glitzy, neon-lit interior, Cordelia caught the bartender's eye. Or, rather, her breasts did.

"What can I get you?" he asked, wiping the counter with a soft cloth.

She pulled out the photo, handed it to him. "You know that guy?"

He took a quick look. "Nope." His eyes snapped back to attention.

"Look at it again," said Cordelia. She'd said the same thing in at least ten other places. "Picture the man a dozen years older. Maybe he has a mustache or a beard. His hair might be longer or shorter, or gray, or whatever. Maybe he wears glasses."

Grudgingly, the bartender took another look. "Now that you mention it, I do recognize him. He doesn't have a beard, but his hair is graying. What's his name. Oh, jeez, it's right on the tip of my tongue." He snapped his fingers. "Bowman. Jack Bowman."

Cordelia did a double take. "Bowman? As in Jack Bowman of DreamScape Builders?"

"Yeah, I think that's right. The guy's in construction."

"He a regular here?"

"He comes in fairly often. Sometimes early, for one of our bar burgers, sometimes late at night, usually with a woman."

"The same woman?"

"Nah, seems like it's a different one every time."

Cordelia didn't need to ask anything else. She already knew. "You're my man," she said, smiling triumphantly.

"I am?" he said, his Adam's apple bobbing.

"It's just a figure of speech. Later."

7

Jane had just come back to her office with a fresh mug of tea when Cordelia phoned.

"Are you sitting down?" came Cordelia's excited voice.

"Why?"

"You need me, Janey. I . . . am . . . freakin' . . . *indispensable*. After this, neither you nor Nolan will *ever* want to sleuth on your own again."

Jane picked up a pencil and drummed it against her mug. "Setting aside the fact that Nolan would never call what he does 'sleuthing,' what did you find out?"

"I solved your case."

"Meaning?"

"I found John Archer."

"You're kidding."

"Think about it, Janey. If you had a playful bent of mind and your name was John Archer and you wanted to keep it essentially the same but change the specifics, what would you call yourself?"

"Don't make me play games."

"What's another name for John?"

"Ian? Sean? Johann? Juan?"

"Stick with English. We have John Kennedy, but lots of people also called him . . . what?"

"Jack?"

"Bingo. And then Archer. What's another name for an archer?"

Jane was losing patience. "Just tell me."

"Bowman. Jack Bowman."

"Cordelia, just because you worked out this little word puzzle doesn't mean you found the guy."

"Of course it does. I took that picture you gave me and did some footwork. I found the bar—just *off* Seventh—that he frequents. And the bartender confirmed it. The guy's name is Jack Bowman. And what's even more important, I know him. That's why he looked so familiar. He's not a good friend or anything, but I did him a favor once."

Jane leaned back in her chair. It never completely surprised her when Cordelia knew someone she didn't. With her connections in the community, and her high profile as part of the arts glitterati in the Twin Cities, she often seemed to have rubbed elbows with everyone.

"He's a contractor. Owns a company called DreamScape Builders. And like me, he's big into charity. A really great guy. And loaded. Remember last year I sat on that board for SecondChance Minnesota?"

"The group that was putting up all that new low-income housing?"

"Right. Your father got me involved. Jack was on the board. He donated materials, time, design help, and a bunch of workmen for the project. I was at one of the sites one day and he was actually there, swinging a hammer. I mean, he heads a multimillion-dollar company and he's out working with the rest of the crew. We got to talking. He'd heard I was the creative director at the Allen Grimby, so he pulled me aside. Like I said, he seemed like a great guy, big smile, easy to talk to. On the other hand, he wasn't above using his considerable pull to get what he wants."

"And what did he want?"

"His daughter, Sunny, is a real theater freak. He'd taken her to New York several times because she's wild about Broadway. He told me she wants to be an actress when she grows up, that she has real talent. Anyway, Jack had heard that we sometimes took on interns at the theater during the summer. Most of the time the kids are college age, generally theater majors. His daughter was seventeen at the time—between her junior and senior year. That was last summer."

"Did you take her?"

"Sure. I pulled a few strings. Why not? She was terrific. Like a sponge. She soaked everything up, never missed a day. So, as I said, I don't know Jack all that well, but I do know Sunny. And I've met his wife. She's a real estate agent, if I remember correctly. They live just outside of Stillwater. I took Sunny home one night, got a tour of the house, and was even invited to dinner. The whole family was there—Sunny, her brother, Jack, and the wife. The brother is kind of the intellectual geek type. Jack took some pictures that night and e-mailed them to me. I'll find them and send them to you so you'll know what they all look like."

"Sure. Do that." Jane wasn't sure how to reconcile what she'd learned about John/Jack from Steve Glennoris with Cordelia's information. Then again, John had been in construction back in Traverse City, and he was still in construction, so that fit. Had he taken the money he'd stolen from Glennoris—and maybe money from an insurance payoff from his first wife's death—and parlayed it into a fortune?

"Sunny's not Jack's biological daughter," said Jane.

"I know. She's very open about it."

"Neither is Annie."

"But I thought you said—"

"Maybe Annie calls him Dad because that's how she thinks of him."

"Yeah, okay, but if she's really his stepdaughter, you'd think she'd mention it to you."

"You're sure this Jack Bowman looks like John Archer?"

"It *is* him, Janey. No doubt in my mind."

"From what I just learned, he's not exactly the fantastic guy you think he is. If he was, he never would have disappeared from Annie's life."

"People are complex. So are relationships. And we can all grow and change, right? Come on, Janey, let's get back to the point. Do I win some kind of award or what?"

"I admit, finding him was a stroke of luck." It was the wrong thing to say. Jane could almost feel Cordelia's hand plunge through the phone line and grab her sweater.

"It wasn't luck. It was my unfailingly astute intuition. I knew that if I showed that picture around, I'd find the right bar. Don't give me up for Nolan, Janey. I'm the real deal."

Cordelia couldn't seem to get it through her head that Nolan had something special to offer. Intuition could blow hot and cold. If Jane really did want to learn the business, Nolan offered her a once-in-a-lifetime opportunity. Not that she intended to take it. "I owe you, kiddo."

"You bet you do. So, are you going to phone Annie? Give her the news?"

"Actually, she's working here today."

"Great. Call me after you talk. As for me, I finally get to take off this hideous Nazi interrogation bra."

"Pardon me?"

"It's a need-to-know kind of thing. You don't. Peace."

Jane spent the next hour chasing down info on Jack Bowman and DreamScape Builders. She located a picture of him on his business website. He looked older, heavier, his temples graying. The photo convinced her, like nothing else had, that Jack Bowman was indeed John Archer.

Reading through the links, she learned that his company employed over a hundred people. Designers, architects, draftsmen, sales staff, plumbers, electricians, drywallers, concrete and patio specialists, excavators, landscapers, and on-site construction workers. The company was full-service: built houses, did remodels, and worked on just about everything else—all high-end.

DreamScape Builders had been founded by Jack Bowman in 1997, the year after he'd disappeared from Traverse City. By accessing local marriage data, Jane learned that Bowman had married Susan Greta Llewelyn in 2000. Susan brought two children into the marriage—Curt, who would now be twenty-six, and Sunny, seventeen. Susan was the branch VP of Northland Realty's Hastings office.

Besides being the president and CEO of a large company, Bowman owned both commercial and residential property in the Metro area. He also served on the boards of several charity organizations, and for the last four years had organized a local golf tournament to raise money for disabled veterans. On paper, at least, he sounded like a model citizen.

So where was the disconnect? Had Jack Bowman, alias John Archer, a possible ex-con, murdered his first wife, Mandy, making it somehow look like a natural death in order to collect on a hefty life insurance policy? Had he stolen from his business partner, Steve Glennoris, and never looked back? Had he changed his name and disappeared, relocating to the Twin Cities, parlaying his newfound wealth into a booming construction business, a new marriage, and a new life? It seemed as if most of it had to be true, but there were still a lot of gaps to fill before Jane would feel she had a grip on who Jack Bowman really was. On the other hand, she'd found what Annie wanted.

Climbing the back stairs to the Lyme House kitchen, Jane found Annie chopping bok choy at a long table with two other prep cooks.

"How's it going?" she asked.

Annie wiped an arm across her forehead. "Honestly? I prefer bartending."

"Are you hungry?"

"I'm always hungry."

"Your shift's just about up. Let's go sit in the pub and grab ourselves something to eat."

Annie reached around to untie her apron. "Let me clean up a little first. I'll meet you."

On weekday afternoons, the Lyme House Pub was generally pretty empty. Today was no exception. With a book tucked under her arm, Jane pulled herself a beer. She took a table in the back by the round copper fireplace.

Annie walked in a few minutes later. She was dressed the exact same way she had been yesterday—cargo jeans and an army green sweater. Her long blond hair was wound into a bun, but without the health department–mandated hairnet, delicate golden tendrils fell on either side of her face. She sat down, her tired blue eyes working their way over the room, from the ceiling beams to the wall sconces glowing amber in the subdued light. "This place is terrific. I almost like it better than the Xanadu Club."

"This was my first baby," said Jane. "I helped design it."

"It's exactly what I want," she said, looking around admiringly. "Someday I hope to be set up just like this. Not with a restaurant, but I want to be my own person, answer to nobody."

"That last part is difficult. I answer to my customers every day. To the bank. To my employees."

"Yeah, I know. But you understand what I mean. I want this kind of stability and accomplishment."

A waiter arrived to take orders.

"We've got some great specials," said Jane.

Annie studied the menu. "I think . . . maybe . . . just a Diet Pepsi."

Jane had the sense that her reticence was another money issue. "It's on the house."

"Really?"

"What do you like? Fish and chips? Irish stew? Shepherd's pie? One of our famous pub burgers?"

"The stew sounds great."

"It's lamb, not beef."

"I know. I saw it being made."

"And bring some soda bread and butter for me," said Jane. "And a bowl of the potato corn chowder."

"Coming right up," said the waiter.

As he walked away, Jane slid the book across to Annie. "You mentioned yesterday that you like to read. I got you a copy of *Too Late the Phalarope*. It's one of my favorites."

"Hey, you didn't need to do that." She studied the cover, then began to page through the interior. "Honestly, this is so nice of you. I'm not reading anything at the moment. I'll start on it tonight." She glanced at the back cover for a few seconds, then put it aside. "Did you get a chance to talk to that PI friend of yours?"

"I did." She felt more guarded this afternoon, knowing that Annie wasn't the open book she'd appeared to be yesterday. On the other hand, there was no reason Annie should trust her.

"I think I found your dad."

"Are you serious? That's terrific."

"He's changed his name to Jack Bowman. It's probably not a legal name change. He owns a construction company in the Twin Cities, lives with his wife and two kids."

Annie's face lost some of its eagerness. "He's remarried? And the kids—they're his wife's?"

It wasn't just an educated guess. "That's right." She waited to see if Annie would admit she wasn't Jack's natural child. When she didn't, Jane decided to play it on Annie's terms. She had a right to her secrets. And yet Jane felt let down.

"Where does my dad live?"

She gave her all the particulars, as much as she'd learned so far.

Annie pulled a small notebook out of one of the pockets of her jeans and wrote everything down.

"He's quite wealthy," said Jane.

"Wealthy," Annie repeated, her eyes drawn to the fire. "Huh."

"I talked to a man he worked with in Traverse City. Steve Glennoris. He said your dad stole from him. A couple hundred thousand dollars. They had a joint business account and your dad wiped it out before he left town."

Annie didn't say anything, just nodded.

"Did you know about that?"

"No. But it doesn't surprise me."

Jane took a sip of beer. "Just so you know, Jack's life seems to be full of secrets. I was told he'd taken out a life insurance policy on your mom. When she died, he may have inherited a sizable sum."

Annie's eyebrows furrowed. "He never said anything to me about an insurance policy."

"He also may have served time in prison."

"Oh?"

Jane could have pegged that reaction as a lie from a mile away. When their food arrived, Annie tucked into her stew as if she hadn't eaten in decades. Picking out some of the biggest pieces of meat, she set them on her bread plate.

"You don't like the lamb?" asked Jane.

"No, it's not that. I want to save some for my dog. He's in the car."

"Has he been out there all day?"

"He likes to snuggle in my sleeping bag in the backseat when he gets cold. But with the sun out, it must be fifty inside the car, so he's fine. Nothing to worry about."

Pulling her soup closer, Jane decided to take a diplomatic tack. "Look, I don't know what went down between you and your father. That's none of my business. But when you consider that your dad may have served time in prison, and that he also may have stolen money from his business partner and received a large life insurance payout after your mother died, and add to that the fact that he's assumed a new, *false,* identity, two questions present themselves. First, are you absolutely sure you want to contact him? He sounds like a guy who wouldn't be particularly happy to have someone from his past pop up out of the blue. In fact, if you do contact him, I'd urge you to be careful. You could blow his present life out of the water."

"What's the second question?" asked Annie.

"You said your dad had nothing to do with your mother's death, that it was completely natural. But do you really have all the details?"

Annie wiped her mouth on a napkin, giving herself a moment to think. "I assumed I did."

"I'm asking because Jack Bowman may turn out to be a great guy, but at the moment, I'm not sure he's the man you think he is. I don't mean to pry, but what is it you really hope to gain from reuniting with him?"

Annie picked up her spoon and stirred the stew. "Answers," she said. "For once in his life, I want him to tell me the goddamned truth."

8

When Jack left the house around eleven thirty, Susan breathed easily for the first time that day. Who knew that fear could be so physically exhausting? She desperately wanted to text Kristjan, but before they'd said their good-byes, they'd promised not to contact each other again. From now on, they had to be scrupulously circumspect. No being alone together until it was over. And even then, they would need to be extracareful if they were going to pull off a murder without getting caught.

Susan spent the rest of the day on the computer in her study. It was her favorite room in the house because it was her retreat, where she could shut the door and lock out the world. She read industry magazines, looked at sales boards, called clients, tried every way she knew to bury herself in work. But all she could think about was how she and Kristjan would accomplish the murder. She made a few notes, worked out a plan that seemed to have promise. But then, feeling frightened, she burned the pages in a crystal ashtray on her desk.

She left her study around four to spend a few minutes in the

65

kitchen getting dinner in the oven. Just a simple roast and vegetables. Tuesday nights were family nights at the Bowman house. That usually meant dinner together, but sometimes, time permitting, they might drift downstairs to the family room to watch a movie. It was hard to get everyone's schedules to match, which was why Tuesday dinner had been designated holy family time. It had been Susan's idea, but as usual, Jack had proposed it to the kids. Thus, they assumed he was the caring parent, the one who wanted to stay connected.

More often than not, it was like pulling teeth to get Jack to honor the commitment. That's why, when he called around five, saying he was running late, she assumed he was going to bail. But he surprised her. He said he'd be home as soon as possible. He asked her to hold dinner until he got there. She found the entire interaction strained but maintained a pose of sweetness and compliance. She promised they'd all be waiting for him when he returned.

Back in her office, Susan watched the light turn the snowy hills in the distance a deep twilight blue. Dinner was usually on the table by six thirty. Sunny was up in her bedroom. Curt generally arrived around six. That meant she had only a few more minutes to herself. Dreading the evening ahead, she felt her resolve begin to crumble. She'd promised Kristjan no communication, but she rationalized that she often talked to him about business matters. Pulling her cell phone out of the pocket of her wool cardigan, she tapped in his number.

He answered immediately.

"Why are you calling? I thought we said——"

"I had to hear your voice. I'm drowning over here."

"This isn't a good time." His voice was just above a whisper.

"Please, just——"

"My wife lost her job today. We've been . . . talking."

She was amazed. Barbara had been working at the same place ever since Susan had known her. "Kristjan, no."

66

"I haven't sold a house in four months. I've only listed three in the last six. I'm not even sure how we're going to pay this month's mortgage, let alone the bills for Anna Lisa's surgery."

"Oh, baby, I can help you. Let me help. Please."

"I can't talk. I've got to go."

"Just tell me you haven't changed your mind."

"Don't call me again."

He sounded distracted. "But—"

Speaking more loudly now, he added, "Thanks so much for your concern, Susan. I'll tell Barbara you phoned." He cut the line.

"Who was that?" asked Sunny.

Susan swiveled around. Her daughter was standing in the doorway. For just a moment, Susan thought she might be sick. She hadn't heard the door open. "It was Kristjan Robbe."

"You called him 'baby.'"

"I did?"

"He's your employee."

"He's not my employee, sweetheart. We're colleagues."

"Right."

"Sunny, you know Kristjan and I go way back. We're friends."

Sunny was a tall girl, like her father. She also had Yale's scowl, his dark, intense eyes, and his sulky nature, although for sheer brooding ability, nobody could beat Curt. Susan had loved Yale, but he'd passed on his gloomy nature to their children, which wasn't always easy to be around.

"I don't like him," said Sunny, scratching at a small stain on her sweatshirt.

"Why's that?"

"I don't know, I just don't. You said you hoped he doesn't change his mind. It was like you were pleading with him."

Susan smiled at her daughter. "You see the world in such melodramatic terms. It was just business. Nothing life or death. Come on." She rose from her desk and reached for Sunny's hand. "Curt should be here any minute. Why don't you help me set the table."

"If I have to," she said with a groan.

Annie stood next to her car in the Lyme House parking lot and watched Dooley chow down on a goodly sized portion of stew. Once he'd licked the bowl clean, she poured him some water. And then they went for a walk.

Annie couldn't believe her string of good luck. Meeting Jane had been a godsend. Jane had even packed a couple sacks of scraps for Annie to take—"For Dooley," she said. When Annie dug into the sacks, she found two thick beef sandwiches along with two plastic bowls of stew, to which it appeared Jane had added a bunch of extra meat. At the bottom of the sack was an extralarge foil-wrapped piece of chocolate cake. Annie was touched, but also embarrassed. Jane must have thought she was starving.

"What an incredible loser she must think I am," she whispered to Dooley.

Even so, Annie was grateful. The sandwiches and stew—and the pay for eight more hours of work—would keep her and Dooley alive for the next few days. And it was the next few days that mattered most.

Finding a stairway that led down to the lake, Annie headed west, toward the setting sun. She needed time to think, and Dooley needed some fresh air and exercise.

A half mile or so on, she stopped at a bench and sat down. She lifted Dooley up on her lap. The lake stretched out in front of her, covered with ice and a thin coating of snow. It was all so beautiful, the chilly air, the blanket of white turning a deep purple in the growing twilight.

Annie had a lot to mull over, and yet she couldn't seem to stop herself from thinking about Jane. Annie was probably doing what she always did—projecting, not seeing the real person. But she was pretty sure that with Jane, what you saw was what you got. She needed to find a way to give something back. Her mother always said generosity was its own reward, but that just seemed trite.

Hugging Dooley, Annie said, "We found Johnny. As soon as we're done here, we'll drive over to his house."

This was the outcome she'd been praying for, ever since she'd walked out of the apartment in Traverse City, slamming the door in Johnny's sneering face.

"He better have some answers," she said, stroking Dooley's fur.

If she had to bring his life crashing down around his ears to get them, she'd do it. With pleasure. Cold and quick, just the way he'd taught her. And like Johnny, without a second thought.

Curt sat hunched over his second glass of chardonnay, looking more morose than Susan had ever seen him. She tried to get him to open up about what was bothering him, but he deflected all her questions, saying he was just tired.

"I'm starving," said Sunny, sitting on the other side of the dining room table from her brother.

"I promised Jack we'd wait," said Susan.

Jack insisted that Curt and Sunny call him by his first name. He wasn't their father and said he didn't want to usurp Yale's position in their lives. He saw himself as a friend. Susan found his perspective odd, but the kids were still fairly young when they'd first started dating, so they just went with the flow.

"I've got a study date with Michael tonight," said Sunny, playing with her water glass. "He's coming by to pick me up. I need to change first. I don't want him to think I'm a total slob."

"Even if you are," said Curt, finishing his wine.

"Bite me."

Susan glanced at her watch. It was almost seven thirty. She'd set the oven to warm an hour ago. The roast had probably turned into a piece of cardboard by now.

"I can't stick around forever, either," said Curt.

"Let's just give him another fifteen minutes."

"Can't we, like, have some cheese and crackers?" asked Sunny. "*Something?*"

Curt pushed back from the table. "I've got midterms this week. Tell Jack I'm sorry, but I had to take off."

"I'm getting out the cheese," said Sunny, following her brother into the kitchen.

Susan put her head in her hands and closed her eyes. Just another happy "family night" at the Bowmans'.

It was going on nine when Susan heard the back door open. She was sitting on the couch in the family room reading *TV Guide,* working on her second Manhattan. The ruined roast had been put away in the refrigerator. She hadn't been able to bring herself to eat any of it. The kids were long gone.

"Suze," called Jack.

"I'm in the family room." She stared at the Navaho rug, heard him thump down the stairs.

His Hawaiian shirt looked rumpled and sweaty. The light from the lamp on the end table next to her made his skin look pockmarked and ghoulish.

"Where're Sunny and Curt?"

"They left."

His hands rose to his hips. "You promised you'd make them wait."

"I tried, but they both had plans."

"That's just great. Just fucking fabulous."

"I'll fix you some dinner."

"I'm not hungry." He grabbed the *TV Guide* from her hands and threw it across the room.

70

"I'm sorry," she said. "What was I supposed to do? Lock the doors? Handcuff them to the dining room chairs?"

"I bust my hump all day for you people and what do I get in return?"

"Jack, please."

"*Jack, pleeeease,*" he mimicked. "I don't even know why I try." He dumped himself in a chair across the room, buried a hand in his hair. "This day has been pure unadulterated shit."

"You want to talk about it?"

He just sat there, glowering.

"I'll fix you a drink."

"No."

"Look, honey—"

"I lost two big clients today. It's this wretched economy. Why doesn't somebody do something about the banks in this country? Nobody can get their hands on a dime." He got up, started to pace.

"Had these clients signed contracts?"

"One had. The other was pending."

"Have you talked to your lawyer?"

"I've talked to three lawyers. You can't trust anyone anymore." Glancing over at her, he added, "Not even your family."

"Come on, don't be mad at the kids. They have their own lives. They're young."

"They're selfish."

"We're all selfish."

"I should know better. Nobody's there when you need them."

Jack liked to play the victim. He seemed to crave pity. She'd learned to play along, soothe his hurt feelings, but tonight she couldn't manage it. "I'm sorry you feel that way."

He pressed the heel of his hand to his eye. "I feel like crap."

"You're sure you don't want a drink? Might take the edge off."

His hulking body prevented her from seeing the TV. "I know what would take the edge off," he said.

71

Struggling to keep her expression neutral, she responded, "What's that?" He'd probably popped a Viagra earlier in the day and was ready for a little action. Lord, she loathed those pills.

"You and me," he said, sitting down next to her.

She could smell his nervous sweat. "I'm not really in the mood."

"I can take care of that." He stroked her cheek, then moved his hand lower.

There was nothing she could do. She couldn't say no. If she pushed him away, his temper would flare again. She was trapped. She had to keep him happy. Until she could make him go away.

Forever.

9

Annie sat at a bar on Hennepin, nursing her second beer and watching a young man in one of the booths slam back tequila shooters. She'd spent the early part of the evening parked outside Johnny's house in Stillwater. Just after six, a red BMW had pulled into the long driveway and a young man had climbed out and gone inside. Waiting for a few minutes to make sure it was safe, she slipped out of her car and crept up to one of the first-floor windows.

The mostly glass house sat on the side of a bluff. It was modern, multiple stories. In the darkness, with lights burning inside, she watched the young man enter the kitchen and give an older woman with dyed red hair a peck on the cheek. The woman was working at an island, cutting up a green pepper for the salad she was preparing. She nodded to a wine bottle on the counter behind her and the young man poured himself a glass.

While they were talking, a dark-haired teenager sauntered in. She was morose, cute, wearing extralarge, round, black-rimmed glasses. She reminded Annie of Marcy in the *Peanuts* comic strip. She lifted the wineglass out of the young man's hand and took a sip. Annie assumed they were brother and sister. The three of them continued to talk until the older woman, most likely Johnny's new wife, finished with the salad. Then they all went into the dining room and sat down at a long table. Annie shifted her position in the darkness so she could continue to watch the scene unfold.

It was possible that the table was painted black, although Annie doubted it. It looked like ebony. The interior was picture-perfect, everything polished and gleaming. It was the kind of home Annie had seen on HGTV, the kind of place only rich people could afford. So many emotions tumbled around inside her that it was hard to pick out which was primary. She was sad for those people, knowing that Johnny was part of their lives. Sure, there was some envy. Most of Annie's clothes came from used-clothing stores. She couldn't afford health insurance. She bought most everything secondhand. She lived in a tiny efficiency apartment, and even with all the scrimping, she still had trouble making ends meet. But mostly, she was overwhelmed by Johnny's betrayal. It appalled her to think she could still feel that way after so many years.

For a half hour she crouched on the cold, dark hillside, playing voyeur. The red-haired woman did most of the talking. Annie wondered where Johnny was. They weren't eating, so she assumed they were waiting for him. But right around seven thirty, the young man stood. In a matter of seconds, he was outside, climbing back into his BMW. As he sped away, Annie raced to her car. It was pure impulse. She followed him all the way back to Minneapolis, to the bar on Hennepin.

What stood out most was the funk he seemed to be in. He sat alone in a booth, making eye contact with nothing but the shot glass in front of him. Every so often he'd lift it up and call for another. He was tall and rail thin, with tiny wire-rimmed glasses, tousled brown hair streaked with blond highlights, and a dark scruff. It was a definite salon look, which made him either vain or just a guy who wanted to appear trendy. He wore a maroon-and-gold U of M football jersey over a white T-shirt, but he hardly seemed like the athletic type. He came across as bookish and sensitive. She doubted many women found him attractive. And yet, she did. Mostly it was the lost look in his eyes that appealed to her. She'd always been drawn to lost.

It took awhile to decide how to approach the situation. Annie was a pro at using her looks to get what she wanted from just about anybody, man or woman. Sex was easy. Once upon a time, it was how she'd paid the bills. It was the only time in her life when money hadn't been a problem. But she hadn't used that route in years. She wanted to make something of herself, so she'd earned a degree. People with degrees had self-respect. They were smart, accomplished. Most, like her, were also living with crushing student debt well into their thirties, but that was part of the deal. Sometimes Annie thought it was a raw deal. The American dream—get a good education, graduate to a good job—wasn't supposed to work like this.

Lifting her beer off the counter, she walked over to the booth and slipped onto the bench across from him. He stared at her for a few seconds with a blank look on his face.

"You seem like you could use a friend," she said, leaning in, her elbows pressed to the tabletop.

"Yeah?"

"Yeah. You look kind of down."

"What's it to you?"

He had a nice voice. Not too low, not too high. But gentle. And beautiful hands. Annie always noticed hands. "I'm alone. You're alone. I think we're both miserable."

"You're miserable?"

"Pretty much."

"Because you're by yourself?"

"No. That's normal."

He licked salt off the edge of his shooter. "Someone as beautiful as you doesn't need to be alone."

"Wish I had a dollar for every time I've heard that one. Listen, I'm not coming on to you, if that's what you think."

"No?"

"Maybe I should leave."

"Don't," he said, reaching across the table. "I'd like someone to talk to."

"Someone who's not part of the problem?"

He looked back down at the empty shot glass, rolled it between his fingers. "Yeah. I guess you could put it that way."

She waited a few seconds. "A girl?" she asked.

He shook his head.

"A guy?"

His lips turned up in a slight smile. "No, not that either. How about you?"

"Nothing romantic." She sipped her beer. "For me, it's life. Just life. I mean, things can get so tangled it's hard to figure out what the real problem is."

"Tell me about it." He held up his shot glass for another.

"So I see you're sending yourself to Pluto on tequila shooters."

"That about covers it."

"You do this a lot?"

"More than I should. You want another beer? Or something stronger?"

She shook her head. "Booze isn't my drug of choice."

"No? Coke? Pot? I can get you anything you want."

"Aren't you the gentleman. No thanks, I'm fine." She nodded to his football jersey. "You in school?"

"Med school."

She raised an eyebrow. "That's pretty cool. What branch of medicine are you interested in?"

"I want to be a heart surgeon, like my dad was."

"Was?"

"He died just before my thirteenth birthday."

She drew a lock of hair behind her ear. "What's your name?"

"Curt Llewelyn. Yours?"

"Annie. Annie Archer."

"Nice to meet you, Annie." He tried a smile. He actually looked kind of handsome when he smiled, but it was a short-lived effort.

The waitress set his fourth shooter in front of him, removed the other glass.

"Here's to you." He tossed half of it back in one neat gulp. His eyes were starting to look glassy.

"You live around here?" she asked.

"Yeah. A condo in the Mill District. You familiar with that part of the city?"

"I'm not from around here. I'm just passing through."

"How long you going to be in town?"

"Not sure."

"You're here because . . ."

"I'm looking for something. My past, I guess you could say."

"A mystery woman."

She laughed. "That's me."

"The condo is old. Historic. Maybe your past is lurking somewhere over there."

"You think?"

"It's possible. Where are you staying?"

"I'm between motels."

He smiled more broadly this time, revealing even, perfectly whitened teeth. "Look, if you need a place to crash—"

"Aren't we moving a little fast?"

"No, I don't mean that. I've got a den with a comfortable couch. Doesn't come with strings. Looking for your past can be hard work. I know, I've been there. Hell, I'm still there."

It was a tempting offer. She and Dooley were scheduled to spend another night in the back seat of her Corolla, packed into the sleeping bag. This sounded much more comfortable. Even if they did end up in the same bed, that was fine with her.

"I've got a dog."

"The more the merrier."

"Are you kidding? You're really offering to let me sleep on your couch?"

"For as long as you want."

She eyed him for a few seconds. "How drunk are you?"

"I know what I'm doing."

"Can I be honest with you?"

"No."

"You shouldn't drive."

He grunted, shifted in his seat.

"I'm not kidding. I could leave my car here, drive you home."

"I don't need a mother. I've already got one, and she sucks."

"I'm nobody's mother."

Sliding his shot glass away with the back of his hand, he sighed, pawed at the side of his hair. "Oh, all right. I am placing my life in your hands, Annie Archer. Drive me." He dug into his pocket and shoved the keys toward her. "As long as you promise you'll still respect me in the morning."

Jack rolled away from Susan, breathing hard.

Susan had kept her eyes closed all through the lovemaking. She tried to go somewhere else inside her head—a beautiful meadow, George Clooney's bed—but with little practice at out-of-body expe-

78

riences, it hadn't worked. It hadn't been rape, but it was as close to it as she ever hoped to come. If anything had proved to her that her life with Jack had become impossible, tonight had. She couldn't live this way much longer.

Now, if he would just fall asleep as he usually did, she could slip out of bed, take a shower, and try to wash the feel of his hands off her body. She desperately wanted to talk to Kristjan, she *needed* him, but he was living through his own kind of hell at the moment. She'd see him tomorrow at the office. They could talk then.

Jack pulled a sheet over the lower half of his body. "Thanks for nothing."

"What?"

He wiped the sweat off his forehead with the back of his wrist. "If you're not in love with me anymore, just say it. I'd prefer the truth to *that,* whatever it was. It wasn't sex. I mean, lying there like a wax statue isn't my idea of a sex partner. I might as well do it myself."

She wanted to ask him how the girls he generally slept with treated him. Jack liked young women. The younger the better, within legal limits.

"Well?"

"I'm sorry, honey. It's all my fault. I told you this morning, it's my job. The economy. Our office sales are way down. My position could be on the chopping block if the numbers don't come up. It's got me so turned around that I can't think about anything else."

"I've got problems, too, but I haven't turned into a block of wood."

"I said I was sorry. You have to believe that I love you more than anything else in this world." The words tasted bitter, but she had to lie. She had no choice.

"I don't know, Suze. Lately, I've been thinking it's not the same with us anymore. Maybe we should think long and hard about, you know, splitting. It happens. People fall out of love."

"No," she said, wrapping her body around his. "That's not what I want. Ever."

This was the worst possible timing. If they were in the middle of divorce proceedings, with that prenup and the life insurance policy on the table, and something even slightly suspicious happened to Jack, it wouldn't take the police long to start looking into her life. "Listen, honey, I'm just preoccupied. And frankly, so are you. We're both a little depressed."

"I'm not depressed. I don't get depressed, I get angry. And then I get even."

"Well," she said, running her fingers caressingly along his arm, "then I guess I'm going to have to learn to be more like you."

10

Annie stuck her head out of her sleeping bag and looked around. It took a few seconds for her mind to focus, to remember that she was in Curt Llewelyn's condo. She'd driven him home last night, poured him into his bed with his clothes and boots still on, and covered him with a quilt. She'd nosed around the place a little, but the two beers had worked their way through her system. She was beat. After examining the bookshelves in the study and seeing that most of the volumes were medical or scientific, she spread out her sleeping bag on the wide leather couch. Dooley slept with her most of the night, but at the moment he was curled up on a brown bear rug across the room. Lord, a bear rug. It had to be fake. She hoped it was a gift. She liked Curt and didn't want to think he had such terrible taste.

"Pssst," she said.

Dooley's eyes popped open.

"Come here," she whispered, motioning with both hands.

He shook himself awake, then trotted over to the couch. Annie lifted him up next to her.

"Morning," she said, cuddling him close. "I suppose you need to go outside."

He twisted his head around and licked her nose.

As she flipped back the top of the sleeping bag and sat up, Curt's desk caught her eye. She hadn't taken much notice of it last night, but today she was appalled by the mess. Books resting on papers resting on more books sat next to empty soda cans, scattered coffee mugs, and several plates of half-eaten sandwiches. What he needed was a maid. Or a blowtorch.

"The Mississippi's right outside," whispered Annie, kissing the top of Dooley's head. "Can you believe that? Maybe we can find a walking path." She pulled on her cargo jeans, her socks, and her hiking boots while Dooley stood looking up at her, wagging his tail.

Tiptoeing past Curt's bedroom, Annie scooped his keys off the kitchen counter and rode the elevator down to the first floor. She was glad Dools could roll with the punches. As long as they were together, he seemed happy. She was still half asleep when they emerged into the morning light. A stiff, cold wind rolling off the river finally woke her.

Annie found a path that took them down to the river. As Dooley sniffed the brush, she stood on the bank, mesmerized by the roiling water. Shafts of sunlight pierced the dark clouds scudding overhead and struck the opposite bank. It was a gloriously beautiful winter day. Minnesota had its own kind of beauty, but nothing could measure up to the mountains. If she was lucky, she'd make it back to Steamboat Springs in one piece. She'd been itching to find Johnny for so many years, and yet now that she had, she saw her revenge and torture fantasies for what they were: impossible or just plain stupid. She needed a better plan.

Back inside, Annie sat down on the couch in the living room. "I must look like a mess," she said to Dooley, who was rolling on his back, snorting and kicking. The fresh air had done them both good.

What Annie needed was a shower. She wasn't at all confident that Curt really intended for her to stay another night. Cracking open his bedroom door, she saw that he was still asleep. In fact, it looked as if he'd hardly moved.

"He's going to have one hell of a hangover, Dools," she whispered.

The condo had two full bathrooms. With Dooley safely shut up in the den, she took a shower in the one farthest away from Curt's bedroom. It felt glorious to be clean again. Standing naked in front of the mirror, she touched the jagged razor scars on her thighs. It was a daily reminder of a time in her life when she'd been, quite literally, too stupid to live. She'd spent years hating herself when, instead, she should have been hating Johnny.

Back in the den, she dug through her duffel and found fresh clothes. Directly off the kitchen was a small laundry room. If Curt didn't immediately toss her out when he woke, she'd use it. Just about everything she'd brought with her was dirty.

Annie wasn't quite sure how to get her car back. The bar on Hennepin was too far away to make it on foot. Even if she tried, she'd probably get lost. Or Dooley would freeze to death.

She drifted around the condo for a while, looking at all of Curt's stuff. He seemed to be a curious mixture of sophistication and adolescence. With all the paintings and sculpture strewn about, he was obviously interested in art. He didn't appear to read much, except for his medical books. The kitchen cupboards were filled with dozens of different kinds of tea, a bag of fresh-ground coffee, some jars of exotic olives and olive spreads, but in general the food on hand wasn't far from what a teenager would eat. Lots of canned ravioli, boxed macaroni, and a stash of Oreos that would have done a five-year-old proud. But he looked like he survived mainly on take-out and pizza, beer and bourbon.

The condo wasn't large, but it must have cost a mint to rent—or buy. The kitchen was long, kind of narrow, but had state-of-the-art appliances—Sub-Zero, Wolf. The furniture was modern and new—lots of leather, some Oriental rugs, a few modern paintings here and there—while the building was old. Some of the walls looked as if they might be the original limestone. The floors and cabinets were solid cherry, the counters in the kitchen and in the bathrooms a gorgeous golden granite. Annie couldn't help wondering why this rich guy, headed for a career in medicine, with everything going for him, seemed so down. Popular wisdom insisted money couldn't buy happiness, but Annie was more than willing to give rich misery a shot.

She picked up the remote and pointed it at the flat-screen TV on the wall but didn't turn it on. She didn't want to wake Curt because she felt there was a better than even chance that she'd get the boot. She liked it here. It was warm, comfortable, and safe. As far as she was concerned, Johnny could wait. He wasn't going anywhere. She had one credit card she hadn't completely maxed out and most of the money she'd made in the last couple of days working for Jane. She still had time. If her job was gone when she got back to Steamboat Springs, she'd find another.

For the next couple of hours, Annie sat on the living room couch reading *Too Late the Phalarope*. Just before noon, she heard stirrings in the bedroom. Feeling suddenly nervous about her appearance, she rushed back to the bathroom and ran a brush through her hair, which had, thankfully, dried. She also retouched her makeup.

She was standing in the kitchen holding Dooley and eating from a jar of peanut butter when Curt lumbered out of the bedroom. He stared at her, bleary-eyed. And then he said, "Annie. Right."

"You remember me?"

"I wasn't that drunk." He stumbled over to the refrigerator, opened the door, and stared at the contents. "Not much to eat."

"Are you hungry?"

He felt his stomach. "Thirsty, mostly." He poured himself a glass of milk and gulped it down. "Better," he said, leaning back against the counter. His jeans and football jersey looked as if he'd been living in them for days.

"I could make some coffee," said Annie.

"Nah, I'll do it." As he filled the coffeemaker with water, he said, "Sleep okay?"

"Great."

"Glad something around here's great."

She sat down at a glass-topped table. "I appreciate you letting me and Dooley stay here last night."

"Like I said, as long as you want."

"Really?"

He looked back over his shoulder. "Why not? You're not going to take advantage of me, are you?"

That drew a smile. "You're a nice guy, you know that?"

He gave a halfhearted grunt.

"Do you have classes today?"

"Nope."

"Tomorrow?"

"Nope."

"Are you on break?"

"Sort of." He turned around as the coffeepot began to gurgle. "I think I'm going to quit."

"Seriously?"

"I'm always serious. That's one of my problems." He pulled out a chair and sat down across from her. "I'm failing."

"You are?"

"Don't act so surprised. It's easy to fail. If you never make it to rounds, or piss off the attending or the nurses, or forget to turn in your write-ups, or generally do a piss-poor job of oral presentations, it's a certainty you're going to wipe out."

She studied him, not sure what to say.

85

"That's a cute dog."

Dooley wagged his tail as Curt lifted him from Annie's arms. "He likes me." He let Dooley lick his face.

"Did you ever have a dog?"

"Yeah, before my dad died, when we were still living at the house on Fremont. When my mom, my sister, and I moved into an apartment, we had to give her up."

"That must have been awful."

"Yup." He set Dooley on the table, stroked his back. "Very awful."

"Why'd you have to move?"

"My dad was a slacker, just like me. We were in major debt because he'd stopped working without telling anyone. He hadn't paid bills in, like, forever."

"Your mom didn't suspect anything was wrong?"

"She knew he was depressed. My sister and I did, too. But Mom had no idea he'd quit the practice. Or maybe he was thrown out. I never knew exactly what happened. And then, one fine April night, he killed himself. The police ruled it an accidental death. He'd been drinking and his car hit a tree. But he killed himself. We all knew it." He said it all matter-of-factly.

"That's so sad. What was he depressed about?"

"My mom is a fucking bitch, that's what. She'd been having an affair with the next-door neighbor. She said it was because she and Dad weren't getting along. My dad, he wouldn't fight back, you know what I mean? I never understood it. She'd scream at him and he'd just walk away. She made his life miserable, always out buying shit, piling up the bills, keeping up the pressure on him to make more money. One day he just cracked. I don't think she ever once really listened to him."

"You don't like her much."

"She's an utter waste of space. I wouldn't care if she disappeared from the face of the earth. My father died because *she* drove him to it."

"That's pretty harsh."

"If you think I hate her, you should talk to my sister. She's still living at home."

"How old is she?"

"Almost eighteen. She may not be happy there, but Mom sure is. She's living the good life again because she latched on to a new guy."

"Did she marry him?"

"Of course."

"He a nice guy?"

"He's paying for this condo, for my school, and he gives me a generous allowance. But he's got the dough. It's no skin off his nose. My sister thinks the sun rises and sets on him."

"What's that mean?" She needed to be careful. She didn't want him to wonder why she was asking so many questions, but she had to find out as much as she could about Curt's sister. She was the one in the most danger.

"Sunny adores him. From the very first, they connected in a big way. For one thing, they both love the same stuff. Expensive cars. Fast motorcycles. Scary snowmobiles. I can't blame my sister for wanting to forge a relationship with a father figure. She doesn't remember our dad as well as I do. But he was the best. Jack isn't even in the same league."

"Huh. Interesting. So what don't you like about this Jack?"

"Well, I mean, he's not the worst guy in the world, but he does stupid, risky things and then brags about it, like he thinks it's cool. Take snowmobiles. He likes to blast around the lakes too early in the winter. It's like he's playing Russian roulette with the ice."

Annie felt a shiver of recognition.

"He sees himself as the kind of guy who helps people. A philanthropist. In some ways, that's what he is. But on a personal level, it can get pretty fucked up."

"Like how?"

"Well, for instance, the summer between my junior and senior years of high school, we were invited to dinner at this big home in Andover. The owners were business friends of Jack's. Before we got there, Jack told me that the husband was a coldhearted asshole who treated his wife like dirt. Jack said she was a 'real looker,' and that she was starved for male attention. I wasn't sure why he was telling me about it, but he made a big point of it when Mom was out of the room. Sunny wasn't there that night. I don't remember where she was, maybe staying at a friend's place. Anyway, these people had a pool, so we all took a swim before dinner. Mom and Jack were drinking pretty heavily, and so were the Middletons. Blake and Connie Middleton. Boy, they were a pair. Somehow or other, Jack managed to get my mom and Blake out of the pool, leaving me and Connie alone. He winked at me before he left. Big, broad wink. God, he was so obvious. You can guess what happened next."

"She came on to you?"

"Like a wild woman."

"Did you fight her off?"

"Are you crazy? I was seventeen. But later, as I thought about it, I felt pretty disgusted. *Used,* you know? I wouldn't be surprised to learn Jack had been behind one of the the Japanese screens, watching. He's an animal. Perfect for my mom. He'll eat her up and spit her out before it's all over. Trust me on that one."

Johnny hadn't changed a bit. "Why don't I pour us some coffee."

"The mugs are in the cupboard right above the coffeemaker."

"Milk? Sugar?"

"Two teaspoons of sugar. There's a sugar bowl on the counter. Silverware in the drawer next to the sink." Turning to watch her, he said, "So what about you? I suppose you're from a Brady Bunch family."

"Hardly. But I loved my mom and dad."

"That's cool. Where are you from?"

"All over, but mostly Michigan."

"Never been to Michigan. What's your dad do for a living?"

"He piloted a boat. Worked at a resort. Both my mom and dad worked resorts. My dad died when I was five."

"Sorry."

"Yeah. But I have good memories. When I was little, he used to read me stories every night before I went to bed. We had this big, brown, fuzzy mohair couch in the living room. He'd sit down and I'd climb into his lap. When we were done reading for the night, he'd lift me into his arms and carry me into the bedroom. Sometimes he'd sit with me until I fell asleep."

"You're lucky."

She set the coffee mugs on the table, resumed her chair.

"You still close to your mom?" he asked, pulling one of the mugs closer to him.

"Sure."

"Maybe I need to move far away from home like you did. Give myself a fresh start. Do you recommend it?"

She shrugged. "Depends."

He held her eyes for a few seconds, then looked out the window. "Whatever. What are your plans for the rest of the day?"

"Don't have any."

"We should go get your car. You'll need your wheels."

"Yeah, I will. Thanks."

"We could find a place to have lunch."

"On the topic of food, I've got a great roast beef sandwich in my car. It was cold last night, so it should still be good. I'd be happy to share it with you."

He cocked his head, scrutinized her face. "I get it. You're broke."

"Pretty much."

"Not a problem. I'm loaded. Let me take a quick shower and change into some clean clothes. I've got an appointment with my adviser over at the U this afternoon. But until then, I'm free."

Before he got up, Annie reached across the table and covered his hand with hers. "I like you, Curt. Not because you're buying me lunch and letting me stay here for a few days, but because you're nice. And honest."

"You like honest?" He stood. As he walked away, he added, "Don't be surprised if you change your mind. Honesty is way overrated."

11

Susan held up a real estate flyer, examining both the front and the back. "This is good. Makes the house look walk-in ready." Her attention shifted to one of the agents walking past her office door. "Hey, Jerry," she called, smiling.

Kristjan sat on the other side of the desk. They'd already established the ground rules. The door to her office would remain open. They would talk quietly, and when anyone came past or needed to speak with Susan, they'd be all business.

"Barbara's in a bad way," Kristjan continued, looking wrung out, dark circles under his eyes. "When her boss called her into his office late yesterday afternoon, she had no idea she was about to get the boot. She cried on and off most of the night."

"You haven't had much sleep."

He shook his head.

Susan hadn't slept much either. She'd tossed and turned all night, alternately excited and appalled by what, it seemed, she was about to do. As the morning light dawned, she was in possession of a rock-solid plan, but she needed Kristjan's help to make it work.

When the phone rang, it startled them both.

Susan looked over at the caller ID and saw that it was Jack. Pulling off her earring, she picked up the receiver. "Hi, honey."

"Listen, Suze," came his rumbling voice. "I've been thinking about last night. I know you don't want to hear this, but we have to face facts. It's not working for us anymore."

She got up, turned her back on Kristjan, and looked out through the window blinds at the parking lot. "Honey, I thought we settled all that. Just give it some time."

"I was thinking about talking to a lawyer."

"No. *Please.* Let's talk first. You owe me that much."

He didn't reply.

"Jack, you've got to promise me. You won't speak to anyone until we've had a chance to talk this out. If I can't change your mind, then fine. I won't stop you."

He said nothing for several more seconds. "I'll be at a work site all day, home around seven. We can talk then. Just don't expect a miracle."

"I'll see you tonight." She hung up, then turned around and sat back down.

"What was all that about?" Kristjan asked, eyeing her warily.

Keeping her voice low, she said, "Jack wants a divorce."

"Jesus, when did that happen?"

"Last night. But it's okay. I've got everything all figured out."

His gaze turned skittish, evasive. "Susan, I don't know. I can't leave Barbara when she doesn't have a penny to support herself, when she's so down."

"I'll help you with money; that's not a problem."

"You don't get it. It *is* for me."

"Keep your voice down."

He looked over his shoulder. "I've had some time to think. This just . . . it's not right."

"Every minute that goes by I'm even more certain that it is the right thing to do."

"People around here are putting two and two together. Randi Malone told me this morning that the other agents are starting to talk. She asked me if there was any truth in it—that we were having an affair. What's it going to look like if Jack dies suddenly? The police will be all over us."

"Not if we do it fast, before Jack talks to a lawyer, and not if we do it right, make sure it looks like an accident."

"But . . . what about Barbara? She's so fragile. I can't leave her. It isn't just the money."

Now she was getting angry. "Come on. You don't love her. You haven't loved her for years. You stay with her because it's easier than getting a divorce."

"Honestly, I'm not sure how I feel."

Another agent walked by the office, glanced inside.

"Hey, Dan." She plastered on a quick smile.

Dan stopped, stood just outside in the hallway. "You two look cozy."

Susan held up the flyer. "Kristjan's got a buyer that's on the fence. We're trying to come up with some strategies to make it work."

"Sure," said Dan, giving her a wink. "Good luck, Kristjan."

Kristjan didn't turn around, just held up his hand. "Thanks."

Dan moved on.

"See," hissed Kristjan. "He knows. They all do."

"You're just being paranoid."

Through gritted teeth, he said, "I think I have a right to my paranoia. My future's at stake. I don't want to spend it in prison."

She pushed back from her desk, crossed her legs in an effort to look less shaken. "So you're backing out?"

"I'm sorry."

"You're weak."

"Maybe. Or maybe I'm just not as ruthless as you are. You want too much, Susan. You always have."

Her world was swollen like a boil about to burst and here he was, sitting across from her, completely useless. "Are you telling me you don't love me anymore?"

"Not enough to help you commit murder."

She felt suddenly cold all over.

"Let him divorce you. You'll get something out of it. And then you can move on. You're still young, still attractive."

"Are you saying we're finished?"

"It's for the best."

Morning sunlight stretched in through the blinds and sliced a pattern of lines across her desk. If she was the kind of person who believed in prophetic signs, she might have seen them as prison bars. But Susan was a realist. The lines were nothing but shadows.

Standing up, she handed the flyer back to him. She spoke more loudly now. "Good luck with the house."

He rose uncertainly. "You're not going to follow through on this, are you? Susan? Are you?"

She was dying inside but refused to let him see it. She should have known that a man with such mild manners would, in the end, prove to be mild clear through. "Close the door on your way out," she said, sitting back down and turning her attention to her computer screen.

12

Late that afternoon, Annie was in her car traveling west along I-94, with Dooley snoring softly in the passenger's seat, when her cell phone rang. She dug it out of her coat pocket and clicked it on.

Even before she said hello, she heard: "Annie? Are you there? Jesus, answer your goddamn phone."

"Curt?"

"There's no pulse. I felt . . . but . . . so I—" His voice moved in and out.

"You're breaking up. Who doesn't have a pulse? Where are you?"

"In Still . . . at my . . . ents' place."

"*Who's* not breathing?"

"Mom. She's . . . and blood all over her. It's freakin' unbe . . . all over the stairs. All over me."

Annie roared off at the next exit and pulled to a stop along the edge of a service road. "Have you called the police?"

"No. I should. I will. She's got all . . . cuts from the glass . . . her eyes—"

"You're saying she's dead?"

"Yes!"

"Call 911. I'm only a few minutes away. I'll be there as soon as I can."

"Hurry. I am *freaking out*."

Annie parked in the driveway between Curt's red BMW and a white Jaguar sedan that she assumed must belong to his mom. Before leaving her car, she folded the sleeping bag over Dooley and gave him one of his favorite toys.

The front door was unlocked. Curt sat slumped on a wood bench in the foyer, his head in his hands, the front of his yellow oxford shirt covered with large red blotches. As soon as he saw her, he jumped up and threw his arms around her, gripping her hard. She could feel his heart beat like an out-of-control metronome.

"You okay?" she asked, backing up, still holding on to his arms.

"Not even in the same world as okay."

"Have you called 911?"

"What? No, not yet."

"Why not? You've got to call them. Now."

She waited, watching his hands shake, hearing the fear in his voice.

When he was done, he led her through the living room to a hallway in the center of the house. He was unsteady on his feet, moving in a jerky way, nearly knocking over a lamp. He stopped in front of a stairway.

Halfway down, the blood appeared on the steps. Just a small spatter at first. Annie stepped in front of him to get a better look. "Are those your footprints?" she asked, glancing down at his running shoes.

"I guess," he said, sounding dazed.

At the base of the steps lay the redheaded woman she'd seen last night through the window. She wore gray sweatpants and an orange flowered tank top. She was lying on her back, one leg bent at an odd angle underneath her, one arm flung out to the side, her body a mass of jagged cuts. Glass shards and cut flowers littered the steps and the floor around the body.

"Listen to me carefully," said Annie, turning around. "This is important. How did you get blood on you?"

He looked down at himself, pinched his shirt away from his stomach. "I . . . I turned her over when I checked her pulse. That must have been it. There's no way I *couldn't* have gotten blood on me." He was close to hyperventilating.

"Right. That makes sense. She must have been headed downstairs holding a vase of flowers when . . . she tripped. See, she's wearing flip-flops." There was no sign of a weapon, or of any foul play. "Were you in the house when she fell?"

"No. I just got here. I was on my way to the family room downstairs when I found her."

"I thought you had some sort of meeting this afternoon."

"I met with my adviser, but it didn't last long. I like to play pool when I need to think. That's why I drove out here."

Annie wasn't sure what to believe. She didn't understand why she had to push him to call 911. For a fraction of a second, she wondered if he was trying out a story on her to see if it would wash. But she decided instead that he had to be in shock. People in shock didn't think clearly or react normally.

She pulled him away from the stairs and into the living room. "Have you checked the house? Are we the only people here?"

He nodded.

"You should call John. I mean, Jack. And your sister. They need to know what's happened."

He sank down on the couch. He'd been so hyper up until now. As he removed the phone from his back pocket one more time, it was as if a heavy weight was pressing down on him, causing every motion—even the blink of his eyes—to slow.

While Curt led the paramedics downstairs, Annie roamed the first floor. She'd never seen a dead person before and couldn't sit still. She'd heard people say that the dead simply looked peaceful, as if they were sleeping. Another piece of bullshit to add to her growing list. Susan's eyes were open and staring, but empty. And far from looking peaceful, the expression on her face could only be described as frozen terror. Annie was afraid she'd be haunted by that expression for the rest of her life.

To get her mind off what was happening on the floor below, she turned her thoughts to Johnny. Meeting him like this would be problematic. She considered taking off, telling Curt she had something she needed to do back in Minneapolis. She fought with herself for several minutes about it but concluded that she couldn't leave him alone. For some reason, he seemed to need her.

Annie jumped when the doorbell rang. Jack would have his own key, so it had to be someone else. Heading back through the living room, she heard voices in the front hallway. A uniformed cop with dark hair and a buzz cut rushed past her and charged down the steps. Another one, taller with curly hair, stood with his back to her, talking to Curt. The two of them spoke for a few seconds and then started for the stairway. When the cop saw her, he stopped.

"Who's she?"

"My girlfriend," said Curt, eyeing her cautiously.

"It was . . . a horrible accident," said Annie, moving over to Curt, taking hold of his hand.

"Don't either of you leave," said the cop. "My partner and I will need to ask you both some questions. The ME will be here shortly."

Annie didn't like the sound of that. She waited in the hallway with

Curt until the cop disappeared down the steps. "Did the EMTs call them?"

"Yeah."

"Why?"

"It was an unattended death, which means it has to be treated as suspicious." He motioned for her to follow him into the kitchen.

"What did the paramedics say?" she asked, easing down on a stool next to the island. The kitchen was bigger than her entire apartment.

"Not much. They mostly talked to each other."

"Did you reach your sister? Or Jack?"

He spoke more calmly now. "Jack didn't answer, so I left a message. But I couldn't tell my sister what happened over the phone. She has to hear it in person. I asked her to come home ASAP. I'll stay here as long as I need to so I can tell her myself."

She squeezed his hand. "I'm sorry. Really, so very sorry."

He nodded. "Want something to drink?"

It seemed wrong to be thinking about themselves when his mom had just died. They both must have sensed the same awkwardness, because their conversation ceased. They sat holding hands, listening to the police and paramedics do their work, until the back door opened a few minutes later.

Annie held her breath as Johnny walked in. Tracy was right; he'd put on weight, but he still looked buff, maybe even more muscular. His expression was stern, impassive. As usual, he gave nothing away.

"You got my message," said Curt.

He tossed his keys into a pottery bowl on the island. And then his eyes found Annie. It took him a few moments to register who she was. When he did, she could see a ripple of apprehension flash across his face.

Before he could give anything away, she was up, her hand extended. "Mr. Bowman? I'm Annie Archer, a friend of Curt's. I'm really sorry about your wife."

He blinked, looked momentarily confused, then he played it just the way she assumed he would. "Nice to meet you," he said, holding her hand a little too long.

The curly-haired cop walked into the room. "Are you Mr. Bowman?"

Johnny nodded. "I want to see my wife." Turning back to Curt, he said, "You're sticking around, right?"

"I need to be here when Sunny gets home."

"Yeah, good idea." Switching his gaze back to Annie, he squinted at her and then left the room.

An hour later, while Annie and Curt were sitting at the island drinking reheated coffee, Sunny arrived. She breezed into the kitchen, a heavy book sack slung over one shoulder.

"What's going on?" she said, dumping the sack, unzipping her black leather jacket. "How come all those cop cars are here?"

Curt got up and faced her.

"What?" she demanded, her eyes searching his.

"It's Mom."

"What about her?"

He held her shoulders. "She fell down the stairs. She's . . . gone."

"Gone?"

"Dead."

Her eyes widened. "Dead? Mom's *dead*? I don't believe you." She glanced at Annie, then back at Curt. "This is crazy. How . . . when—"

"I don't have many answers," he said, "but it happened sometime this afternoon. I found her. I thought I'd stop by to play some pool."

She pushed him back. "You found her?"

"Yeah."

Something silent and fleeting passed between them. Annie didn't know what it was, only that it was important.

"The police will want to talk to you," said Curt.

"Me? Why?"

"It's an unattended death. Nobody was here when it happened. That means the medical examiner will need to review it. We all know it was an accident, but they have to treat it as suspicious until they can make an official determination."

She listened, her expression becoming more and more agitated.

"They'll probably want to know where you were earlier this afternoon."

"Where were you?"

"Over at the U. I had a meeting with my adviser. Do you have any idea where Jack was?"

"Why?" It took a few seconds, but the light finally dawned. "Oh, no you don't. I see where you're headed. He had nothing to do with it."

"Sunny, listen to me."

"No." Her eyes slid to Annie. "Who's she?"

"A friend." He grabbed her arms. "Listen to me. Are you listening?"

She tried to squirm away.

"What are you going to say to the police?"

"What do you think?"

"Sunny? Are we on the same page?"

"Sure. Let go of me."

He dropped his hands. "Sunny?"

"I'm not an idiot." Giving him a defiant look, she stormed out of the room.

Later that night, after they'd been questioned by the police and told they could leave, Annie and Curt stood in the kitchen of his condo, passing a bottle of wine between them. Curt kissed her for the first time. She had so many questions she wanted to ask but understood that now might not be the best time.

"I don't think I could have made it through the day without you," he said, smoothing back her hair.

"I'm glad I could help."

"You didn't just help, you saved my life."

She found the comment a little melodramatic.

"Annie?"

"Yeah?"

"I want to make love to you. How do you feel about that?"

Her answer was another kiss.

Reaching for her hand, he led her into his bedroom, drawing her down on the bed. They undressed each other, exploring each other's skin. Ever since the night they met, Annie had wondered what it would feel like to be with him.

Covered by a warm quilt, Curt kissed her again, this time more passionately, more deeply.

Annie closed her eyes as he moved over her.

"You're so beautiful," he whispered.

"So are you."

He kissed her neck, her shoulders.

And then, with an abruptness that startled her, he rolled away.

She turned to find him curled into a fetal position, hands covering his face.

"I can't," he whispered.

This was hardly the first time Annie had been with a man who couldn't perform. But all of those guys had been middle-aged or old. Completely out of shape. Curt was young, vital, healthy.

"It's okay," she said soothingly. "Today was a huge blow. Any man would be affected by it."

He looked at her, his eyes wet. "I'm such a freakin' mess. You deserve so much better."

"Quiet down," she said. She turned on her side and leaned on her elbow, caressing his face, wiping away the tears.

"Something's wrong with me. Something's *always* been wrong with me."

"Stop it. This is just a tough time in your life."

"Will you hold me?"

It was a request she'd never heard pass a man's lips before. Women, sometimes, but never a guy. "Sure," she said.

"All night? You'll stay here in my bed?"

"Of course I will."

He uncoiled and laid his head next to hers. "I'll be better tomorrow, I promise."

"You don't have to be anything but who you are," she said. "Ever."

"You're an angel," he whispered, his lips close to hers. "My beautiful, unexpected angel."

13

Kristjan got the word that night from a coworker. When Amy Lahto, Susan's administrative assistant, called, he was in the kitchen loading the dishwasher. He was on cleanup duty tonight because Barbara was resting on the couch in the family room. The children were upstairs playing video games. For the moment, his life had returned to manageable proportions.

"I just talked to one of Susan's kids," said Amy.

Kristjan lowered himself onto a kitchen chair. "Which one?"

"The daughter. Sunny. She said it was an accident. That Susan must have been carrying a vase of flowers downstairs when she tripped. I guess it was pretty awful. Lots of blood."

He pressed a hand to his forehead.

"It takes your breath away, doesn't it?"

He didn't like Amy and didn't think the question required an answer.

"Anyway, I thought you of all people would want to know right away."

"Thanks." He caught the implication in her words and it sent a charge of electricity clear down to his toes.

"I mean, you two were so close."

You nosy bitch, he thought to himself. "Yes, Susan and I have been good friends for years." The reply was stiff. False. He didn't care.

"Accidents happen so fast, you know?"

He suppressed the urge to hang up.

"That's all I've got to say, except that the medical examiner was at the house to make sure it was really an accident."

"There's some question?"

"Apparently." She let the word hang in the air. "Well, I guess I better call the other agents, give them the news. Unless you want to."

"No."

"Maybe you should call her supervisor?"

"Since you're phoning everyone else, why don't you."

"Whatever you think is best."

Some people got a charge out of passing along juicy news—good or bad, didn't matter. Amy was like that. Kristjan was reminded again of why he didn't like her. "Thanks again, Amy."

"Sure thing. See you at the office."

He sat hunched in the chair until Barbara appeared in the doorway.

"Who was that on the phone?" she asked.

Her voice seemed to come from a great distance. Without looking up, he said, "Susan Bowman's dead. She fell down the stairs at her house." When she didn't say anything, he looked up.

"How terrible. Are you upset?"

He wrapped his arms across his stomach, forcing himself to stay calm. "Of course I'm upset. Aren't you?"

She moved into the room and sat down at the table.

He saw now that she was holding a scotch and soda. Not her first of the evening, and definitely not her last. Once upon a time Barbara had seemed like the dark beauty in a Titian painting. Plump, sensual, earthy, with rosy cheeks and large, luminous brown eyes. She never needed makeup to cause a man's head to turn. After the twins were born, unlike many women who put on weight, she'd lost and kept losing. All her plump, youthful beauty seemed to waste away, replaced by a face that appeared haggard, older than her years. Some of the color had returned to her cheeks when the kids started sleeping through the night, but the worn-out face remained. He had to look closely now to see the woman she once was.

"No, I'm not particularly upset," said Barbara.

"That's a cruel thing to say."

"Is it?" She shrugged. "I guess."

Disgusted, he got up and finished loading the dishwasher. After switching it on, he said, "I'm going out for a while."

"You were gone all afternoon."

"I was working."

She lifted the scotch and soda to her lips. "Okay, leave. But before you go, maybe this is a good time to mention something."

He turned back to her. "What?"

"I know about your affair."

He stopped breathing. "How long—"

"Does it matter? You know, Kristjan, you're not terribly good at breaking rules. You never have been. And you're not as clever as you think you are."

He shot her a fierce look.

Standing up, she faced him. "I am sick to death of being the cross you have to bear. Sick of being tolerated, endured. I've spent years trying to deconstruct our marriage, trying to decode your fragile feelings. Oh, I know. You think women are the fragile, emotional ones, but we're not. We're the pragmatists. We do what needs to be done. While you're off in la-la land with your needs and your slutty girlfriend, we take care of business. We do the laundry, the dishes, take the kids to doctor's appointments, clean up the dog shit, and wait for a little thanks."

"Barbara—"

"Shut up. What I'm trying to tell you is that, even with all your flaws, I love you and I refuse to lose you. While you're out thinking, think about *that*."

14

On Thursday morning, Jane sat at the small mahogany desk in her upstairs office at the Xanadu Club, reading over a revised financial projection. The cost of building the new restaurant on the St. Croix River had risen into the stratosphere. In the next couple of weeks, she'd need to meet with her two partners—Judah Johanson, her financial partner at the Xanadu, and the executive chef for the new restaurant, Maynard Lawrence. She'd heard from Judah already and knew his feet were as cold as hers, although Lawrence was still making plans. He insisted there was significant fat that could be cut from the construction costs. Jane's response was, essentially, show me. She'd have to see it on paper and talk at length with the construction manager before she agreed to move forward. In many ways, she hoped this unexpected jump in the building cost would be the end of it, that she could bow out without too many recriminations—or legal ramifications.

Jane had expected Annie to stop by yesterday, looking for more work. When she hadn't, Jane began to get worried. Annie didn't seem to understand that because she posed a threat to Jack Bowman, he posed an equal threat to her. Looking at Annie's W-4 form, Jane punched in her cell number. After several rings, voice mail picked up. She left a brief message, asking Annie to give her a call. She felt frustrated and concerned for Annie's safety, not that there was much she could do about it now. She spent the remainder of the morning working with her executive chef on the new spring menu.

Just before noon, the door to her office flew open. Jane didn't even need to look. The only person who ever sailed in without knocking was Cordelia.

"What's up?" she asked.

A copy of the *St. Paul Pioneer Press* was thrust in front of her face. "You should read the newspaper, Janey."

"I know, but I don't have time."

"Make time. Newspapers in this country are about to go the way of the pig-footed bandicoot because of people like you."

"Did you come to harass me generally, or is there a point?"

"I'm here for lunch. You're buying."

"Some special reason?"

"Because I solved that case for you."

Jane swiveled around to look at her, amused to find that she'd made yet another one of her periodic transformations. Once again, it involved her hair. "What do you call that?"

"A rooster. Kind of Rod Stewart meets Tina Turner. Except my hair isn't long enough yet to do a full Tina."

Cordelia's hairdresser had died her auburn hair black. The front and top were short and spiky, with layers in the back. Red highlights made her look as if her head had caught fire. Everything had been ratted for maximum fullness.

"I'm speechless," said Jane.

"Yes, that's the proper response. Now, quit working and pay attention to me. If you're nice, I'll tell you what you missed in today's paper."

"Where do you want to eat?"

"In the main dining room. We can make a grand entrance." She patted the side of her hair. "I'm in a white tablecloth mood. Oh, and I'd like to sit somewhere near a potted palm."

"I think we can accommodate that."

Once they'd found the perfect table, Jane ordered coffee for both of them, and an appetizer for herself. Cordelia ordered the grass-fed beef carpaccio, which came with a creole sauce and mixed greens. For dessert, she asked for the molten chocolate cake à la mode. "I'm eating light today."

"I can see that."

She rumpled the paper in front of her. "Okay. Listen to this. 'Hastings Realtor Dies in Tragic Home Accident. Susan Bowman, wife of well-known Twin Cities builder and philanthropist Jack Bowman, died Wednesday afternoon at her home near Stillwater. Mrs. Bowman fell down an interior stairway. The exact cause of death has not been determined. Mrs. Bowman is also survived by two children, Curt and Sunny, and a sister, Grace Lee Ingersol, a longtime resident of Fort Worth, Texas.'" Cordelia glanced up, an expectant look on her face.

"That's awful," said Jane.

" 'The exact cause of death has not been determined.' "

"What are you suggesting?"

"Annie Archer returns to Jack Bowman's life and two days later his wife is dead."

"You think there's a connection?"

"Don't you?"

"Why would she want to murder her stepfather's second wife?"

"I don't *know*," said Cordelia, eyes bulging. "That's just it. We may be the only ones who know what's really going on. Things are happening behind the scenes that virtually shriek for our attention."

"Then you'll be glad that I've done a little more checking around."

"I am all ears."

The coffee arrived. Cordelia added cream to hers; Jane took hers black.

"Okay, so I phoned resorts near Traverse City yesterday afternoon. I found a woman who knew Mandy Archer, Annie's mother. Her name is Helen James, and she works at the Bell House Resort on Lake Ann, which is about twelve miles west of Traverse City. She's in her early sixties now, still employed at the resort. Years ago, she said she considered Mandy a friend. Apparently, Mandy was fired from her job at the end of ninety-five."

"How come she was fired?"

"Helen wasn't sure about the particulars, but she said that Mandy had become extremely erratic. She'd always been superconscientious and was well liked, but early that year she started missing work. Sometimes she didn't even call in with an excuse. And when she did show up, she'd blame other people for the things she'd forgotten to do. Helen said that by the time she got canned, she was acting hyper, nervous, sometimes almost paranoid, and at other times she was overconfident, almost pompous."

"So what causes someone's personality to change abruptly?" asked Cordelia.

"Drugs?"

"That would be my guess. Did this Helen mention anything about the way Mandy looked?"

"Just that she'd always been very neat and tidy—and pretty. But by the end of ninety-five, when she was fired, she said she looked awful, like she'd aged ten years."

"Meth," said Cordelia.

"Was meth around back in the midnineties?"

"Probably."

"I was reading up on the symptoms, and you know what? Taking meth can cause strokes and heart problems, even heart attacks."

Cordelia tapped a finger against her chin. "You think Jack was giving it to her?"

"It's possible."

"Man, I don't know. The Jack I met doesn't seem like the type to get involved with drugs."

"There is no type. Remember the guy Jack swindled? His partner in Michigan? He said Jack had been in jail. I asked Helen about it. She said that after Mandy died and Jack took off, she'd heard some people talking. They said he spent time in prison for possession and sale of illegal substances, specifically cocaine."

"Seriously?"

"The guy is as sleazy as they come. If he did have something to do with Mandy's death, and was selling drugs on the side, it explains why he needed to get out of Traverse City fast—and why he needed to change his name and disappear."

"But look at all the good he's done in the Twin Cities, all the charity work."

"People are never all good or all bad. That's why neighbors of serial killers can say 'He was such a decent guy, so helpful.'"

A waiter arrived with their food.

"This looks fabulous," said Cordelia, slathering a slice of the raw beef with creole sauce. She closed her eyes and took a taste. "Ambrosia."

"The thing is, from what I can tell, Annie doesn't have the full story on what happened to her mother. Helen told me Mandy didn't die in a hospital, she died at home. I should have a copy of the death certificate later today."

"Could be another one of Annie's lies. You said she lied about Jack, said he was her real father."

"I don't believe I used the word 'lie.'"

"Well, that's what it was. If you want my opinion, I think we should stop focusing all our attention on Jack and start focusing on her."

When it came to Annie, Jane was totally confused. "Maybe."

15

Towers on the Green, where DreamScape Builders had its offices, was located in Apple Valley. The office park was ultramodern, with a man-made lake snaking through the campus. Annie parked her Corolla in the lot next to building 5490. On the way to the front entrance, she passed several huge metal sculptures, beams balanced on beams, all of them looking uncomfortably precarious. Spending four years with the Greeks and the Romans during college had left her with a distaste for modern art. This was a prime example. She couldn't see the point in it. Where were the beauty and the craftsmanship? It was nothing but an exercise in physics.

The first floor was an open court, with soaring ceilings and acres of polished granite. She stepped up to the reception counter and asked what floor DreamScape Builders was on. A young woman stood and pointed to a block of elevators. She told Annie to get off on six.

Riding up alone, Annie felt that same knot of apprehension in her stomach she'd first felt yesterday. She'd seen Johnny only once more at his Stillwater house—for a few seconds as she and Curt were leaving. She could feel his eyes on her all the way out to her car.

Up on six, she approached the receptionist, a middle-aged woman in a yellow paisley dress.

"My name's Annie Archer. I called earlier to see if Mr. Bowman was in. I need to talk to him."

"Mr. Bowman's not doing any business today," said the woman in a hushed tone. "There was a tragedy in his family yesterday afternoon. You'll need to come back another time. I could set up an appointment for you if you like."

"He'll see me," she said. "Just give him my name." She repeated it.

The woman appeared skeptical. She pressed a button on the intercom, picked up the phone, and spoke softly. "Mr. Bowman? There's an Annie Archer here to see you."

Annie waited, the knot in her stomach tightening.

After setting the phone down, the woman scrutinized her. "I guess you were right." She explained how to find the office.

Proceeding down a quiet hallway to the corner office, Annie found a burled wood door with Johnny's new name on it. She pushed it open.

Johnny was seated behind a Japanese-inspired inlaid wood desk, leaning back in a casual pose, dressed in a green, yellow, and orange Hawaiian shirt, much like the one he'd had on yesterday. The look on his face was impassive, but it was a forced aloofness, one that no doubt cost him.

The office was suitably extravagant. A matching inlaid wood credenza spanned one entire wall. It was filled with crystal glasses of every type and size, various wines and assorted bottles of alcohol. Along the other wall were a creamy brown leather sofa and two matching chairs. The remaining two walls were glass. His desk sat at the point where the two glass walls converged. The view of the parkland behind him was nothing short of breathtaking. There was a message in the arrangement, of course: Jack Bowman, in his own small way, was king of all he could survey.

Without speaking, he nodded to one of the chairs in front of his desk.

She sat down. Folded her hands in her lap. Smiled at him. She'd used smiles for years to mask her emotions. That was why she never trusted smiles in others. "It's been a long time."

"What do you want?"

"We'll get to that."

"Tell me how you found me?"

"No, I don't think I will. But I'm sure you're curious. If I found you, that means others could."

"Have you told anyone from Michigan where I am?"

"No."

"Have you told Curt about . . . us?"

"Not yet."

"You swear it?"

"On my mother's grave."

That seemed to relax him. Arranging his face into something more friendly, he said, "You have no idea how much I've missed you. It killed me to leave like that. I wanted to tell you my plans when we buried your mother, but you were so angry at me. I couldn't trust that you wouldn't use it against me."

"You mean like telling Glennoris where you'd gone? I hear you stole two hundred thousand from him."

His eyes narrowed. "Who told you that?"

"Is it true?"

"Of course not. That was *my* money, Annie. Not his." He watched her for a few seconds. And then his face softened. "God, you're even more beautiful now than you were back in Traverse City."

"So I'm told."

He picked up a pen and tapped it nervously against a coffee mug. "How'd you meet Curt?"

"In a bar."

"Okay, it's none of my business. But tell me this much. Are you two serious?"

"About what?"

He tossed the pen down. "You're still angry. You've come to make me pay. Fair enough. Tell me what you want and let's get this over with."

She didn't respond.

"You want money, right? You deserve something for the way I treated you."

"Think so?"

"Just stop with the attitude. All you're doing is making me mad."

"We can't have that."

"Annie, goddamn it, I love you. I always have."

For the first time, his words penetrated. "Liar."

"My life . . . it's a mess. It was a mess back in Traverse City and it still is. I've made so many mistakes. I try to learn from them, but I seem to dig myself in deep wherever I go. Do you have any idea what I'm talking about? Have you lived long enough to understand what life is really like?"

"I got the part about you not being able to learn."

He rubbed his forehead, looked around the room. "I deserve that. I deserve anything you want to dish out. Just . . . don't hate me. That would kill me. If you'll let me, I'll try to make it up to you. I've got so much now. I can give you anything you want."

The intercom buzzed.

"Go ahead," said Annie, shifting in her chair. "Answer it."

"We're not finished," he said, pressing a button. The receptionist's voice purred, "Two police officers are here to see you, Mr. Bowman."

"Did they say what they wanted?"

"Just that they need to speak with you right away."

He scratched the side of his face. "I guess you better send them in."

"I'm forgetting my manners," said Annie. "I should have offered my sympathy on the death of your wife."

His eyes filled with suspicion. "Thanks."

"Terrible accident."

"Yeah, it was."

"Have you got a life insurance policy on her, too?"

His mouth opened.

"I know about the one you had on my mom."

"It doesn't mean anything. I took one out on me, too. We were always strapped back then. If one of us died, the other wouldn't have been able to pay the rent on the apartment and have any money left over."

"Makes sense."

A knock on the door interrupted them.

"Come in," he said, rising.

Two plainclothes officers walked into the room. One was short, gray haired, and stocky, the other a bit taller and bald.

"Mr. Bowman?" asked the gray-haired cop.

Jack nodded.

"I'm Sergeant Ramos. This is Sergeant Sterling." He motioned to his partner. "We'd like to ask you a few questions. Probably best to do this privately."

"I already talked to two officers yesterday."

"Right," said Ramos, unzipping his leather jacket. "That was the Washington County Sheriff's office. We're Stillwater PD. My partner and I are taking over the case."

Jack circled around his desk and extended his hand. "Nice to meet you both." Turning back to Annie, he said, "We'll have to continue this another time."

"Fine," said Annie. Nodding to the officers, she crossed to the door. She left it slightly ajar on her way out. Standing in the hallway, she listened.

"We won't get the official autopsy report back on your wife for another few days," said Ramos. "However, after examining her yesterday, the ME said it looked like her death may not have been accidental."

"Sit down," said Jack.

Annie heard some rustling.

Ramos continued, "Your wife sustained a matrix of severe injuries yesterday afternoon. A shoulder fracture. Multiple contusions and lacerations on the head and body. As I said, we don't have the final report back yet, but preliminary indications suggest some of the injuries were inconsistent with a fall down the stairs."

"Inconsistent?"

"There's a good chance her death will be ruled a homicide."

Nothing was said for several seconds.

"Officers are on the way to your house as we speak with a search warrant."

"But . . . don't I have to be there?"

"That's certainly your right. However, I did call a few minutes ago and your daughter's home."

"I need to be there. I don't want anyone questioning her unless I'm with her."

"Legally, that's not necessary. She's over eighteen."

"She is not. Who told you that?"

"She did."

"She's seventeen. Her birthday isn't until next month. I don't want you talking to her unless I'm with her. *Is that understood?*"

Annie bent her head closer to the door. She wondered if Sunny knew something Johnny didn't want her talking about. That was certainly the implication. Surely the cops had picked up on it.

"Of course, Mr. Bowman," came the other man's voice. Sergeant Sterling. It was the first time he'd spoken. "We're just beginning our investigation. We're not accusing anybody of anything. But we have to ask questions."

"What questions?"

"Well, for one, where were you yesterday afternoon between one and five?"

"*I'm* a suspect?" He sounded indignant.

"At this point, we have to question everyone."

"If you'd just answer the question," said Ramos.

"I . . . I was at a job site in Bloomington. I was there all afternoon."

"What time did you arrive?"

"Around noon."

"And what time did you leave?"

"After I listened to my voice mail. My son called to tell me what happened at the house."

"What time was that?" asked Sterling.

"I don't know. Five? Five thirty?"

"Can anyone verify that information?"

"I suppose. I *didn't* murder my wife."

"No one is saying you did," said Ramos, trying to sound conciliatory.

"I'm not trying to be difficult. I'll help any way I can."

"That's good to know, sir."

Fearing they were all about to file out, Annie made a beeline for the elevators. Johnny had told the truth about one thing. He never learned.

16

Annie returned to Curt's condo around dinnertime, still feeling keyed up by the leftover adrenaline from her conversation with Jack. Dooley met her at the door, wagging his tail.

"Hey, little guy," she said, picking him up. "I missed you. Where's Curt?" she asked, kissing the top of his head. In the kitchen, she found a note propped against the coffeemaker.

> Annie—
> Took Dooley out just after three.
> Filled his water dish in the kitchen.
> Home by seven, promise, with takeout.
> Hope you like Thai food.
>
> C.

Annie had no intention of telling Curt where she'd been today, but she was hoping he'd be home. She needed something to take her mind off the conversation with Johnny——or Jack. She had to remember to call him Jack now, even in her thoughts.

"I feel totally . . . slimed," she said, smoothing the fur on Dooley's chest. "You know? Polluted. Like I've been wading through a sewer. That man is so slick I'm surprised he doesn't slide right off his chair."

Dooley looked up at her, cocked his head.

She'd received a call from Jane and thought about calling her back but decided against it. She did want to talk some things over with her, but figured she'd stop by tomorrow and do it in person.

"This place is a mess," she said, striding into the bedroom. Curt, as usual, hadn't made the bed or removed any of the dirty dishes from the matching nightstands.

Annie spent the next half hour working off her adrenaline buzz by cleaning. She found some fresh sheets in the laundry room and changed the bedding. As she carried the second load of dishes out to the kitchen, the landline rang. She checked the caller ID and saw that it was security. Someone was downstairs asking to be let in.

"Hello?"

"Buzz me in," came an excited female voice.

"Ah——"

"Curt?"

"No, Annie."

"Oh, shit. Look, it's Sunny. Let me in, okay?"

Annie pressed 4 on the phone pad and held it down for a good twenty seconds. She loaded a few more dishes into the dishwasher, then went to the door and opened it. Sunny stepped off the elevator a few seconds later. Her eyes looked red and puffy, as if she'd been crying.

On her way down the hall, she said, "Where's my brother?"

"Out."

She stopped halfway to the door. "Out where?"

"I don't know. But he'll be back by seven."

"Shit, shit, *shit*." She backed up against the wall and doubled over, as if she'd been kicked in the stomach.

"You're welcome to come in and wait." Annie felt sorry for her, but even more than that, she wanted a chance to talk to her.

Sunny crossed her arms and pressed them to her midsection. "What's that?" she asked warily, eyes zeroing in on Dooley.

"My dog."

She adjusted her oversized round glasses. "He's cute. Is it a he or a she?"

"A he."

"He bite?"

"No. He's very gentle."

She moved closer, offered her hand for him to sniff. "I like dogs. Curt and I had one once."

"Yeah, he told me."

"You two must be pretty tight. How long have you known him?"

"A few days."

She appeared to digest that as she entered the condo. Dropping down on the couch in the living room, she unzipped her motorcycle jacket. She looked lost. "What time is it now?"

"A little after six."

She tapped a few fingers over her small, plump mouth. "I had to leave the house. I couldn't stand being there another minute." She lowered her chin, watched Dooley circle and flip down on one of the Oriental rugs.

Annie wanted to cut through all the bull and ask her about her relationship with Jack, but she held back, knowing she needed to handle this first conversation carefully.

"My mom's death. You probably haven't heard. It might be ruled a homicide. The police were crawling all over the house today. I didn't know what to do, so I came here."

"You did the right thing."

"It's like . . ." Her mouth convulsed and she began to cry. "I can't even explain it," she said, wiping the tears off her cheeks with the back of her hand. She removed her glasses and set them on the coffee table. "My mom and I, we didn't get along. But . . . she's not *there* anymore. I can't talk to her. She's really gone . . . forever."

Annie wasn't sure if she should move closer, try to comfort her, or if she should keep her distance. She settled for taking a seat on the other end of the couch. "My mom died when I was twenty. I'm not sure I hated her. Maybe I did, I don't know. It took me years to get to the point you are now, to where I missed her so bad I knew it was an ache that would never go away."

"Yeah," Sunny whispered, choking on a sob. "That's exactly how I feel."

They sat on the couch for a while, Sunny crying, sniffing, batting at her eyes, crying some more. Annie hoped that her presence and the fact that she did understand—more than Sunny would ever know—would be a comfort.

"She was having an affair," said Sunny finally, pulling some tissues out of her jacket pocket and blowing her nose. "Nobody knows but me."

"With who?"

"A guy she works with. His name's Kristjan Robbe. They've been friends for years."

"How do you know?"

"I heard them talking on the phone."

"You think Jack knew?"

She shook her head.

"If she was cheating on him—"

"What? You think he pushed her down those stairs. Is that what Curt told you? No way. *No way.*"

"Then who?"

Her shoulders slumped. "I don't know. I don't want to know."

126

Annie's cell buzzed in the pocket of her painter pants. She pulled it free but didn't recognize the name or the number. "Hello?"

"Is this Annie?" The man had a thick Indian accent.

"Speaking." She could hear loud music in the background.

"My name is Raj Banerjee. I am the bartender at McGill's on Washington. There is a guy here who must leave. He gave me this number. His name is Curt."

"What's wrong?"

"He is falling-down drunk, that is what is wrong. We stopped serving him half an hour ago, but he will not go."

"Just a sec." She glanced over at Sunny. "Do you know McGill's on Washington?"

"Sure. Why?"

"Is it far?"

"No, it's just down the block."

Returning to the bartender, Annie said, "We'll be there in a few minutes." She flipped her cell phone closed.

"Something wrong?"

"Your brother. He's drunk and the bar wants him out."

"Drunk? Curt?"

"You think that's unusual?"

"Well, *yeah.* All he ever thinks about is med school. He's doing rotations this year. Between that and studying, he hardly has time to eat."

"Well, whatever's going on, we need to go get him. If he's really as wasted as this bartender says, I can't get him back here by myself."

"Sure, I'll help." On her way to the door, she kept shaking her head. "It's Mom's death. They were always so close. More like friends than mother and son."

No, they weren't, thought Annie. *What the hell was going on?*

A riot of bodies and loud music met Annie and Sunny as they entered McGill's a few minutes later. Annie scanned the crowd, spotting Curt sitting at the bar. His head was bent, resting against his hand. He looked about as depressed as she'd ever seen him. She pointed him out to Sunny and then began to press her way through the crowd.

Sunny was even more aggressive than Annie, pushing people out of the way in order to get to him first. She whispered something in his ear. Curt rocked back, nearly falling off the stool.

"Robbe?" He said as he tried to right himself.

When he looked up at Annie, his eyes were swimming. "Oops," he said, grinning like a little kid who'd been caught stealing a cookie.

"Let's get you out of here," said Annie, helping him to his feet.

"Yeah," he said, stumbling forward. "Good idea."

They half carried, half dragged him back down the street. As they rode silently up in the elevator, he teetered next to Annie, his eyes closed. Back in the condo, he tripped over an end table and landed flat on the floor.

"Did I miss a step?" he said, looking confused. He started to laugh, but the laughter turned quickly to tears.

"God, what happened to you?" asked Sunny, shrugging out of her jacket and trying to help him up.

Annie moved over to give her a hand and together they maneuvered him into the bedroom.

"I am *so* fucked up."

"Shut up," said Sunny, pulling off his Nikes.

Annie covered him with a quilt, realizing that this was the second time in three days that she'd poured him into bed.

"Don't go," said Curt, grabbing Annie's hand. "Stay with me. Here?" he said, fumbling with the quilt, trying to find the edge so he could lift it up.

Sunny crooked her finger, motioned Annie over to the door. With their heads together, Sunny whispered, "I don't want to tell Curt that Mom's death might be ruled a homicide until tomorrow. He's too out of it tonight. Don't you tell him either, okay? I want to be there when he hears the news."

"Sure," said Annie. "I won't say anything."

"I'm spending the night."

"Okay. You know where the extra blankets are?"

She gave Annie a pained look. "I'll be in the den if anyone wants me."

"Aren't you going to call Jack? Tell him where you are?"

She gave her head a tight shake. "He'll be okay."

"I'm sure he will. I was thinking he might be worried about you."

"He won't. He gives me a lot of space." Studying Annie for a moment, she said, "You know, you're the only person I've ever met who didn't assume I call him Dad."

"Is he your dad?"

"No."

"Did he adopt you and Curt?"

"Nope. We have no legal or biological relation to him."

"That okay with you? You never wanted him to be your father?"

"Never. He's something better. He's my best friend."

The words made Annie's stomach clench. "You two . . . do a lot of stuff together?"

"Sure."

"I'll bet he's got a fancy motorcycle."

"He collects them."

"And you go riding with him?"

"All the time."

Annie couldn't stop herself. "He ever take you riding in thunderstorms? You know, when there's lots of thunder and lightning?"

Sunny gave her a baffled look. "How'd you know that?"

"You think it's fun?"

"I love it."

If Annie had harbored hopes of convincing Sunny that Jack was a predator, this little interaction had just dashed them. It felt for all the world as if Jack had won all over again. But he wouldn't. Not this time. Because one way or another, Annie was about to drop a lighted match on his life.

17

At noon the next day, Jane was behind the bar at the Xanadu Club when Annie walked in. Jane waved and smiled, surprised at how glad she was to see her. "What are you doing here?"

"I got your phone call yesterday," said Annie, easing onto one of the stools. "Sorry I didn't call back. I stopped by the Lyme House a few minutes ago. One of the bartenders said he thought you were working over here today."

"You hungry?"

"You need to ask?"

"Have lunch with me." Jane grabbed a menu and led her to a booth. "The food here's a little different from what you had at the Lyme House. This is more American traditional. A steak house with pretensions."

Annie laughed. As she studied the menu, Jane studied Annie. She wondered where she'd spent the last couple of nights. She'd changed her clothes. The cargo pants had been replaced by black jeans, the wool sweater by a red corduroy shirt over a black scoop-necked tank top. She looked wonderful.

After they'd ordered, Jane said, "I found out a few more things that might interest you."

Annie leaned forward. "Like what?"

"Well, first off, did you know your mom was fired from her resort job at Lake Ann at the end of ninety-five?"

"She was? Why?"

"She'd become erratic, sometimes not even showing up for work."

"That doesn't sound like my mom at all."

"I was told that she'd begun changing well before that."

Annie's eyes rose, searching her memory. "Okay, yeah. She never missed any work that I knew about, but I did notice a change. I assumed it was me, that my behavior was setting her off. She'd lose her temper over the smallest stuff. A few times I felt like she was pushing me out the door, like she didn't even want me around. I didn't understand it and I let her know. And then, sometimes, she'd get supertalkative, superfriendly. She just wouldn't shut up no matter what I said, and she'd get all gushy, tell me how much she loved me and that I could tell her anything. It was weird. But I figured it was all in reaction to me, to the crap I was pulling."

"Do you remember her physical appearance changing?"

Annie shook her head.

"Do you know why your dad was in prison?" Jane put the question that way to see if Annie would deny any knowledge of it, as she had earlier.

"Nothing violent. That's all anybody would ever say about it."

Her heart sank. Annie didn't even remember the lie. "It was drugs. He was selling cocaine. Did you ever see him with any?"

"No. Honestly, I didn't."

"Your mom?"

"Are you saying she was doing drugs?"

"Meth. It was found in her blood during the autopsy. I've got a copy of the death certificate upstairs if you want to take a look."

"I can't believe it," said Annie, shaking her head, looking stunned.

"Didn't anybody comment on the change in your mom at the funeral?"

"There was no funeral. We had a small service at the cemetery. Just Dad and me. Like I said, my dad didn't have a lot of friends. Mom had some, nobody I ever paid much attention to. I didn't like any of them because I thought they were all judging me. That's why, when Dad said he wanted to keep it just family, just the two of us, I thought, great." She shook her head. "Meth. I can't believe he'd do that to her."

"How much do you know about meth?"

"Plenty. It destroys people. Rots their teeth, their bodies, their minds."

"Exactly. It also can cause strokes and heart problems. In fact, if you take too much of it, it can give you a heart attack."

"You're saying my dad *killed* her?"

"I wish I could tell you I knew for a fact what happened, but nobody knows that—except your father. I'm guessing again, but I think things were closing in on him back then. Maybe the cops suspected he was buying, or buying and selling meth. Or maybe he was just sick of his life and wanted to move on. Either way, he needed money."

"He was always restless, always looking to score big."

A waiter set a cup of coffee in front of Jane and a Diet Pepsi in front of Annie.

Jane nodded her thanks. "There's something else you need to know," she said. "Your mom didn't die in a hospital. She died at home."

"Are you serious?"

"It's all in the death certificate."

"Why did he lie to me?"

Jane had to wonder once again why Annie was lying to her.

"I could kill him for what he did." Her eyes shifted, drifted over the heads of those sitting at the bar. "You heard about his new wife.

Susan? She fell down the stairs at their house on Wednesday and died. I'm pretty sure that he pushed her."

"Why?"

"Susan was having an affair with another real estate agent. His name's Robbe. I'll bet anything Dad found out and blew a gasket. The police are calling it suspicious, but I don't think it will be long before it's ruled a murder."

Jane took a sip of coffee. "Have you talked to your father?"

"Yeah. Yesterday."

"Annie, listen to me." She pushed the mug away. "The reason I did that extra research on him was because I'm afraid. For *you*. I think he's dangerous. Maybe it's best if you just leave, go back to Colorado."

"Not until I get what I came for."

"Answers."

"Yes."

"That's all?"

"What else would there be?"

"I'm concerned for you. I don't want you to get hurt."

"What's it to you?"

"I'm not sure I could live with myself if something happened to you because I found your father for you."

"Don't worry. I'll be fine."

"Will you?"

"I'm only going to stick around a few more days."

"Do you have enough money to get home?"

"I'm okay."

"If you need more cash, you could work the bar here this afternoon."

"Really? You need the help?"

"Fridays are always busy. If you're interested, I'll have our head bartender show you the ropes."

"You're incredible, you know that?"

Jane felt a flush climb her cheeks. "Just . . . earn what you need and then go home. Go have a good life and forget about Jack Bowman."

"Good advice," said Annie. "You know what? For once I'm going to do the smart thing and take it."

No, you won't, thought Jane. *No way on earth.*

18

Kristjan and his wife were a sorry pair. While their kids were off at school, they were left alone, each trapped in silent, solitary misery.

Barbara was too depressed to do anything other than lie on the couch and watch her daily dose of adultery, duplicity, betrayal, and deception, otherwise known as the afternoon soaps. Kristjan stayed in his study, his feet propped up on a footstool, looking out the window at the snow-covered hot tub in the backyard, trying to understand how everything had gone so wrong.

In between moments of panic, Kristjan mourned the death of the woman he once thought he would be with forever. And yet, as hard as he tried to remember the path they'd taken in their minds, he couldn't understand how they'd reached the conclusion that the only way for them to live the life they wanted was to end Jack's. Hearing those words from Susan had been an out-of-body experience. It was like being an actor in a movie. *He* hadn't agreed to help, the reckless stranger inhabiting his body had. But when that one, brief moment of madness turned into cold reality the next day, he knew, at all costs, he had to stop her. With or without his permission, she would drag him into it—of that he had little doubt.

As dismal as Kristjan felt, he had to keep his wits about him. The police had ruled Susan's death suspicious. That meant they would start digging into her life. It wouldn't take long before Kristjan's name popped up. There was no proof of their affair, no smoking gun, just innuendo and office hearsay. Even if it could be proved, the fact that he and Susan were having an affair didn't mean he'd murdered her. If anything, it argued against it. Jack was the obvious suspect. He was the wronged husband who lost his temper. It was such an age-old equation that the police had to put it together.

Barbara appeared in the doorway. Her frizzy light brown hair was pulled back into a ponytail. The dark smudges under her eyes were evidence that she hadn't been sleeping well.

"A car just drove up," she said. "I think it's the police."

He dropped his feet to the carpet. "A squad car?"

"No, but two men got out. They look official."

Her words were interrupted by the doorbell.

"If you want me to," said Barbara, "I'll tell them you're not home."

"Don't be ridiculous. I haven't done anything wrong." The questioning was inevitable and he wanted to get it over with. He followed her out into the living room. When the doorbell rang again, he was the one who answered it.

The men stood outside, holding open their wallets to show off their badges. One was gray haired, kind faced, and Latino; the other younger, balding, and dour.

"Mr. Robbe?" asked the gray-haired cop.

"Yes?"

"I'm Sergeant Ramos. This is Sergeant Sterling. Could we come in?"

"Is this about Susan Bowman?"

"Yes, sir, it is."

Kristjan returned to the living room. He took a seat on the couch next to his wife—a show of solidarity he didn't feel. The cops sat across from them on matching blue velvet wingback chairs. They glanced around, taking in the furnishings, the artwork, the family photos. Kristjan assumed they were making judgments about his general wealth and income, not one of which was accurate. Once upon a time, this had been a half-million-dollar house. If they tried to sell it now, they wouldn't get half that amount. Add to that their massive credit card balances, car payments, and the two mortgages they'd taken out to pay medical bills—and other various and sundry crap they thought necessary to maintain their lifestyle—and debt, in all its modern variety, was about to swallow them whole.

"My partner and I spent the morning at the real estate office in Hastings, where Mrs. Bowman worked," said Ramos, patting his pocket and removing a notepad. "Talking to some of her coworkers—"

Barbara cut him off. "You learned about my husband's affair."

Kristjan froze. He turned to stare at her, trying to stifle his look of shock. What the hell was she doing?

"Yes," said Ramos. "We did hear about that. Is it true?"

"It's over," said Barbara. "My husband ended it several days ago."

"Is that correct, Mr. Robbe?"

Kristjan wondered how his wife knew it was over. He'd never told her that. Maybe she was just bullshitting on his behalf, trying to put a better spin on it. If so, he wasn't sure it was a smart move. "It's actually been over for quite some time, it just took me a while to say the words."

"So you were the one who wanted to end it? Or would you say it was mutual?"

"No, it was me."

"Why?"

"Because I couldn't stand all the sneaking around. It was getting too complicated." The words came out sounding false. Panic rose in his chest as he realized that if the cops thought Susan had called off the affair, it gave him a motive. He pushed himself to say more. "I guess . . . I realized I love my wife and that what I was doing was wrong." *Too weak,* he thought. *They can see right through me.*

"So you knew about the affair?" asked Sterling, watching Barbara with his chilly cop eyes.

"That's right. When it comes to manipulative bitches, my husband is very much the innocent."

Kristjan felt his neck heat up.

"Susan's been working her wiles on him for years, although I doubt he saw it that way. Kristjan wasn't her first affair, you know."

"Are you saying she was unhappily married?" asked Sterling.

Kristjan leaned back against the couch, away from his wife. "She was," he said. "Jack Bowman is a brutal man. A womanizer. You've probably already heard, but Jack wanted a divorce."

"How do you know that?"

"Susan and I had a meeting in her office on Wednesday morning. Jack phoned while I was there. I heard her talking to him about it, pleading with him not to speak to a lawyer until they could discuss it."

Ramos kept his eyes on Kristjan. "Mr. Bowman never mentioned anything about a divorce."

"Well, he wouldn't, would he? If Susan decided to fight him on it, it could have cost him millions. That's the one thing in the world that's most important to Jack. If he did murder her, that's why."

"Do you have any proof that he was asking for a divorce?"

"No. But I'm not lying. Why would I make it up?"

"Did Bowman know about your affair with his wife?" asked Sterling.

Kristjan shook his head.

"Then I don't understand. Why did he want the divorce?"

"He said he was unhappy in the marriage. He'd fallen out of love."

"Did you talk to Susan at any other time on Wednesday, the day she died?" asked Ramos.

"No. We never spoke."

"I'm thinking," said Sterling, sliding a cell phone out of the holder on his belt and checking it, "that it makes more sense that Bowman did know about your affair. He wanted a divorce because Susan was cheating on him."

"That's not what Susan told me. She said it had come out of the blue. She was completely shocked." Kristjan's mouth felt suddenly dry.

"You and Mrs. Bowman were friends for many years," said Ramos, flipping back in his notebook. "When did the affair begin?"

"About five months ago," said Kristjan. Next to him, he could feel his wife's back stiffen.

"Any particular reason?" asked Ramos. "I mean, you'd been strictly platonic friends for a long time, right?"

"Yes. Just friends."

"So why the sexual involvement?"

"Boredom" was the first word that came to his mind, though he didn't say it out loud. "I'm not sure I know how to answer that."

"She wore him down," said Barbara. "She was good-looking. Sexy, I suppose. I'd use the word 'slut,' but men view the world differently."

Kristjan's gaze rose to the ceiling.

"So the two of you have worked things out?" asked Ramos. "You've forgiven your husband?"

"It's been hard," said Barbara. "But we're trying. For the sake of the kids."

"How many children do you have?"

"Three," said Kristjan.

"Where were you Wednesday afternoon between one and five, Mr. Robbe?" asked Sterling.

"Here with me," said Barbara, pulling Kristjan's hand into her lap. Kristjan wanted to yank it away but gritted his teeth and restrained himself. "Actually, I was showing a house at one, but"—he looked over at his wife—"I was home by three, I think."

"Yes, three," she said. "I misspoke."

"Are you employed, Mrs. Robbe?" asked Ramos.

"I was. I'm an LPN. The hospital where I work has been cutting staff because of the economy. I was let go recently."

"I'm sorry to hear it," said Ramos.

"Thanks. I'm not usually home during the day, but I was on Wednesday."

"Did your husband leave the house after he arrived home?"

"No."

"What kind of car do you drive, Mr. Robbe?" asked Sterling.

"A Camry."

"What color?"

"Black."

"And you, Mrs. Robbe?"

"Me? Why would you want to know that?"

"We need to get an idea of the cars Mr. Robbe has access to."

She seemed put out. "An Accord."

"The color?"

"Gray. But Kristjan never drives my car."

"That's fine, Mrs. Robbe," said Ramos. "We just need the information for our report."

"Any particular reason?" asked Kristjan.

"One of the Bowmans' neighbors said she saw a dark sedan out in front of the Bowmans' house around three on Wednesday afternoon."

"It wasn't my husband," said Barbara, caressing Kristjan's hand.

"Just curious, Mrs. Robbe," said Ramos. "What kind of a relationship did you have with Mrs. Bowman?"

"None at all."

"You never saw her, even at company events?"

"Well, sure, I saw her, but I didn't like her, so I kept my distance."

"Didn't she find that odd?"

"She did," said Kristjan, sitting forward and extracting his hand from his wife's grasp. "She thought Barbara was rude."

"That's nothing compared to what I thought of *her*."

"You hated her?" asked Ramos.

"You bet I did. I had a right."

"Even before the affair started?"

"I knew what she was up to, knew where their friendship was headed."

"Even though your husband maintains he didn't?"

"That's right."

"Did you ever warn him about her?"

"He doesn't listen to me. He thinks I always take the negative side."

"So you're still in love with your husband?" asked Sterling.

"Very much."

"You'd do anything for him?"

"I wouldn't lie for him, if that's what you're suggesting. I don't need to. He didn't do anything wrong."

"Except cheat on you."

"That's it," said Kristjan, pushing off the couch. "We're done."

Ramos held up his hand. "We're not accusing you of anything, Mr. Robbe."

"Glad to hear it."

"We're just doing our jobs. We have to ask these questions, even though they're difficult."

"I would never have hurt Susan. I loved her."

"Even after you broke it off with her, you still cared about her?"

"Of course I did. Now, I'd like you to leave." He stalked into the front hall and opened the door.

On their way out, the officers nodded to Barbara and then to Kristjan. "We'll be in touch," said Ramos.

Closing the door behind them, Kristjan stood in the hall at the edge of the living room. "Why'd you do that?"

"Do what?"

"Lie about me being home Wednesday."

"To protect you."

"How utterly perfect that my wife feels it necessary to lie to the police so they won't think I murdered my lover."

"Ex-lover. And I don't think you murdered her. But you weren't home. I got scared. You were doing so much blathering I had to say something to back you up. Can anyone verify where you were after you showed that house?"

"No," he said grudgingly.

"Then? I helped. I did it for you."

"You've never had an unmixed motive in your life."

"How can you say that?"

The hurt in her eyes cut him deeply, but he was too embarrassed to show it. "Just . . . leave me alone." He walked back to his study and slammed the door.

19

Annie worked at the Xanadu Club until seven that night. Before she left, she asked around, hoping to find Jane. She located her sitting at the bar next to an attractive but frighteningly thin middle-aged woman. Jane introduced her as Julia.

Annie and Julia shook hands, spoke briefly about nothing in particular. When the conversation died abruptly, Annie turned to Jane and thanked her again for the job, said she'd worked five hours. Jane promised that's she'd have cash for her if she stopped by in the morning. Annie told her she'd be back, and if Jane could find more work for her to do—in the bar, the kitchen, just about anything—she'd be grateful. Jane seemed pleased. She gave her a hug and sent her on her way.

Stepping out into the frosty night air, Annie actually felt happy for the first time in weeks. She drove home listening to a CD, singing along with the Indigo Girls' "She's Saving Me," one of her favorite tunes. It didn't take long for the irony to penetrate.

As she rode up in the elevator at Curt's condo, she was still thinking about Jane. At one point during the afternoon, the bartender she'd been working with let it slip that Jane was gay. Annie had taken it in silently. She figured that the guy thought she disapproved. Not even remotely true.

Annie was beginning to realize that she was attracted to Jane. It didn't happen often with women. Most of the time, Annie stayed with guys. It was easier. Men were less complicated. If they liked you and wanted to have sex, they let you know. Annie appreciated the straightforwardness. Women were head trips. But sometimes, they were worth the effort.

Annie liked Curt, but he was young—six years younger than she was. And he was turning out to be his own kind of head trip. Not that Annie didn't owe him. She was drawn to him, for sure, to his complexity, to the hurt inside him. If Annie had an Achilles' heel, a fundamental flaw that got her in trouble over and over again, it was her empathy. She identified too easily and quickly with people who were in pain. Sometimes it impaired her ability to reason, even though, in the throes of that empathy, she always thought she was making the right decisions. She wanted to help, to comfort Curt, to be a port in the storm. There'd been an important man in her life once who'd been that for her, but at the same time she didn't want the compassion she felt for Curt to take over her life.

Unlocking the front door, Annie stepped from a bright hallway into total darkness. It took a few seconds for her eyes to adjust. When they did, she saw Curt lying on the couch in the living room, dressed in his striped flannel bathrobe and gray sweatpants. She wondered if he'd even been out today. He told her that when he had a study day at home, he sometimes took breaks up on the roof. He'd taken her up there yesterday to show her what a beautiful view he had of the river. The lock on the stairway door was cheap and opened easily with a credit card. He laughed about it. Said that his second career option was breaking and entering. Annie didn't like it up there. It scared her being up that high without railings. Curt didn't seem to notice.

Sunny sat cross-legged in the deep window well smoking a cigarette. A brittle blue light drifted in through the windows.

"You're home," said Curt. He didn't get up, just waved a couple of fingers.

"I called you a couple of times," said Annie, leaning down as Dooley hopped out of Curt's arms and trotted over to greet her. "You never answered."

"My cell's out of juice."

Annie perched on the arm of a chair opposite the couch. Dooley scrambled out of her arms and resumed his place with Curt.

"I see that you and Dools have bonded."

"I'd forgotten how much I missed having a dog around."

"How's your hangover?"

"I'll live."

Looking over at Sunny, Annie asked, "Am I interrupting something?"

"We were just talking about Mom."

"Sunny gave me the news," said Curt, "that the cops think it might be a homicide. It's kind of hard to believe, you know? I mean, who would want to hurt her?"

"According to the crime shows I watch on TV," said Annie, "the cops always look pretty hard at the husband."

"Jack had nothing to do with it," said Sunny, coming to his defense with such swiftness that even Curt looked over at her.

Somewhere in the loft, Annie heard a cell phone trill.

"If you never plan to answer your goddamn phone," said Curt, "why don't you turn it off? I'm sick of listening to it."

"Oh, for Pete's sake," grumbled Sunny, stubbing her cigarette out on a plate and then stomping past Annie into the kitchen. Coming back into the living room, she flipped it open and said hello directly into Curt's ear.

"Oh, hi, Jack." She listened for a second. "Come on, don't be mad.

I must have turned my cell off by accident. What?" She listened. "That's why I left. I wasn't ready for an interrogation." She drifted back to the window well, where she picked up her pack of cigarettes and shook one out. "Curt's place. Yeah, I told him. Sure, she's here." Turning her head away, she listened for almost a minute. "Look, I said I was sorry. Why are you so worked up?" Another pause. "You *know* I don't think that. Jesus, Jack. Yeah, yeah, I hear you. I'll leave right now. What? Sure, I'll get it. I'm hanging up now."

"Boy, he's on the warpath," said Curt, sitting up, rubbing his shoulder.

"I've never heard him that pissed before."

"Is he angry at you?"

"Nah. It's got to be the whole situation." She lit the cigarette, took a deep drag, blew smoke out the right side of her mouth.

Wake up, thought Annie. "Sunny?"

"Huh?"

"Has Jack ever hurt you?"

Even in the darkness, Annie could see a look of irritation cross Sunny's face. "Of course not. In fact, this is the first time ever that he's totally lost it with me."

"Just be careful."

Still annoyed, Sunny stood up. "God knows why, but Jack wants your cell phone number. Write it down for me."

Annie went to find a pad and pencil as Sunny and Curt said their good-byes.

"Call me tomorrow," said Curt.

"If I live through the police interrogation."

"Just . . . use your head."

"Give it a rest."

"You never know what they might have dug up."

She flicked ash onto the plate. "It's ancient history. Everyone's forgotten about it."

"There's probably a record somewhere that the cops can access."

"You were a juvenile. Juvie case files are sealed."

On Sunny's way to the front door, Annie handed her the paper with her number on it. "Be careful," she said again, not caring if it made Sunny mad.

"And call me tomorrow," called Curt.

"Yeah, yeah, yeah. When do I ever not call?"

Once they were alone, Curt pulled Annie down on the couch next to him.

"Didn't know you had a juvie record," said Annie, curious to learn what he'd done. "I've got one, too. You show me yours and I'll show you mine."

"No thanks." He played with the fingers on her left hand. "I know why Jack wants your phone number."

"Yeah?"

"First of all, he wants to do a little question-and-answer session. He's always used my friends to find out what's going on with me. That way, he doesn't have to ask directly."

"That's bizarre."

"That's Jack."

The real reason Jack wanted her number had nothing to do with Curt, but Annie played along. "Does he know you quit school?"

"No. So don't tell him. Sunny doesn't know either." He tipped his head back and gazed impassively at the city lights outside. "As soon as Jack hears I'm failing, he'll yank the condo, take back my car, and stop sending those wonderful monthly allowance checks."

"He owns it all?"

"Everything down to my underwear."

"What will you do?"

"Go find an ashram in Tibet that doesn't require underwear and become a monk." Glancing at her sideways, he added, "You think I'm kidding?"

"I hope so."

He grinned, shook his head. "The second reason he wants to connect with you is that . . . he wants to *connect* with you. He's tried to hustle every girlfriend I've had since I graduated from high school."

"Has he ever been successful?"

"A couple of times."

"Gross. What a loathsome creep."

"There's something wrong with him, that's for sure. Then again, who am I to judge?"

"Meaning?"

He shrugged. "There's something wrong with me, too."

She turned and slipped her arm across his stomach. "Don't say that."

"Why not? It's true."

"Does Sunny know he tried to seduce your girlfriends?"

"Hell, no."

"Why not tell her?"

"Because it would hurt her for no good reason."

"I'm not sure that's true. Has he ever hit on Sunny?"

Curt backed away from her. "Hell, no."

"You know that for a fact?"

"Jesus, why would you even think something like that?"

"How would you describe Sunny's relationship with him?"

"Hero worship. She idolizes him."

"That's not healthy."

"I'm the last person to make judgments about emotional health."

Annie laid her head against Curt's chest. "You're too hard on yourself."

"I'm not hard enough."

"I don't get why you're so critical of everything you do. I mean, your mom just died. You've got to give yourself time to recover." But as she thought about it, she realized that the night they first met he was also down, and at that point, his mother was still alive.

He brushed a tear away from his cheek. "I can't seem to stop crying. It's been like this all day."

"Have you eaten?"

"I'm not hungry."

"You need to eat. I'll make us peanut butter and jelly sandwiches."

"If it comes with a large glass of bourbon, I might be able to choke it down."

Annie was about to get up when he pulled her back into his arms.

"Stay here," he whispered, holding her tight.

Annie's heart broke for him. "Should we go in the bedroom?"

"No. Beds demand too much. Let's just stay here."

She could smell alcohol on his breath.

"Don't ever leave me, promise?"

"I won't leave," she whispered.

"Ever?"

"Ever's a long time."

"I know. It's okay if you want to lie."

"Curt—"

"Annie, just *lie* to me."

"I'll never leave you," she said.

He closed his eyes. "Thank you."

20

By nine that night, Jane was home, sitting at the computer in her study, digging into Annie's past. She refused to remain in the dark any longer.

Checking her e-mail, she found that Cordelia had sent the photos Jack had taken at their spur-of-the-moment dinner party last summer. She studied the photos of Susan, Sunny, and Curt. It was good to put a face with a name. Susan was pretty. Diminutive. Red-haired. Professional looking in her gray slacks and navy blue blazer. Both Sunny and Curt had dark hair. Sunny's was cut in a classic pageboy with straight bangs. Both were thin, but while Curt appeared bookish, intellectual, and not terribly attractive, Sunny's good looks, round glasses, and bright red lipstick made her seem almost glamorous.

There was only one photo of Jack. He was seated at the table with his arm around Sunny. He looked bloated and tired. Jane dragged the photos to her iPhoto application. She could study the pictures of the house later.

With the room lit only by the computer screen, Jane Googled "High School Traverse City Michigan." Up popped several sites. She clicked on various links until she narrowed her search to the three schools Annie might have attended. Checking the individual home pages, she found that none gave information about former students.

Clicking on the links to various reunion pages, she searched for the year Annie would have graduated—1995. In a section of the Central High School reunion site, she found e-mails from alumni who had attended a tenth reunion event a few years back. One of the notes said:

Great to see all my old buddies. Casey, still the jock. And Britt, that baby is gorgeous. Too bad so many people didn't show. Bummer. Thought maybe Annie Archer might come. What the hell happened to her? Anybody know? I was totally surprised when she just disappeared like that. I wonder if she finished high school somewhere else. If anybody's heard, e-mail me. She was cool and I'd like to get in touch.

Aaron Dunne

Jane began a mental list of Annie's lies. First: She said she hadn't left home until after she graduated from high school. Second: By inference, she'd let Jane think that Jack Bowman was her natural father. Third: She'd said her dad had never been in prison. The question in Jane's mind was: What else had Annie lied about?

Jane brought up Intelius.com, deciding to save herself some time. She paid for a background summary of Annie in Colorado. Included in the report would be current and previous addresses, a criminal background check, bankruptcies and liens, small claims and judgments, and relatives and associates. In a few minutes she would have it all. Everything she never wanted to know.

"I miss you *so* much," cried Cordelia. She was going for pathos but ended up just sounding shrill. It was a sorry day when she couldn't even get pathos right. She was lying on her bed, her three cats all reclining on various parts of her body, talking to Melanie in Kansas City. "When are you coming home?"

"The middle of next week."

"I won't last that long. I am completely . . . overwrought."

"I can tell. But then, you always have been."

"True. It's part of my idiom."

"I miss you, too, babe, but you know what it's like here in February. Everyone in my family—with one significant exception—was born a Pisces. I'm drowning in balloons and being poisoned by cheap marble cake."

"Tell me again why you were born in August?"

"My parents took a cruise that December. I was conceived in the Caribbean, and dedicated to the proposition that all humans should stay out of boxes, especially those of a totalitarian nature."

"I miss your wordsmithery."

"I miss your lips."

"Oh, baby!"

"Give Hattie's picture a kiss from me."

"I will."

"Gotta go. My mom is hollering. It's time to wrap more presents. You staying put tonight?"

"I thought I'd join Robert and Andrew for a late movie."

"Well, I love you. Talk to you tomorrow."

"The morrow, yes. Good-bye, my love, and flights of angels—"

But before she could finish, Melanie had hung up.

Floating down the stairs from her loft-within-a-loft bedroom, encased, as it were, in a cloud of longing, Cordelia was just about to slip into her down parka when there was a knock on the door.

Visitors had to phone up to be allowed in, unless they had a key that would get them past level three in the freight elevator—or unless they lived in the building. Or, and this was the big or, some moron let them ride up without asking if they lived in the building, thus circumventing the security system.

The knocking grew louder, more frenzied.

"Hold your horses." Whipping open the door, Cordelia found her sister, Octavia, standing outside in the hallway.

Cordelia's mouth dropped open. "What . . . what are you doing here?"

"Frankly, it's a tangle."

"That's a line. I can't place it."

"*The Lion in Winter.*"

"Of course." Coming to her senses, Cordelia nearly knocked her sister down rushing into the hall. "Is Hattie with you?"

"Hattie?" said Octavia. "Why would you think I'd bring her? This isn't about Hattie. It's about me and my crumbling marriage." Swinging her hips like a fashion model, she undulated into the loft. She wore a mink coat over a beaded black camisole, black wool slacks, and open-toed sling-back spikes. She dropped her mink on one of the sofas and draped herself over a chair by the newly installed wet bar.

Cordelia watched all this, stunned. She felt faint. Waving air under her nose, she leaned against the door to steady herself.

"You don't look well," said Octavia. "Something wrong?"

"If you're here, who's taking care of Hattie?"

"The nanny, of course."

Of course. "Is she a good person? Trustworthy? Kindly? Loves kids?"

"I assume so. Radley hired her."

"You *assume*?"

"Hattie's fine, Cordelia. But her mother's marriage isn't."

In Cordelia's opinion, Octavia was an amalgam, but one with a theme. She'd taken her moral imperatives from two sirens of literature—Becky Sharp, the manipulative, amoral anti-heroine of Thackeray's *Vanity Fair,* and the amoral, manipulative, deceptive, and ultimately mad Lady Macbeth.

"Why do you think I give a rip about your marriage?" said Cordelia, pressing her lips together in order to keep from strangling on her own exasperation.

Octavia continued on as if she hadn't heard the comment. "You're my sister. You've got to help me think this out."

"After what you've done?"

"Done? What have I done?"

Cordelia felt seasick, or airsick, or carsick, or just plan giddy and dizzy. "I must be dreaming."

"Well, if it's a dream, it's a nightmare. Now come in here and sit down. Sit."

The scene was pure David Lynch—the juxtaposition of the banal with the grotesque. Cordelia had always hated David Lynch movies. Now she understood why. They felt too much like home.

With a frigid midnight wind wheezing through the porch screens, Jane opened the kitchen door and let Mouse, her brown Lab, back into the house. He trotted behind her to the living room, where she'd built a fire. As the wood snapped and blazed in the hearth, she resumed her seat on the rocking chair and picked up her second brandy of the evening. Mouse curled up on the rug at her feet.

"You haven't met Annie," she said, confiding, as she often did, in her dog. "The whole situation has me mystified." She took a sip, mulling over what she'd learned from her Internet search. "On the one hand, Annie seems so decent, so likable. But she's secretive. And, as much as I hate to say it, she hasn't been telling me the truth."

Mouse stretched out on his side, gave a deep sigh.

"You still listening?" asked Jane.

His tail thumped the rug a couple of times.

"Good. Now, here's the real story. Annie's birthday is October ninth. She turned eighteen at the beginning of her senior year in high school. Two weeks later, she applied for a driver's license in Boulder, Colorado. That means she never graduated, even though she said she didn't leave home until she had. She did earn a degree from the University of Colorado at Boulder in 2005, so she must have gotten a GED somewhere along the line. Now, here's the really troubling part.

"Annie was picked up for prostitution three months after she arrived in Boulder. It's a class 3 misdemeanor in Colorado. Since it was a first offense, she got off with a hundred-dollar fine. But she was picked up again eight months later for the same thing. That time, she was fined five hundred dollars. And then, a year later, she was arrested a third time. Again, for prostitution. She paid another fine but also had to serve a month in jail. After that, her record is clean."

Jane looked down at Mouse and saw that his eyes were closed. "That's okay, boy. You don't know her."

Jane had learned something else in the last couple of days. Background searches were frustratingly silent about everything you really wanted to know. Had Jack molested Annie as a teenager? Was that part of the reason she'd fallen into prostitution? Was she still a prostitute? She did work at a resort in Steamboat Springs, but it was part-time. Jane doubted she earned much money.

"How much pressure does it take before a young mind fractures?" she asked Mouse, watching his sleeping eyes flutter. "Who *is* Annie Archer?"

Nolan would tell her to back off, leave it alone. He might be right. Humans were never simple. Or logical. And there was never just one. Of anyone.

21

Curt was still asleep the next morning when Annie left for a meeting with Jack. He'd had a rough night, tossing and turning, unable to get much rest. They held each other for a long time, but Curt never tried to take it any further. Around one, they got up to watch TV in the living room. Annie went back to bed an hour later, but Curt stayed up, drinking directly from a bottle of Maker's Mark. As far as she could tell, he rarely fell asleep, unless he was dead drunk, until the early morning hours.

It didn't take a doctorate in psychology to see that Curt was in trouble. He was erratic, dependent on alcohol to mellow his moods. He refused to talk about what was bothering him, except to say that he felt empty. But he was quick to point out that Annie's presence in his life made him feel less alone. In just a few days he'd gone from offering his place as a pad to crash, to pleading with her never to leave. He didn't seem to understand the pressure he was putting on her.

Jack was waiting for her at a table by the windows when she walked into Dunn Bros coffeehouse around ten. She could tell he was having a serious problem with his face. He didn't know how to arrange it. It was actually kind of funny, watching him move through various emotional postures—from sternness to anger to concern to hurt to affection and back to sternness again. She ordered an espresso, suppressing a smile as she waited by the counter for it to come up. She had on sunglasses, so she could watch him easily, her head toward the barista but her eyes on him. All the while, Jack sat at the table running through his rather limited gamut of emotions.

"You're late," he said as she approached.

She took off her sheepskin jacket and hung it on the back of the chair. "You're early."

That earned a slight smile. He'd always liked spunk.

Once she was settled, her sunglasses resting next to her espresso, he put his elbows on the table and leaned toward her. "I'm sorry, honey. I hurt you and I deserve your anger. I should have tried harder to find you."

Conciliation. Interesting move.

He nodded out the window. "Nice wheels over there."

She looked. "Which one?"

"Across the street. The black Cadillac Escalade."

"Is it yours?"

"No," said Jack, sliding the title and the keys across to her. "It's yours. It's a V-8, with a Bose sound system, interior leather and wood trim, and it's OnStar ready."

"You sound like a car salesman."

"It's a beauty, isn't it? Just a little gift to show you how happy I am that you're back in my life."

"Are you?"

"Absolutely. But, honey, I need to know what else you want from me. The car's just the beginning. Like I already said, I want to make it up to you. But you've got to tell me how."

"Okay." She folded her hands on top of the table. "Tell me the truth."

"About what?"

"My mother."

"What about her?"

"How she died."

He shifted back in his chair. "You know how she died. A heart attack."

"What caused it?"

"How the hell should I know?"

"She was a meth addict."

"Who told you that? Where are you getting all this ridiculous information? That I stole from Glennoris. That your mother took meth."

"From a friend."

"From that Lawless woman? You shouldn't hang around with people like her. She's a notorious dyke, in case you didn't know."

It never occurred to her that he'd have her followed, but it shouldn't have come as a complete surprise. "My mother was doing meth when she died. It was in the toxicology report submitted with the autopsy. Death records don't lie, Johnny. Did you get her hooked on it? You took out that insurance policy on her knowing you could send her to heaven or hell anytime you wanted. How'd it work? Did you give her an extra bump the night she died? Meth causes heart attacks if you take enough."

"You're way off. That's bullshit."

"Oh, and by the way, I found out Mom died at home, not in a hospital."

"Of course she died at home. Where'd you get the idea she died in the hospital?"

God, he was good. He could twist just about anything and make it come out the way he wanted. Simple denial worked like a charm when you were backed into a corner. She'd have to remember that. "You play with people, Johnny, try to confuse them. But you're not confusing me. I know what you told me. I saw my mother changing before I left, but I figured it was all my fault."

"Look, honey, if your mom was doing meth, she wasn't getting it from me."

"You didn't notice something was wrong when she got fired? When her personality started changing?"

"I knew, sure. I kept telling her to go see a doctor, but you remember what she was like. She refused. Absolutely flat-out refused."

"And Susan. You murdered her, too. You found out about the affair she was having."

His frown deepened. "I didn't know—not until yesterday when the police asked me about it. Susan was a high-priced whore. I should have seen it years ago. I'm too gullible."

"You're the victim, all right. Poor Johnny. But you get even. With my mom. With Susan."

"That's just crazy, honey. But if it's what you think, then we're back to my original question. What do you want?"

"*The truth.*"

He played with his coffee cup, rubbed the back of his neck, gave himself some time to think it over. "Okay, okay. So I gave your mom the meth. I was selling it back then, making a bundle, too. The drug was pretty new; nobody took it very seriously. It was a great high, and it was fairly cheap compared to other drugs. Your mom loved it. I mean, I didn't force her to take it, but I could always count on it to make her feel, you know . . . in the mood. What's not to like about that? It took the edge off, made her happy, made her feel beautiful. She lost a bunch of weight and thought it was fantastic."

"Were you using it?"

"Nah."

"Were you selling cocaine, too?"

"Too dangerous. But the meth sales made me a ton of money. Your mom was happy and so was I. You know how strapped we were back then."

"Mom knew you were dealing?"

"Hell, no. Well, not at first. But later, yeah. By then she didn't care, as long as she got hers free of charge."

"And the night she died?"

He ran a hand over his unshaven face. "She took too much. Simple as that. I came home and found her in bed. She wasn't breathing."

"I don't believe you. You wanted that insurance money so you could get out of town. You planned to clean out the joint bank account you had with Glennoris. You were going to put together the biggest bankroll you could and then disappear. My mom wasn't part of the picture."

"No, Annie, listen to me. This is the absolute truth. I swear. Your mom and me, we couldn't afford the condo any longer because she wasn't working. We were planning to move to one of the places I was rehabbing. She was sick. I did push her to see a doctor, but she wouldn't go. When she died like that, out of the blue, I panicked. I thought the cops would figure out I was dealing again, so after the funeral, before they could put together a case against me, I got out of there. I had to disappear. And yes, okay, I did take the money Glennoris and I had in that bank account, but I was scared to death. You may not believe it, but I loved your mom, more than any other woman I've ever known. You asked for the truth and that's it."

Annie looked down at her espresso, fingering the tiny handle, forcing back the urge to toss it at him.

"Stop judging me for a second and listen. It's hard for me to admit it, but when it comes to personal things, I've always been a complete screwup."

"A screwup?" He was letting himself off way too lightly. Under other circumstances, she would have challenged him harder, but she had a specific reason for asking for this meeting. She'd needed to hang on to a shred of his goodwill. Jane was right. Jack was a danger to her. If he thought she was about to tell the police what she knew, he'd react to protect himself. She needed to buy herself some time because she didn't want to leave yet. She had three big reasons: Jane, Curt, and Sunny. Also, if the police were about to arrest Jack for the murder of his wife, she wanted to be around to watch. Hell, she wanted a front-row seat.

"Tell me about Sunny," said Annie.

"What about her?"

"You know what I'm saying."

He looked confused. "No, honestly, I don't."

"What happened last night when she got home? You were pretty pissed."

"Sure I was angry. I called her all day, but she never called me back. I didn't know what to think."

"She's okay, right?"

"Of course she's okay. Jesus, what do you take me for? Come on, Annie. We're just spinning our wheels here. Tell me what the hell you want."

She paused for effect, then dropped the bait. "Money."

Like the sun coming up over the mountains, a smile spread across his face. "Now we're getting down to it. How much?"

"You're not going to like it."

"Just give me the figure."

"I want half a million dollars now, the other half in, say, two years."

He folded his arms, ready to bargain. "Too much."

"It's not enough."

"I don't have it."

"Of course you've got it. In fact, I doubt you'll even miss it."

He stroked the side of his face with the back of his fingers. "In return, I get what?"

"My silence."

"Why should I trust you? You could use me as a bank for the rest of my life."

"Would that be so bad? You owe me, Johnny. This way, we both get what we want. You get to be Mr. Big Shot and I get some stability. I'm not greedy. I just want a little financial peace. I plan to live in the mountains. As far as I'm concerned, that's where I'll stay for the rest of my life. I need that money, Johnny. I'm not leaving without it."

He seemed pleased, as if they'd ventured at last into territory he could understand. "Maybe you did learn something from me after all. Let's say I could get it in a few days. You'd leave?"

"Not right away. Because of Curt. He's hurting. I want to stick around until he has a better grip. Susan's death hit him hard."

"And you know just how to help ease the pain."

She clenched her teeth, rose from the table, and slipped her jacket off the back of the chair. "Do we have a deal?"

"Let me think about it."

"You've got one minute. I'm not playing games."

This time, he grinned. "All right, already. I'll call you when I've put it together. With the police crawling all over my life, I have to be careful. Just . . . stay calm. Play with Curt. You're not in love with him, are you?"

"No."

"Didn't think so."

Sliding the title and the car keys back across the table, she said, "You can keep the bribe. What's it get? Two gallons per mile? Takes a real meathead to buy a car like that these days."

He smiled, stretched his arms over his head. "Sticks and stones, Annie. Sticks and stones."

22

Cordelia had been hiding in her bedroom since the wee hours of the morning, when Octavia had fallen asleep midsentence. She took the momentary lull in her sister's soliloquy as her cue to tiptoe up to bed and hope like hell that Octavia kept on snoring. On the off chance that she could get her to listen to reason about Hattie, Cordelia decided not to drop-kick her through the front windows, though remaining cool in a situation like this was not part of her usual idiom.

But now, lying in bed staring up at her semi-Sistine ceiling—the hand of God reaching out to touch the gloved finger of Minnie Mouse—just thinking about Octavia's sudden appearance sent her into paroxysms of outrage.

Jane had once called Cordelia and Octavia "two peas in a very strange pod," but Octavia surpassed even Cordelia when it came to strangeness.

Hearing footsteps on the stairs, Cordelia pulled the quilt up past her nose. "Vampira wakes," she whispered to no one in particular, her eyes zigzagging from one side of the room to the other. There was nowhere to hide.

"So, back to what I was saying," said Octavia, lifting the quilt and flumping down. "What am I going to do?"

Cordelia heard a crunch. She turned and saw that Octavia was eating an apple.

"Well?" said Octavia, examining the fruit for imperfections. "You think you're the heir to the Dear Abby franchise. Give me the benefit of your accumulated wisdom." She elbowed Cordelia in the ribs. "And don't hog the quilt." She yanked it over her, revealing Cordelia's red flannel pajamas.

"You are *such* a blanket hog," said Cordelia, yanking it back. Octavia had on her mink coat. She didn't even *need* a blanket. Oh, the selfishness. The narcissism. "Not to change the subject, but I'm not sure that's the best hair color for you."

"It's called Chocolate Raven."

"Seems more like a pelt than a raven."

"Just stay on point. What am I going to do?"

Cordelia bunched the quilt up under her chin and asked the most obvious question. "How many husbands did Elizabeth Taylor have?"

"Ah, good point. Let me think." She counted on her fingers. "Eight marriages to seven husbands."

"Richard Burton twice."

"Of course."

"Well, then, at that rate, you've got two more to go before you reach her. I'd say she's the gold standard, wouldn't you?"

"But," said Octavia, turning on her side, "is that really a record I should shoot for? Or will my fans think ill of me for being so incurably romantic?"

"Or unlucky."

"Yes, luck has a great deal to do with it."

168

"Most women," said Cordelia, warming to the subject much more than she had last night, "don't marry everyone they have affairs with. That's your basic problem."

"Too true. But I've always been essentially monogamous, until it was clear there was no hope. You can't fault me there." She propped her elbow next to Cordelia's pillow. "You know, Radley wants to adopt Hattie. He adores her. But that was where I drew the line."

Cordelia had already heard some of this from one of the private investigators she'd hired, the woman who'd infiltrated Octavia's house in Northumberland as a cook. "I agree, it wouldn't be wise to allow the adoption." She tried to keep her voice calm. "But if you divorce him, where will you and Hattie live? You've still got that mansion in Connecticut."

"That mausoleum?" She shivered. "No way am I ever going back there."

"Okay, then there's your apartment in New York."

"Ah, New York." She sighed. "How I long to return to civilization. But the apartment is too small. And I've sublet it. No, that wouldn't work. Another apartment, perhaps. Something overlooking the park?"

"Where would Hattie go to school? She'll be entering kindergarten next fall."

Octavia frowned. "Will she?"

"Do you ever spend *any* time with her?"

"Well, of course I do. But I've been very busy this past year. I did that film in Italy. And then the radio work in London for the BBC. When it hit me that my marriage wasn't working, I took a long trip back to the Italian countryside to think about my life. You can't expect me to do that with a child hanging around my neck."

"You know," said Cordelia, trying to be as low-key as possible, "Hattie could always come back here to live with me." As soon as Hattie was under her roof again, Cordelia intended to petition for custody.

"No," said Octavia, waving away the idea. "I don't think that's such a good idea. She got awfully attached to you while she was here. You're not her mother, you know. I am. It was confusing for her."

Octavia was so gargantuanly jealous of Cordelia's relationship with Hattie. "I've always thought of myself as the Auntie Mame in Hattie's life."

Octavia reared up. "What does that make me? Mame's ward was an orphan."

One could only hope.

"You're not helping. Do I or do I not divorce Radley?"

"Do you love him?"

"Not anymore. He's let me down, just like every other man has when it comes right down to it. And he's become so judgmental. He used to worship me, but now it's nitpicking from morning until night. I mean, does *anyone* expect *me* to live with *that*?"

"I don't know much about English law," said Cordelia. "Is nitpicking grounds for divorce?"

Octavia flew off the bed and began to pace, fists pressed to her hips. "I want out. You've helped me see that. But he's going to fight me, I just know it."

"Does he still love you?"

"Of course he loves me. What's not to love?"

"Does he want your money?"

"Thank god, no."

"Then what?"

"Hattie. He wants Hattie. Even if we divorce, he wants to keep her with him."

Cordelia sat up because her heart had lodged so firmly in her throat she thought she was going to choke. "But you're not—"

"Of course not."

Closing her eyes, Cordelia asked, "Have you found someone else?"

"There are always men buzzing around me, pursuing me."

"Anyone in particular?"

A dreamy, faraway look passed across her face. "Oh, I can tell you're going to drag it out of me sooner or later. Yes. An Italian count. Penniless, of course. They all are. But so beautiful."

In other words, thought Cordelia, *another playboy loser.*

"He wants to marry me. Desperately." She whispered his name. "Conte Giacomo Basalmo."

"And you want to marry him?"

"At his family's villa in Abruzzi. Next spring. You know what that means, don't you? I'd become a *contessa*. It suits me, don't you think? I spent a week at the villa with him in January. I could hardly tear myself away. England is so dreary."

"But back to planet Earth. What if Radley won't give you a quick divorce? What if he threatens to string it out for years?" Steeling herself, Cordelia continued, "Would you allow him to adopt Hattie as a last resort?"

"No. Never."

Meaning, yes, probably.

"Why don't I fix us some breakfast," said Cordelia, planting her bare feet squarely on the wood floor.

"Breakfast would be nice. You always know how to cheer me up. But then I must get going. I have a plane to catch. I stopped here on my way to California. I have a meeting with a producer next week in Hollywood."

And if you don't make it, thought Cordelia, *if you disappear without a trace, who really cares?*

Kristjan spent Saturday morning at the Maplewood Mall, drifting around with no particular purpose other than getting out of the house and away from Barbara. They'd barely spoken since yesterday afternoon. He still couldn't believe she'd inserted herself into the conversation with the police the way she had, lied about him being home. She might have thought she was being helpful, but in truth, she was only digging him in deeper.

Shortly after the police left, Kristjan remembered that he *had* bumped into someone he knew on Wednesday afternoon. It was another agent, Morton Alseth—not an agent from his office but a man he'd taken his initial training with many years ago. Kristjan had been on the way into the Caribou Coffee in Stillwater as Morton had been on his way out. They'd spoken for only a few seconds, but if Morton found out that Kristjan was maintaining he'd been home from three on, Barbara's lie would blow up in both their faces.

For the past two nights, Kristjan had slept on the couch in his study. He was bewildered and angry, grieving for Susan, but also wondering if his relationship with Barbara had finally gone off the rails. The fact that she insisted she still loved him only made things more difficult. The irony was, the stress from their tanking financial situation had damaged their relationship, perhaps beyond repair, while at the same time had been the major impetus for keeping them together. Why think about divorce if you couldn't afford to live apart?

Kristjan ate an early lunch in the food court, sitting alone at a table. He arrived at his car dealership in West St. Paul shortly after noon. His intent was to keep his life as normal as possible. It wouldn't be long before Jack was arrested. A circumstantial case could easily be made. But patience had never been Kristjan's strong suit.

While his car was hoisted up in one of the bays and the oil changed, he sat in a room directly off the showroom floor and read a magazine. It always took longer then expected because the mechanics always found something extra that needed to be repaired. Free oil changes were the most expensive thing going. It was nothing short of a scam. And that set him off on another internal rant. In fact, his temper had barely been under control since the morning he'd met with Susan in her office.

After writing out a check for $374.19, he drove around for a while, again with no real purpose, ending up at the Mall of America. He parked on the south end by the movie theaters and took the elevators up to the top floor. Nothing much appealed to him, but he eventually decided on *Jumper*, mainly because Diane Lane was in it.

Two hours later he walked out of the theater and glanced at his watch. It was still early. Too early to go home. His goal was to get back after the kids were asleep. If there was another argument, at least they wouldn't hear it.

Scanning the list of movies, he found another one that sounded okay—*Cloverfield*. He'd always liked monster flicks, but this one didn't hold his interest.

Fifteen minutes after the movie started, he found himself at a McDonald's buying a chocolate shake and cursing Barbara. With her sulking stares, she'd driven him out of the house and forced him to waste a perfectly good day, one he'd never get back. He might not be all that philosophically inclined, but he did think about his life. He knew all actions were motivated. That raised a particularly puzzling question. Knowing Susan as well as he did, knowing her history with men, why had he allowed himself to get involved with her? What made him think their relationship would be different?

Susan was the only middle-class person he'd ever met who insisted—actually believed—that her family was poor. He'd visited the family home in Fort Worth once a number of years ago. It was a spacious sixties rambler in a lovely middle-class neighborhood. Her father was a personnel manager at one of the major utility companies, and her mother was a grade school teacher. There was nothing deprived about them. And yet, for Susan, who went to school with oil men's daughters, it must have felt like poverty in her teenage soul.

When she met Yale Llewelyn, a young surgeon with a promising career ahead of him, she allowed herself, for the first time, to become serious about a man. Kristjan didn't doubt that she'd loved Yale. He had no doubt that she'd loved Jack in the beginning, too. But with Susan, cold calculation was never off the table. Deep down, Kristjan admired that quality in her. It meant she could be ruthless, even conniving, but at least she'd been honest about what she valued.

Susan took what she wanted and rationalized away any personal guilt. Yale had been a good husband, but distant, often absent. Jack had been a lousy husband, but demanding of her time and attention. She'd used them both to make her dreams come true, but in the final analysis, something was still missing.

To Kristjan's way of thinking, the missing ingredient was a man she could truly love, one who returned her love wholeheartedly, a man who was neither a brute nor a depressive. The life they both yearned for might have had a chance to become reality if they hadn't both been blinded by the notion of having it all. Kristjan was grateful that he'd come to his senses before they went through with their plans, but in the end, his attempt to get Susan to listen to reason had come too late. With her feelings of entitlement leading the charge, she'd gone ahead full tilt. It was possible that her actions—and his—could still drag him over a cliff.

Kristjan had dinner at a steak house in Woodbury. He felt better after he got a couple of Manhattans under his belt. He lingered over the meal, his thoughts dulled by the alcohol, until he figured he'd waited long enough.

He walked in the front door a few minutes after ten. The lights were off in the living room. One dim light burned in the kitchen. He could smell that Barbara had burned dinner, whatever it was. He stepped over to the stairway and looked up, seeing a light on under the master bedroom door. He assumed Barbara was up there watching TV. Feeling beat, he decided another Manhattan was the cure. But before he could make it to the kitchen, a light snapped on behind him. He turned to find Barbara in the hallway.

"What's going on?"

She raised the nose of her father's hunting rifle. "I packed your clothes." Nodding to several pieces of luggage by the living room couch, she said, "Take them and leave."

"Why—"

"You shouldn't have left your laptop in the study."

His face blanched. "We had an agreement. You don't use my laptop and I don't use yours."

"All your rules made me wonder what you were hiding. I'm glad I took a look. Otherwise I wouldn't have known you were planning to murder me."

The comment caused him to move back a step.

"Those websites you've been looking at? It's all there. Howto murderyourwife.com. How to make a murder look like a suicide. Or an accident."

"I wasn't . . . no, no. I never—"

"You're incredibly stupid, you know that? What kind of imbecile looks at those sorts of websites on his own computer?"

"I . . . I—"

"Get out."

"Just . . . wait. I need to explain."

"What's to explain? I don't even know who you are anymore."

"You've got to believe me. I never intended to harm you in any way."

She waved the rifle toward the luggage. "I've already called a lawyer. He advised me to keep the laptop."

"But . . . no, you can't. It has all my business information on it."

"Tough. My lawyer thinks we may have an attempted murder case against you."

Kristjan's mind reeled. How could he tell her the truth, that he'd been looking at those sites because Susan had asked him to?

"If nothing else, I won't have any problem proving you're an unfit parent. You'll never see those kids again."

"Barbara, *please*."

"You're a passionless man, Kristjan. A coward and a fool. You were under her spell, I understand that. Who's to say what you two were planning?"

His mind latched on to a thought. "You lied to the police for me. But there's a snag. I ran into someone the afternoon Susan died who could identify me, verify that I wasn't home when you said I was. If I call him, I can prove you lied. I never asked you to do that. I didn't need your lie because I didn't murder Susan."

She held the rifle steady, her feet set wide apart. "Maybe you did, maybe you didn't. But if the police want to know why I lied, I've got all the proof I need on that laptop. I was afraid for my life. You made me do it."

"But Barbara——"

"No more," she said, her voice quiet but menacing. "You'll wake the kids." She waved the rifle toward the door. "If I see your face around here or anywhere near me or my children, I'll call the police. Either that, or I'll use the rifle."

There was nothing he could do. He picked up the suitcases and hefted them over to the door. Stopping for just a second in the entryway, he took one last look around him. He glanced back at Barbara, hoping she might take pity on him, but all he saw in her eyes was contempt.

23

"All I can say is, her showing up like that was a real beaker of acid in the face." Cordelia sat amid the pillows on Jane's office couch, fussing with her gold lamé turban.

Jane had propped one of her legs on an open bottom desk drawer. She was concerned, although she'd never voiced it to Cordelia, that after a year and a half away, Hattie might have forgotten Cordelia. She was awfully little—only five.

"Octavia acted like we'd been cut off in the middle of a sentence and she'd come by to resume it. She didn't want to talk about Hattie—or anything else, for that matter. Just her. She never asked a word about you—or me."

"You didn't learn anything about Hattie?"

Before she'd barreled into Jane's office, Cordelia had stopped to scoop up a bowl of fresh buttered popcorn from a cart in the pub. She popped a kernel into her mouth and looked miserable. "Hattie has a new fish tank. Radley, apparently, likes fish. I mean, what a cold, un-huggable sort of pet. And how incredibly *boring*. What can you do with a fish? You watch through the glass as it swims to the right, swims to the left, swims up, swims downs, swims behind a plant, swims out from behind the plant. And then what? You watch the same thing all over again. I suppose if one fish eats another fish, a little drama is injected into their little fishy universe. But, I mean, *really*. Why not just watch mold grow on a rotting tomato. It's about as exciting."

"Has anyone ever said that you're too timid with your opinions?"

Cordelia tossed a fistful of popcorn at Jane's head.

Sensing a food opportunity, Mouse got up from the rug in front of the cold fireplace, shook himself, and came over to see if anything had fallen on the floor.

"She left right after breakfast," said Cordelia, her chin sinking to her chest. "I'm no closer to getting Hattie back than I was before she came."

"Do you think there's a real possibility she'll let Radley adopt her?"

Cordelia's eyes rose to the ceiling. A few tense seconds passed before she erupted. "Yes. He'll make sure it happens before they divorce. That way, he can petition for full physical and legal custody as part of the final decree. Octavia will demand that the details be kept quiet. She can't let the world know what a disaster she is as a mother."

"Maybe world opinion will prevent her from allowing Radley to adopt Hattie."

"Nothing stands in her way when she's got a new man in her sights. At least Radley seems to love Hattie. If Hatts ended up leaving with Octavia, what happens then? Octavia drags her along to the villa in Abruzzi? And when the relationship with the count bites the Italian dust, what next? She gets dragged to a feed bin in Bohemia where Octavia consummates her next love affair with a cheese maker?"

Jane crunched down hard on a popcorn kernel to keep from laughing. "A feed bin in Bohemia?"

"An ice rink in Far Rockaway with a Zamboni driver? A rice

paddy in Mongolia with one of the hordes? Octavia likes to couple in the unusual, out-of-the-way places. She finds it stimulating."

"She told you that?"

Waving the subject away, Cordelia said, "Oh, she's been that way forever. We both enjoy the occasional oddball trysting site."

"You do?"

"Lower your eyebrow, Janey. You're looking way too Midwestern."

"God willing and the crick don't rise."

"Stop it."

Jane's phone buzzed. Glancing over, she saw that it was the reception desk. "Just give me a second."

"Can't. I'm already late. It's almost eight and I was supposed to be over at the theater half an hour ago." Rising, she said, "Call me anon."

"I will," said Jane. She hadn't mentioned anything about her Internet search last night—what she'd learned about Annie. Cordelia would want to know, but there wasn't time tonight.

Leaning sideways, Jane pressed a button and picked up her phone.

"Jane, hi, it's Edward." Edward Sandberg was one of her evening hosts. "There's a man on the phone looking for someone named Annie Archer. He says she works here."

The Lyme House pub was short a bartender tonight. Since Saturday was the busiest night of the week, she'd offered Annie the evening shift.

Curious to know who might be calling, Jane said, "Did you get his name?"

"Curt Llewelyn."

"What line is he on?"

"Two."

"Thanks. I'll take care of it." She pressed the lighted button and said, "Hi. I understand you're looking for Annie?"

"Yeah," came a tentative-sounding voice. "She told me she was working there. This is a bar, right?"

"Restaurant and bar."

"I need to talk to her. I tried her cell, but she doesn't pick up."

"We don't allow bartenders to use their cells while they're working. I can have her call you back. Does she have your number? Is there a message?"

"Just tell her Curt called. That she needs to come home right away."

Home, thought Jane. Last she'd heard, Annie had been between motels. "Sounds serious."

"If you could give her the message, I'd really appreciate it."

"Will do." Jane dropped the handset in its cradle, then sat back and considered the situation. It appeared that Annie was staying with Jack Bowman's stepson. How on earth, she wondered, had that come about?

Jane found Annie standing by a row of beer pulls, talking to a customer. Motioning her aside, she said, "Curt called. He wants you to come home right away. Sounded like an emergency."

"That's all he said?"

"That's it."

Looking around, Annie seemed to be thinking. "Can I leave?"

"Sounds like you better. Don't worry, I'll pitch in."

Annie stepped into the storage room behind the bar and came back with her coat.

"Let me walk you out to your car," said Jane. "I need some fresh air."

Outside, fat, dreamy snowflakes swirled into cones beneath the yellow lamplights. The tang of woodsmoke from the restaurant kitchen drifted through the darkness.

"You're limping," said Annie, moving away from Jane and looking down at her leg.

"It's an old injury."

"Are you in pain?"

"Yeah. I'm not sure what's going on." Her leg hadn't hurt this much in years. The pain only added to a general undertow of anxiety. "So, you're staying with Curt Llewelyn," she said as they reached the Toyota.

"Yeah, I am."

"How'd that happen?"

She dug into her pocket for her keys. "It's kind of a long story."

"Annie . . . I think we need to talk."

She drew her hair back away from her eyes. "I'm not sleeping with him."

"Whoa, kiddo. None of my business."

"No, but I wanted you to know. We're just friends."

"Listen," said Jane, folding her arms over her stomach. "I like you. I think you know that. I've tried to help you."

"You have helped me."

"But from the very beginning, you haven't been honest with me. You don't owe me anything, least of all honesty, I realize that, but—"

"But I do," said Annie. "I owe you so much. You're . . . maybe the kindest person I've ever met."

Kind, thought Jane. *Wonderful.*

"Maybe we could get together tomorrow?" said Annie. "Just the two of us?"

"Unfortunately, tomorrow's pretty busy for me."

"How about tomorrow night?"

"That might work. I'll be here at the restaurant until at least midnight."

"I'll stop by."

"Good," said Jane. "And . . . Annie, whatever the emergency is, I hope you and Curt can resolve it."

"Me, too." She hesitated. Leaning close, she brushed Jane's lips with hers.

"Annie, I—"

The second kiss was long, slow, ineffably tender.

Snowflakes fell lightly against Jane's face as she drew back, searched Annie's eyes. "Why did you do that?"

"Because I wanted to." She touched Jane's cheek. "Was it a mistake?"

"No," said Jane, reaching up for Annie's hand. "No," she said again, this time more firmly.

"See you tomorrow night. And I promise. No more lies."

24

She promised me she'd call," said Curt, pacing back and forth in his living room. "You heard her. I told her to call me today and she said she would."

"Does she always keep her promises?" asked Annie. The soft feel of Jane's lips still lingered in her memory. She tried to shake it off, to concentrate on what Curt was saying.

"If I ask her to call, she calls. So I called her—about a dozen times. Left that many messages. Something's wrong, I know it."

Five feet away she could smell the booze on his breath. "You called Jack?"

"Hours ago," he said, throwing himself down on a chair. "He told me she was still in bed when he left for a breakfast meeting this morning. He hasn't seen her since."

"He's not worried?"

"Not as much as I am. Sunny's erratic. Sometimes she stays at a friend's place and forgets to let anybody know."

"Have you tried calling her friends?"

"Everyone I could think of. But since it's Saturday, most of them were out. I left messages."

Dooley lay on his back in Annie's arms. He seemed extra glad to see her, making little happy snorting sounds when she pressed her face to his fur.

"Her car's still at the house," added Curt. "It makes no sense. If she wanted to run away, she would have taken it. She's lost without that Saab."

"Did the police talk to her today?"

"Jack said he didn't want her talking to them unless he and his lawyer were present. The lawyer couldn't do it until Monday or Tuesday. I don't think they set a specific time because the funeral is set for Monday morning. Jack pulled some strings and got my mom's body released to him today."

Annie let go of Dooley and crouched next to Curt. "Are you helping with the plans?"

"He's taking care of everything. Which is good, because I don't want anything to do with it."

"Still can't forgive her?"

"I'll never forgive her."

She hesitated. "Curt?"

"What?"

"Is there a specific reason Sunny doesn't want to talk to the cops? Like, maybe she thinks they'll force her to talk about something she'd rather keep secret."

"You're partly right. She thinks cops can read minds, that they'll try to trip her up, make her say something that isn't true. She's terrified. I can't explain it. It's just the way she is."

She guessed that he was covering, that knew more than he was saying. "Did you talk to the police today?"

"They called, but I was out."

"You were?"

184

"I walked over to a liquor store to buy more bourbon."

That she believed. "Jack was in a pretty lousy mood last night when he more or less demanded that Sunny come home."

"Yeah. So?"

"Maybe they got into a fight."

"It's possible."

"She got pissed and stomped out."

"Without taking her car? She's dramatic, I'll give you that. But I can't see her getting angry and then calling someone to come get her when she has a perfectly good set of wheels in the garage. It doesn't make sense. And remember, Jack said she was still home this morning."

"We've only got Jack's word for that."

"Jesus, you're more paranoid than I am. I need another drink." He pushed off the chair and crossed into the kitchen. He came back a few seconds later with a glass filled with ice and bourbon.

"It's just after nine," said Annie. She didn't entirely understand why he seemed so panicky. It wasn't very late. "She might still come home."

Curt's phone rang. "Maybe that's her," he said. He lunged to grab the cell off the coffee table, spilling half his drink in the process.

Annie went to get some paper towels.

"Hello?" he said eagerly. "Oh." His voice dropped a good octave. "Brianna, hi. Yeah, I left you a message. Hey, did you see Sunny today?" He listened. "Okay. But does she have any new friends I might not know about?" He lowered his head. "Yeah, nobody new in that group. Well, if she calls, will you tell her I need to speak with her? It's important. Thanks, Bri. Yeah, bye."

When Annie returned with the paper towels, she saw that Curt had turned on the TV. He stood in the center of the room, staring at the screen.

Annie wiped up the spilled bourbon while Curt downed what was left in the glass.

"Brianna said she was at the mall today, but she didn't run into Sunny." He pointed the remote at the TV and switched it off.

"This friend, Brianna. She'd tell you the truth, right? If she knew where Sunny was, she'd let you know?"

"Why wouldn't she?"

On his way back to the kitchen to refill his glass, Annie stopped him. "You don't need another drink. What you need is to sit with me on that couch and calm down."

"Do I?" He slipped his arms around her waist. He looked deep into her eyes. "God, I'm glad you're here. Thanks for coming home."

It wasn't her home, and yet it was as close to one as she'd had in years. The problem was that the more time she spent here, the harder it was going to be to say good-bye to Curt—and to Jane.

For most of her life, Annie had kept others at a distance. If necessary, she forced them away. If people got too close, they'd find a way to hurt you; that's just the way the world worked. But somehow both Curt and Jane had breached her defenses. It made her nervous and, at the same time, oddly grateful. She'd never had the courage to admit it before, always projecting an image of the self-sufficient loner—someone who didn't need people in her life to make her happy—but ever since her dad had died, she'd felt profoundly alone.

"Let's trade stories," said Curt, holding her hand as they sat down on the couch. "Tell me something about your family. No . . . your dad. You were pretty little when he died, right?"

"Five."

"Okay, tell me something you remember the two of you doing together. Something nice." He leaned back and closed his eyes.

"Well," said Annie, reaching back into her past, "he took me on a boat ride a few months before he died."

"What did he die of?"

"Cancer."

"Did you know he was sick?"

"If I did, I don't remember. But I doubt it. I was pretty little."

"Keep going."

"He loved boats. The one we were on that time was fairly large, I think, but it was just him and me. No other passengers that day. I remember standing in the back watching the wake as we cut through the water. It looked like root beer—frothy, foaming root beer. I can still see it. At one point, we pulled up to a dock. I remember people walking around on shore, and hundreds of birds, probably gulls, dipping and swooping over our heads. It was that golden late afternoon kind of light, you know? September or October. Chilly, but not cold yet.

"I loved being on the water as much as my dad did. Didn't matter if it was a canoe, a rowboat, a big motor boat, a pontoon, or the kind of large charter fishing boat we were on that day.

"My dad was up front, high up in the captain's chair, when this big wave came crashing over the side and swamped me. It scared me and I started crying. I had on my favorite sweater. I still remember it. Blue wool with darker blue and red snowflakes on the front. I thought it was ruined, and I imagine that added to my misery. I was huddled against the side of the boat when my dad picked me up. He carried me down into the cabin and took off my sweater and the white cotton shirt I was wearing under it. He dried me off, then removed his own sweater and wrapped it around me. He rolled up the sleeves until my hands poked out. I remember how much the sweater smelled like him—and how much I loved it. And then he carried me up to the pilot's chair, telling me that he'd let me drive when we got farther out into the water. I adored it. He held me the entire way home. I felt so warm. I don't think I've ever felt that warm again since."

Curt was silent for a few seconds. "He sounds like a great guy."

"He was."

"Your life could have been so different if he'd lived. That's what I always think. If only my dad hadn't driven into that tree. I mean, why didn't he love Sunny and me enough to work through his problems?

Why did he have to end his life? Sometimes I get really mad at him. I scream at the wall or the sky that he was a selfish bastard and wasn't worth loving. But mostly, I just miss him. Quietly. To myself. If I could only talk to him one more time, man, what I would give."

"I know it wasn't my dad's fault that he got cancer, but I can get so mad at him because he left me and Mom all alone." She squeezed his hand. "We're a lot alike. Both of us lost our fathers when we were young."

And both, thought Annie, *ended up living with the same pathetic substitute.*

"I've never said this to a woman before," said Curt. He stopped, then rushed on as if he were afraid that if he didn't get it out quickly, he'd never say it at all. "I think I'm falling in love with you. Not the optimum time in my life, I realize. But I won't be like this forever. I don't suppose you . . . feel the same way."

"I don't know," said Annie. It was an honest answer. "I'm six years older than you are."

"So what? Is it because . . . because I can't—"

"No," she said, slipping her arm over his stomach. "In fact, if anything, not having sex has made me feel closer to you. It's not the only reason you want to be with me."

"Hell, no," he said, kissing her forehead. "It's my mother's death. That's what has me so down."

"But you were depressed the first night we met."

"Yeah, but that was school."

Was it? thought Annie. Maybe she should have pursued the issue, but she didn't have the heart to upset him any more than he already was.

25

After the brunch crowd thinned on Sunday afternoon, Jane left the Lyme House for home. It wasn't the way she'd planned to spend the day. She dug out an old silver-handled cane from an upstairs closet and limped around the house leaning on it, worried that the pain and weakness in her leg seemed to be growing worse. Mouse was put off by the heavy stick. He watched her silently from the middle of the living room rug. They often took a midday walk, but that wasn't going to happen today.

By evening, Jane was sitting on the couch in front of the fire, wondering if she should call her doctor. It wasn't exactly an emergency. She had some pain pills upstairs in the medicine cabinet, but they were old, most likely ineffective. She'd been reading for hours but now felt restless. She'd left a message for Annie with her manager at the Lyme House, telling her that something had come up and that they'd have to reschedule. If it hadn't been for her leg, the kiss they'd shared last night would have completely dominated her thoughts.

Pulling her cell phone out of her pocket, she thought about calling

Annie, but instead she punched in Kenzie's number in Nebraska. She'd called her dozens of times since the breakup, but assumed because of caller ID that Kenzie saw who was phoning and refused to answer.

Tonight was no different. The phone rang exactly six times, after which Kenzie's voice mail picked up. Jane had never left a message, it just didn't feel right. Neither did e-mail. She'd tried writing a couple of letters, but both were still in her desk drawer. She listened to Kenzie's voice ask her to state her name and leave a message. At least it was a different message this time. In this one she sounded more upbeat. Happier. That was probably good. She was getting on with her life. Maybe she'd found someone else, someone who could spend more time with her. Jane recalled something Kenzie had once said referring to Jane's penchant for helping people with their problems, getting too involved in criminal matters. It was a comment Annie, with her background in Greek and Roman myth, could appreciate. "You're like Atlas, Lawless. The man who held the world on his shoulders. His fatal flaw was that he couldn't find it in himself to put the world down. That's you."

Jane held her breath as the voice mail beeped. *Hang up,* she told herself. *Hang up.* "Kenzie, hi. It's me."

Now she was stuck. She had to say something, even though she hadn't thought it through. All her emotions tumbled together with no focused thought emerging. "I guess . . . I thought—" She took a deep breath. "I just want you to know how sorry I am. For everything. I never meant to hurt you. If we could just talk sometime, if I could just know what you're thinking—not what I *think* you're thinking. It's hard, you know?" She was starting to cry. This hadn't been one of her best ideas. "That's all I wanted to say, I guess. Except . . . I'll never forget you. I wish you . . . everything good."

She hung up. She loathed people who wallowed in self-pity, but since that seemed to be the direction she was headed, she might as well do it up right.

Mouse followed as she limped into the kitchen with the help of the cane and took down a bottle of Jameson and a glass tumbler from the cupboard. The whiskey would help both the pain in her leg and the deeper one in her heart.

By eleven, she wasn't exactly pain free, but she was well on the road. When the doorbell rang, she wiped tears from her eyes and got up to answer it. Her leg did feel a little looser, but then so did the rest of her. Those Irish distillers knew what they were doing.

She drew back the door without looking through the peephole because she was sure it had to be Cordelia. It wasn't.

"Annie?"

"I took a chance that you might be home by now. Can I come in?"

She hesitated. "Sure."

"You've got a fire going. Wow, this is a really great house." She rubbed her hands together for a few seconds, then bent down to greet Mouse, who seemed to be particularly interested in her hiking boots. "What a sweet Lab."

"Let me take your coat." Jane hung it up in the front closet as Annie crossed into the living room and took a seat at the end of the couch. She warmed her hands near the fire.

"I opened a bottle of Irish whiskey. Want some?"

"Sure."

Jane returned to the kitchen and came back with another tumbler. She was almost past the point of caring what she looked like—almost, but not quite. She'd undone her French braid when she first got home, so her hair tumbled around her shoulders and probably looked a mess. She'd spilled some soup on her shirt at dinner. She'd wiped it off halfheartedly, but the stain was still there.

"It's been a brutal day," said Annie, staring into the fire.

"Really? Why?"

"You're still limping."

"I'm okay. Tell me why it was such a bad day." She poured Annie a drink and then sat down on the rocking chair opposite her.

Annie took a swallow. "Sunny, Curt's younger sister, is missing. Nobody's seen her since Friday night. Curt left a couple dozen messages on her cell phone in the last two days. He's called all her friends, got them out looking for her. We spent the day doing that ourselves."

"Have you called the police?"

"Jack did. Curt thought he'd pitch in and help us look for her, but Susan's body was released to him yesterday. He's planning the funeral for tomorrow morning at St. Jude's Catholic Cemetery in Woodbury."

"Isn't he worried about her?"

"Apparently not as much as we are. He thinks she'll show up sooner or later."

"Is Jack Catholic?"

"Susan was. Normally, I think there should be a Mass before someone is buried, but Jack's arranging everything and probably couldn't be bothered. He's having a catered gathering at his house after the service. You're welcome to come. In fact, I wish you would. I'll be going with Curt, but it would be good to have a friend there."

"Of course I'll come," said Jane.

"Anyway, I was hoping that, maybe, if you had any free time, you could help Curt and me find Sunny. I can't pay you—"

"Don't worry about money. You think she ran off?"

"That's Curt's theory. I think she didn't want to be interrogated by the police. I'm not sure, but it might have something to do with Curt's past. He has a juvie record, although I can't imagine why the police would be interested in that. Curt thinks something bad happened to her."

"Something like . . ."

"I don't know. All I can say is, it really bothers me that my dad was the last person to see her."

The words "my dad" caused Jane to wince. "He's not your dad. He's your stepfather." Maybe it was a good thing that she'd had a few drinks. It meant she could cut to the chase a lot faster than she normally would have.

Annie thought about it for a few seconds as she gazed at the fire. "Not even that."

"Why all the secrets? Why lie about when you left home? I know you didn't graduate from high school in Michigan. I know all about the arrests for prostitution in Colorado. Who *are* you, Annie?"

"I'm nobody."

"That's too easy. You said you came here to get answers from Jack Bowman. Is that the truth? I feel like, from the moment we first met, you've been playing me."

"I warned you. We talked about it when I helped you clean out that storage room. Masks. Mirrors. Sometimes I try to reflect back to people what I figure they want to see. I'm good at it. Most of the time I hide behind a mask. I'm so used to lying about Jack, about my past, that I do it without even thinking."

"Why?"

"Oh, come on. Use your imagination. You think I'm proud of what I've done? You think I liked sleeping with guys with six-word vocabularies? Besides, I don't get you either. Why do you care so much?"

"You don't see yourself as worth caring about?"

"Truthfully? Not really."

"You think *that* little of yourself?"

"If you knew who I was, you would, too."

Jane got up and sat down next to her. "What did Jack do to you?"

"Not what you're thinking."

"He never . . ."

193

"Molested me? No, he never touched me."

"Then I don't understand."

"I would have done anything for him. When he came to live with us, he said he wanted to be my friend. And then later, as we got to know each other better, he called me his best friend. I believed he was. He made me part of his dreams. He's good at that. He painted a picture of our future that I wanted, desperately. Mom and I had always been poor. The apartment we were living in when Johnny got out of prison was the nicest place we'd ever had. But Mom had to work all this overtime just so we could stay there. Almost everything went for living expenses. Johnny showed me pictures of mansions, said that when he got enough money together, he'd start building ones just like them. We'd have our pick. We'd be rich. He'd buy me a new car, all new clothes. We'd travel. We'd have our own pool, maybe even our own tennis court. I bought into it. I was absolutely mesmerized by the picture he painted. But mostly, I just wanted him to be happy and for us to be together. I loved him more than anyone else in my life. My mother was all rules and regulations, but Johnny didn't care if I did my homework or smoked pot. He was all about living in the moment, taking risks, living your dream. And he was fun, always doing something exciting—at least, exciting to a teenager. In some ways, I think that's what he was. He never really grew up."

"But you left before you finished high school. What happened?"

"Reality happened." Annie downed another gulp of whiskey. "See, because Johnny was a felon, he had a terrible time finding jobs. I felt sorry for him. I've always thought of myself as streetwise, cynical, but really I'm kind of a soft touch. Johnny was good at playing the pity card. He hooked up with Glennoris, a real lowlife, and they started rehabbing houses for this other guy. After a couple of years, he and Glennoris formed a partnership and started their own company. But neither of them had two cents. They had to find financial backers, fat cats who needed to be charmed to part with their cash."

Jane closed her eyes. She knew what was coming.

"Johnny and I were sitting around one afternoon. I'd just turned sixteen. He started talking about a guy who might lend him some money to buy a HUD house. The poor guy was really lonely because his wife had just died. Johnny said he felt sorry for him. He asked if I'd like to go out to dinner with the two of them that night. I said, sure, why not? Mom worked a lot of evenings. Johnny suggested that I get all dressed up. He even picked out the clothes he wanted me to wear. Half an hour into the dinner he excused himself to go make a phone call. When he came back to the table, he said there was an emergency at one of his job sites and he had to get over there right away. He told me that Don—that was the asshole's name—would bring me home. He brought me home, all right, after he basically raped me in the backseat of his car. Don told me that Johnny had promised him that I'd be cooperative, that I liked older guys. That's why I said he 'basically' raped me. I never consented, but I didn't fight him as hard as I should have."

"It was a rape, Annie."

"I know."

"Did it happen more than once?"

"What do you think? For the next two years, I served as bait for Johnny's get-rich-quick schemes. I went along with it because I thought I was doing it for him, for the family, for our future. After the first time, I learned how to shut my eyes and grit my teeth until it was over. After a while it stopped hurting so much." She took another swallow of whiskey, wiped a hand roughly across her mouth. "I'm so fucking stupid."

"Don't say that," said Jane. "You were young. It wasn't your fault. What Johnny did was child abuse."

Annie refused to make eye contact. "Sex is easy. It's meaningless. A way to make money. A way to get what you want."

"Is that what that kiss was all about last night?" asked Jane. "Just a way to manipulate me? Is there something I have that you want?"

The muscles along Annie's jaw line tightened. "Sure. I want your life. Can you give it to me?" She stood, set her empty glass on the mantel. "Poor dumb Annie, right? Stupid, but pretty. What a waste of a human being."

Jane carefully pushed off the couch, afraid to put too much pressure on her bad leg. She wanted to say something to help, to make Annie's past fade to a distant memory, but words couldn't change what had happened.

"I have to go."

"Don't. Stay with me tonight."

"Why? So you can feel sorry for me? I don't need anyone's pity, especially yours."

"It's not that," said Jane, reaching for Annie's arm.

She shook the hand away. "It would feel like pity to me."

"I care about you. Not just as a friend, as someone I tried to help. But more than that."

Walking quietly to the front closet, Annie found her coat and put it on. Before she left, she said, "I care about you, too."

26

Wearing a basic black dress with a revealing neckline, the only dressy piece of clothing Annie had brought with her, she stood in front of the bathroom mirror in Curt's condo, applying the last of her makeup. Curt, dressed in his best dark blue suit, the one he said he reserved for weddings and funerals, stood in the doorway watching.

"You look like a million bucks."

"You do, too," said Annie. She'd never seen him in a suit before and could easily imagine him as a doctor. He looked older, somehow. More substantial. It was still early, not quite ten, but already she could tell by the glassy look in his eyes that he'd been at the bourbon. His mother would be buried at St. Jude's Cemetery in Woodbury in a few hours. He seemed preoccupied and probably needed something to dull the pain, which under the circumstances was understandable.

"Sunny should be there this morning," said Curt. "I can't think about anything else."

"Maybe she'll turn up at the cemetery."

He shook his head. "At least the police are taking her disappearance seriously. What if something really bad happened to her? What if she's . . . dead?"

Annie turned to him. "You can't think like that."

"How am I supposed to think? Nobody's seen or heard from her since Saturday morning. She wouldn't just take off, not without calling me. That leaves two options. She's alive but unable to communicate. Or she's dead."

Annie didn't know what to say. "You have to stay positive."

"Why?" He stuffed his hands into his pockets. "Why'd you go see that woman last night? Lawless, right? Jack told me she's a dyke."

Annie turned back to the mirror, sprayed herself with perfume. "She's a friend."

"How'd you meet her?"

"I needed money. I walked into a restaurant she owned and asked her for a job as a bartender."

"And she gave it to you? Just like that?"

"No, she let me work at some other jobs first. Cleaning up a room that had been flooded. Restocking. Some prep work in the kitchen."

"And all the while she took the opportunity to get a good look at how gorgeous you are."

"What's that mean? That I slept with her to get the position of head celery chopper?"

"Did you?"

"You're pissing me off. What I do is my own business. You don't own me, just because you're letting me stay here." She tried to move past him, but he blocked the door.

"You didn't get home until after three. What were you doing all that time?" He grabbed her hand.

She tried to twist it free. "You're hurting me."

"Tell me."

Shoving him away, she said, "We only talked for a few minutes.

I spent the rest of the time driving around. I needed to think." She went into the bedroom and started folding her clean clothes.

"About what?"

"Look, you keep grilling me like this and I swear, I'm out of here. I don't want to leave you today of all days, but I will. Back the hell off."

Turning away from the door, he said, "I need some air."

"If we're going to make it to the funeral on time, we need to leave soon."

She waited for a response, but instead heard the front door shut.

"Damn it," she muttered. She sat down on the bed and put her head in her hands. She should have known this would happen. Everything was getting way too complicated. This was where she usually checked out.

"Dooley," she called. "Come here, boy." She needed to take him outside before they left. "Dools? Come on. Front and center." When he didn't show, she went into the living room. His favorite spot was the end of the couch, tucked into a bright red feather pillow. But the couch was empty. "Dooley," she called again, searching each room. "Dooley, *come*," she said, standing in the middle of the kitchen, feeling her heart begin to race. Had he somehow managed to get out without anyone noticing?

Grabbing her coat, she charged down the outer hallway to the elevators, calling Dooley's name the entire way. On the ground floor, she hurried out the front door, looking in every direction. "Curt?" she shouted. "Curt, where the hell are you?" She noticed a man leaning against a minivan, smoking a cigarette. She asked if he'd seen a little black dog with a red collar—or a man in a blue suit—leave the building. He said no, that he'd been standing there for a few minutes and no one had come out.

Annie rushed back inside and took the elevator down to the parking level, thinking Curt might have left and taken Dooley with him.

But his BMW was in his parking space. Standing in the damp cold of the underground garage, it occurred to her where they both might be.

She took the elevator up to six, raced to the door that led up to the roof. Sure enough, the door was open. Charging up the stairs, she found Curt sitting on a low, narrow ledge about fifty feet away. He was holding Dooley. The sight of the two of them, perched so precariously, with the far bank of the Mississippi beyond and nothing but air in back of them, made her stomach lurch. Curt's head was turned away, but Dooley saw her and tried to wiggle free.

"Time to go," she called, trying to keep her tone casual.

Curt gripped Dooley to his chest and turned a cold gaze on her.

"Curt? Come on. I'll drive." She wondered how much he'd had to drink. If he was even the slightest bit dizzy, he could easily lose his balance, fall backward. With a quick intake of breath, she realized that *that* was the point. All he had to do was shift his weight just a fraction and they'd both be gone.

"Curt?" She crouched down. "Let Dooley go, okay?"

He glanced up at the sky. "It's a beautiful day. People shouldn't be buried on beautiful days." He paused. "You remember the day my mom died?"

"I'll never forget it."

"You remember I called you and asked you to come to the house."

"Yes."

"How did you know where the house was? I never gave you the address."

"I—" She rose slowly from her crouching position. He must have been holding the question back, waiting for just the right moment. She hated him for that calculation. All the time she'd spent with him, he'd been saving this juicy little question to spring on her when he needed it. "After the night we met at that bar, I did some research on your family, drove out to your parents' home just to take a look."

"Why?"

200

"Curiosity."

He stroked Dooley's head. "Because I was thinking, maybe you're a lot like my mother. Maybe you were looking for a meal ticket. When you saw how rich my family was, you decided to be nice to me."

"It was nothing like that."

"You're less obvious about it than my mom. That was a smart move a few minutes ago, threatening to leave. But you wouldn't do it, would you. That's not how you see this playing out."

"Curt, just let Dooley go. Give me five minutes and we'll be gone."

"You're good. You're really very good."

"And you're an asshole." Her fists clenched inside her coat pockets. "I thought you were a nice guy, that you might be worth the trouble, but you're just like every other jerk I've ever known. You want to own me. And if you can't, then you want to punish me. Go ahead. End your useless, fucking life. It'll hurt like hell if you take Dooley with you, but I refuse to beg."

His face was impassive.

She didn't see the tears until he turned his head and sunlight glinted off them. Dropping his arms, he set Dooley on the ground.

She bent down and gathered up the little dog.

"Do you love me?" he asked.

"You said honesty was overrated."

"I want the truth."

She hugged Dooley, sinking her face into his fur. "Not now, that's for sure."

He started to get up but teetered backward.

Annie held her breath.

And then he fell forward onto the cold tar roof.

Dooley struggled to go to him, but Annie wasn't about to let him out of her arms until they were off the roof.

Curt rolled onto his back and stared up at the sky. Slowly, he got to his feet. Tears flowed in rivulets down his cheeks. "I *am* an asshole," he said, weaving toward her. "I don't deserve someone like you." He draped his arms over her shoulders with Dooley between them, his body heaving in deep, guttural sobs.

"You need professional help," said Annie, repulsed by the smell of booze, by his bottomless need.

"I know." He took out a handkerchief and wiped away the tears. "If you stay, just a few more days, if you go to the funeral with me, I promise I'll find a therapist."

"That's blackmail."

"It's all I've got to make you stay." He dropped his arms to his sides. "Please stay."

He seemed so fragile. She hated the manipulation, but at the same time, she knew what desperation felt like. It could make a person do ugly things. "You have to keep your promise."

"I will. You'll stay?"

"For a while."

27

In one week, Kristjan's life had completely fallen apart. He'd been staying at a cheap motel since Saturday night, much the worse for wear. Living out of a suitcase had never been his idea of a good time. But the worst part of it was, he was desperate to see his kids. He even missed Barbara, if that was possible at such a late stage in their broken relationship. He couldn't work; he barely had the energy to leave the room when he was hungry. He was at the lowest point in his life and didn't see any way out. He needed to make it through one more event—Susan's funeral. After that, he wasn't sure what would happen.

Standing in front of the mirror in the bathroom, using a cheap razor and shaving foam because Barbara had forgotten to pack his Norelco, he thought about the phone conversation he'd had yesterday with his lawyer.

Dave Chen was a real estate attorney and a good friend. Kristjan explained what had happened. Dave listened, asked a lot of questions, but in the end said he wasn't qualified to help with either the criminal or the marital matters. He advised Kristjan to find lawyers who could—fast. Kristjan lied to him about the sites Barbara had found on his laptop. He said he'd read about them in a magazine and couldn't believe something like that existed. He said he had to see it for himself. Even though Kristjan figured he was getting better at lying, he had the sense that Dave didn't believe him.

While they were talking, Dave mentioned that a lot of people had come through his office lately who were having both financial and marital problems. With the recession, the two seemed to go together. He said that money insulated people. It kept them happy and occupied with playthings, vacations, entertainments. Take away the money and allow people to get a good look at the guts of their relationship—and at each other—and many ran screaming for the door. Top that off with multiple mortgage obligations, houses that had sunk in value, and hefty credit card balances, and some marriages simply fell off a cliff of their own debt. Kristjan didn't tell Dave about his own financial problems. After the picture Dave had painted, what was the point? The image was straight out of Kristjan and Barbara's own living room.

Once he was done with the call, Kristjan got to thinking. If it was possible to take Susan's death off the table—he hoped it would be ruled an accident or that Jack would be arrested—and if he could get Barbara to believe she wasn't the target of a murder plot—another big if—what then? The first thing on the block when they considered a divorce was the house. But selling the house, with two mortgages attached to it, and the fact that it wasn't worth anywhere near what they'd paid for it, would mean only more crushing financial woes. Barbara's job loss meant that Kristjan and the kids had no medical insurance, at least until they could work something out with Northland Realty. And without their combined incomes, they'd never be able to cover the bills, which would only sink them deeper. What if they did sell the house and get divorced, where would they live?

Some cheap little apartment? What kind of life would that be for the kids?

Kristjan wiped his face with a towel, assessing the damage he'd done with the razor. Three nicks. He slapped tiny pieces of toilet paper over the cuts and walked out of the bathroom. At least Barbara had thought to pack his black suit. It was a little wrinkled, but he could live with it. He dug through the suitcase until he came up with a tie that didn't seem too flashy for the occasion. And then he sat down on the bed, completely enervated. He wasn't the kind of guy to cry in public, but he had a feeling he'd be crying today. "I miss you, Susan," he whispered, his gaze drifting out the window. "I'm so sorry. Can you ever forgive me?" "I'm sorry"—the most useless words in the English language.

As he unbuttoned and flipped up his collar, his cell phone rang. It was lying on the nightstand right next to him. "Hello," he said. His voice was devoid of emotion. He hoped it wasn't one of his clients.

"Mr. Robbe? This is Sergeant Sterling."

"Oh, hi." He ran a hand over his mouth, sat up a little straighter.

"I need you to come down to the police station this afternoon. Say, three o'clock?"

"Why?"

"I have a few more questions I need to ask you."

"Can't we do it over the phone?"

"No, afraid not." Sterling gave him the street address, which Kristjan wrote on the edge of yesterday's *USA Today*. "Has something happened?"

"Susan Bowman's death has officially been ruled a homicide."

The word ricocheted inside Kristjan's head like an echo off a canyon wall. "Do you have a suspect?"

"We have several. I'll see you at three, Mr. Robbe."

28

I've got the money," said Jack, keeping his voice down. He kept glancing over Annie's shoulder, nodding to the mourners as they streamed down the winding paths from the parking lot.

Some days were like feature films inside Annie's head, with the past unwinding like a movie reel. She remembered her mother's funeral—if you could call it that. Just a few words spoken when she and Johnny had been left alone with the urn. Annie's eyes had been dry. So had Johnny's. The memory of that day was a wound, one that had never healed.

"Something wrong?" asked Jack.

"Do you have it all?"

"I have what you asked for." Moving in closer, he added, "We need to set a time when we can meet."

"Just name it."

"Tomorrow morning. At the same coffeehouse where we met last time. You haven't said anything to anyone? About me?"

"What do you think?"

"Good girl."

"I'm not a girl. And there's one other condition I didn't mention before." She stopped, waited until he looked at her. "Tell me what you did with Sunny. No bullshit. I won't leave until she's found."

He gazed at her stonily. "I didn't *do* anything with her. I've got two PIs out looking for her. What more do you want? She'll turn up. She's just high-strung, and . . . scared."

"She knows something you don't want her to talk to the police about. Something you did. That's it, right? You're hiding her."

"You're determined to think the worst of me. You want to believe I'm capable of murder. Well, I'm not. Now get the hell out of my face. The priest's here."

Curt stood at the head of the coffin, staring fixedly at the spray of white lilies. When Annie moved up next to him, he took hold of her hand and leaned close to her ear. "What were you and Jack talking about?"

"You," she said, hoping to stanch the flow of questions.

"Is he hustling you?"

"Oh, stick a cork in it. You think everyone's hustling me. You're delusional, you know that?"

As the graveside service began, Annie's eyes drifted over the crowd. She quickly spotted Jane standing next to an unusually tall, wide woman in a red cape. Annie had been hoping that Jane would change her mind and decide not to show. But no such luck. Jane's eyes remained on her throughout the service. It left her feeling off balance, exposed.

Annie had made the same mistake last night with Jane that she'd made many years ago with an important man. She told the truth. Up until that time, she thought she might actually marry this guy, a grad student, several years older, poor but full of plans for their future. Before meeting Jane, he'd been the kindest, most giving person she'd ever known. He'd been her port in the storm. He believed in her, even when she didn't believe in herself. She felt she owed him the truth. But as soon as she told him about Johnny, about what she'd done for him, and then about the years of prostitution, his feelings changed. He began to pull away. They had sex only once after her night of truth telling, and it had been so awful Annie had left his apartment and never gone back. Quickly, inexorably, he'd removed himself from her life. Just as Jane would. Annie wasn't about to stick around and watch it happen. Tomorrow morning, when she was supposed to be meeting with Jack, she'd be spilling everything she knew to the police.

And then, just as Johnny had done twelve years ago, she'd vanish.

By twelve thirty, most of the crowd had moved to Jack's house. This was the first time Jane had been inside. With so much glass, almost every room commanded a magnificent view of the St. Croix River valley.

"I suppose," said Cordelia, giving Jane a minitour of the place, "that you filled Nolan in on everything you learned about Annie."

"I got a lecture on the perils of becoming personally involved."

"That way lies madness?"

"I believe he used the term 'psych ward.'"

"Piffle."

They entered the great room off the dining room. Kilim rugs covered the dark wood floors. Adding to the sense of lively, almost riotous color were antique Deruta jugs and plates, which were scattered around like confetti.

Standing next to a potted ficus tree, Cordelia told Jane, sotto voce, that she couldn't believe how badly she'd misjudged Jack. "I'm usually such an excellent judge of character."

By what Escherian leap of logic she'd come up with that conclusion, Jane would never know. On the drive to the cemetery, she'd filled Cordelia in on everything she'd learned in the last couple of days.

"But, *Sunny,*" continued Cordelia, her eyes pulsing. "I thought for sure she'd show up today at the funeral. This is just appalling."

The only person Jane had recognized back at the cemetery, other than family, was Kristjan Robbe. She'd found a picture of him on the Northland Realty site. He was handsome in a pale, blond, Scandinavian sort of way. He'd stood apart and alone, his back to an oak, a good twenty feet from the rest of the mourners. The news of his affair with Susan was undoubtedly an open secret within the assemblage. He was an outcast and knew it. He hadn't come back to the house.

Cordelia walked Jane over to the stairway where Susan had died. Jane counted twenty-two steps. A long way to fall. The treads were made of textured, red-tile colored concrete, a hard surface for soft flesh to crash against.

When Cordelia was cornered by a man from the St. Paul Theater Guild, Jane drifted off, glad to be on her own. She'd seen Annie only once, when she'd gone into the dining room in search of food. Curt had been standing with his arm around her. The arm was probably a protective gesture, and yet to Jane it smacked of ownership. They were talking to the priest who'd performed the graveside service and a woman in an ankle-length tartan skirt. The woman held a crystal tumbler, sipping from it between slurred outbursts. Under other circumstances, Jane might have tried to stick around to overhear the conversation, but seeing Annie and Curt together turned her stomach.

On her way upstairs a few minutes later, she met Annie coming down. They were both alone. Annie was about to pass Jane without saying a word when Jane stopped her.

"Just give me a minute."

"There's nothing to say."

"I want to apologize. You owe me that much."

Annie looked around, seeming to think it over. She motioned for Jane to follow her. They ended up in one of the upstairs bedrooms.

"Make it quick. I need to get back to Curt."

"I want to apologize. I was way too pushy last night."

"Fine. Apology accepted."

"You're still angry."

"I am *not* angry."

"What did I do that was so awful?"

Annie focused her eyes everywhere but on Jane. "You made me care about you. You gave me the impression that it would be okay if I told you the truth."

"I'm not judging you, you are."

"Yeah, right."

"Annie, look at me. What you said changes nothing."

"You may not think it does, but it will. I'm damaged goods. A hooker. A whore. You and all your money and all your fancy restaurants—you've got no clue what it's like to live in my world."

"You're right," said Jane, her voice softening. "I don't. But I know what I see. And what I see is a good woman who refuses to forgive herself."

Annie stared straight ahead. "I tell people the truth and they go away."

"That won't happen with me. I promise, I'm not going anywhere."

"You don't know how much I'd like to believe that."

"Then do. I thought we . . . connected the other night. That it meant something."

"It did mean something, but so what? Connecting is easy. The hard part is what happens inside here." She pointed at her head.

Jane felt a wave of tenderness. "I don't want to leave it like this."

"I'm not staying in Minnesota. I'm heading home tomorrow."

"I'm glad to hear it. You're not safe here. I just wish—"

Annie stepped closer. "You don't hate me? Truly?"

"I could never hate you."

Closing her eyes, Jane felt Annie's hair fall softly across her face.

"I want to be with you," she whispered. "Just once."

"I want that, too."

The moment seemed to wrap itself around them, leaving them suspended, not quite anywhere except with each other.

"Will you be home later this afternoon?" whispered Annie, her fingers tracing the outline of Jane's cheek.

"What the hell's going on in here?" came a stern voice. Curt stood in the doorway, his hands drawn into fists.

Jane's surprise quickly turned to fury that he could make such an important moment vanish into his anger.

"This is great. Just fabulous." With an abruptness that punctuated his disgust, he turned and steamed off down the hall.

"I'll call before I come," said Annie, giving Jane's hand a squeeze. Without another word, she ran after him.

It took a full minute for the crushed feeling in Jane's stomach to go away. She didn't know what Curt's connection to Annie was, but it was enough to make her rush after him. Jane was able to subdue her concern only by telling herself that Curt wasn't dangerous, just mad as hell.

On Jane's way to the stairs, the woman in the long tartan skirt passed in front of her and stumbled into an open doorway. "Out of my way," she mumbled.

The sound of crashing glass drew Jane into the room right behind her. The woman teetered by the bed, holding a bottle of Beefeater gin. Across the room, large chunks of a crystal tumbler littered the floor.

"My glass broke," she said matter-of-factly.

"I see that," said Jane, watching her sway and sink backward onto a yellow satin duvet.

"Nobody listens to me," she muttered, trying to straighten her frilly white blouse.

"Listens about what?"

The woman eyed her. "You're that friend of Susan's, right? The one she went golfin' with every week. Can't remember your name."

"Jane."

"Right. Jane," she slurred.

"And you are?"

"You know me," she said. "Grace Lee Ingersol, Susan's older sister from Fort Worth."

"Oh, sure," said Jane. "I remember you now." She recognized a gift when she saw one. "I'm happy to listen to anything you have to say."

"You are?" Grace looked around aimlessly. "Shoot, where's my glass?"

"I think it broke."

"Oh, yeah. Well, hell." She took a slug straight from the bottle. With her head wobbling from side to side, she continued, "My sister was murdered."

"I was told the death was ruled suspicious."

"Uh-uh. Jack got word this mornin'. It was murder, all right."

Jane took a seat on an upholstered bench just inside the door. "Really."

"Yup. And I know who did it." The alcohol mixed with the Texas accent made her words almost unintelligible.

"Who?"

She pawed at the collar of her blouse. "This family is in crisis. We got to find poor Sunny."

"I agree," said Jane. "Do you know what happened to her?"

Grace teared up. "It's that boy. It has always, *always* been that sorry boy. When they were young . . . they were like my own."

"Curt and Sunny."

"Yes, Curt and Sunny," she snapped. "You're kinda dim." With the glacial concentration of the truly blitzed, Grace leveled her gaze at Jane. "I know what's been goin' on around here. I wanted to tell that priest a few minutes ago, but how could I with Curt standin' there givin' me the evil eye?" She swayed forward. "Anybody ever tell you you got a big nose?"

"I've heard that."

"Well." She brushed a piece of lint off her skirt. "I believe I shall lie down for a while."

"First tell me who murdered Susan."

"I already did. Find me a quilt. Or a blanket. I don't know how anybody lives in a place this cold."

Jane opened a closet door. Two wool blankets were stored on a top shelf. She pulled one down. When she turned around, Grace was lying flat on the bed, arms flung out, eyes closed.

"It's all there in the court records," she muttered, letting go of the gin bottle. It teetered on the mattress until Jane grabbed it just before it fell over.

"What court records?" she asked, looking around for the bottle cap.

"Curt's. Don't any of y'all up here ever listen?"

"I'm a little slow. Tell me again." Jane set the bottle on the floor.

"He tried to kill his mama about a year after his daddy died. He blamed her for his daddy's death. The boy simply lost his mind. But he was young, so the records were closed. Con-FI-dential. Nobody was told except the family."

Jane covered Grace with the blanket. "What did he do to her?"

"He . . . he got his hands right there around her scrawny neck." She reached toward Jane with perfectly manicured fingers. "He was a string bean, but tall for his age. And strong as the dickens. He tried to strangle her, and he woulda, too, if she hadn't fought him off. It was one hell of a brawl, and that's God's honest truth. Where'd I put the bottle?"

"It's on the floor," said Jane, sitting down on the edge of the bed. "What happened to Curt after he attacked his mother?"

214

"He was arrested, a course. Spent some hard time in one of those private mental facilities. We all tried to help. But I tell you, he never forgave his mama, I know that for a fact. I warned her to be careful a him, but she would not listen. Nobody listens." She opened her eyes wide, stared at the ceiling. "The kid's a nutcase. So much promise down the crapper. He's going to be a doctor, you know. Just like his daddy. A crazy doctor." She sighed. "So many of them are. I can tell he knows I know he pushed his mama down those steps. Everyone thinks it was Jack, but it wasn't. Why doesn't anybody believe me?" Her eyes pleaded.

"I believe you," said Jane.

"You do?"

"I do."

"Well, hell." Her eyes drifted shut. In less than a minute, she was snoring.

29

After a fight about who should drive—which Annie won by grabbing the car keys and refusing to give them back—Annie and Curt rode home in silence. Inside the condo, however, the gloves came off.

"I can't believe you and that Lawless woman were . . . were—"

"Oh, grow the hell up," said Annie. Nothing infuriated her more than sexual naïveté.

"It's disgusting. What's wrong with you? Haven't you ever read the Bible?"

She threw the keys at his head. He ducked. She walked past him on her way to the bedroom to pack. Dooley hopped up on the bed and nestled in the tangle of sheets and blankets to watch.

Annie had just about finished when Curt appeared in the doorway holding a bottle of vodka. "You've been sleeping with her. Admit it."

"Not that it's any of your business," she said, pulling the top of her duffel closed, "but I haven't."

"You're a liar. Just like—"

"Like who? Your mom? What's the deal with you, Curt? Do you

think every woman is an exact replica of your mother?" Hands rising to her hips, she waited for a reply. When none appeared to be forthcoming, she nodded to the bottle. "And what's with you and your family? Your aunt was totally blitzed at the reception. Are you all drunks?"

"Shut up. Shut the fuck up."

"You're pathetic." She motioned for Dooley to follow her.

"Where are you going?"

"I'm leaving. Isn't that what you want?" She bumped past him into the hallway. Her backpack was leaning against one of the leather chairs in the living room. She swung the duffel over her shoulder and picked up the pack, ready to go. When she turned around, she saw that Curt had sunk down against the hallway wall, his knees pulled tight to his chest. His face was red and streaming with tears.

"No," he cried, choking on his sobs. "That's not what I want."

Lowering the duffel to the floor, she said, "I don't know what's going on with you. You think I can help, but I can't. You need to see someone. A therapist. A priest."

"I said I would and I will." He pressed the heels of his hands to his eyes. "Can't you cut me a little slack? I walk in on you and that woman and . . . shit." He wiped his forearm across his face, struggling to regain his composure. "I feel like someone took a flamethrower to my life. Can't you stay, just for a few more days? Would that *kill* you?"

She didn't want to stay. She had only a little time left and she wanted to spend it with Jane. She'd had it with his drinking, his depression, and his secrets. But the sight of him there on the floor, so miserable, got to her in spite of herself. He was so enormously, cavernously lost.

Dooley trotted over and pawed his leg. Curt lowered it slightly and Dooley crawled into his lap. "Thank you," whispered Curt.

Annie hesitated a moment more. "Okay. I'll stick around one more night, just as long as it's clear I'm leaving tomorrow."

"I give you my word. I won't pressure you. Sure, I wish you'd stay longer, but if you can't, you can't. Maybe . . . hey, let's go out to dinner tonight. Somewhere special. Are you hungry? I'll make reservations."

Making reservations was the one thing he was good at. Annie glanced at her watch. It was going on three. "I ate at the reception."

"But you'll be hungry by seven, right?"

She sat down on the arm of the couch. "Yeah, I suppose." She was exhausted. She hadn't had a good night's sleep since the first night she'd stayed with him. "But you've got to promise me something. No more booze. I'm not going out with you later if you're drunk."

"Deal." He kissed the top of Dooley's head and scrambled to his feet.

"I've got some business I need to take care of this afternoon," she said, thinking of Jane.

"You're leaving?"

"In a little while. I'm taking Dooley with me." She wanted to take a short nap first. "What are your plans for the rest of the afternoon?" It was a dumb question. He didn't make plans.

"Don't know."

"If I laid down on the couch in your study, would you wake me in, say, half an hour?"

"Sure. Maybe I can go with you, wherever you're going."

He was turning into the human equivalent of glue. "We'll see, okay?"

As she walked toward the back room, he pulled her into his arms. "I love you, Annie. I just need you to know that. You don't have to love me back, it's okay."

"Curt—"

He put a finger to her lips. "Go take your nap."

Kristjan was surprised to find Barbara on her way out of the police station just as he arrived. She tried hard to appear brisk and purposeful but couldn't quite pull it off. Her frizzy brown hair had been pulled back into a loose, haphazard ponytail. She seemed ragged, worn out. Her eyes flashed angrily at him, but as he came closer, she seemed to deflate.

"What's wrong?" he asked.

She fell against him, shivering. It felt so good to have her in his arms again that for a moment, he didn't care about reasons.

Holding on to him tightly, she said, "The police called me in for an interview. I . . . I brought your laptop."

He pushed her away. "You did what? I thought you'd at least give me another chance to explain."

"They needed to know that you . . . might . . . have been planning to . . . to—"

"*Why*, Barbara?"

"I was scared."

"I wasn't planning anything, I swear it. I'd never hurt you. I'd never hurt anyone."

"Ramos and Sterling have been gathering evidence. They found some scraps of paper in Susan's briefcase with website addresses written on them in her handwriting. The same ones you were looking at on your computer. They also pulled a bunch of recent text messages off her cell phone."

"God in heaven, didn't she erase them?"

"They found one you sent the morning of the day she died telling her not to do it. That it was wrong. Too dangerous. You never spelled out what the 'it' was, but one theory is that Susan was planning to murder her husband. That she used your laptop to search those sites."

"That never happened. They're dead wrong. What are their other theories?"

Her face had turned ashen. She looked back over her shoulder. "I don't want them to see me talking to you."

"You've got to tell me. I need to know what they're thinking before I go in there. Honey, *please*. This is life or death."

"They, ah . . . they think that I was the one using your laptop to search out those disgusting websites."

"My god, why?"

"Because . . . because"—she struggled to find the right words—"they think I was trying to figure out a way to murder Susan and make it look like an accident. Because of the affair."

He was so stunned, he couldn't speak.

"They asked if I'd take a polygraph. I refused. I told them I had to talk to a lawyer first."

"But you've got nothing to hide."

Her gaze darted away. "I have to go."

"Barbara?" He reached out to her, but she was too quick. She ran off into the parking lot and disappeared down a stairway.

The cop at the reception desk told Kristjan to take a seat, that someone would come out for him shortly. Ramos appeared a few minutes later and led him to one of the interview rooms, a depressingly small, windowless space with a wood table and four corporate-looking chairs. Sterling was already seated, a file folder open with papers spread out in front of him. Kristjan guessed that dour was his permanent expression.

Ramos asked if he'd like something to drink. "Coffee? A Pepsi?"

Kristjan hated cola, but his mouth was dry. "Sure. A Pepsi would be great."

Ramos left the room. When he returned, he set a can in front of Kristjan and opened another one for himself.

"Why'd you call my wife in here without me?" asked Kristjan, pulling the can toward him. "I ran into her on my way in."

Ramos smiled pleasantly. Mr. Nice Cop. "Did your wife say anything to you?"

Kristjan could tell he was fishing. "Yeah, she told me everything." That was sufficiently vague. He hoped it caused the cop a few problems.

Ramos glanced at his partner. "Well, I suppose there's nothing on the table here that's a secret. You know, then, that the car parked outside Susan Bowman's house the afternoon she died belonged to your wife."

Kristjan tried to hide his shock by casually opening the can and taking a sip, but he wasn't much of an actor. "You're sure about that?"

"Your wife admitted it," said Sterling. "She said she went there to have it out with Susan about your affair. Which means you and your wife were both lying about your whereabouts the afternoon Mrs. Bowman was murdered."

Kristjan folded his arms over his chest, mainly so the cops wouldn't see his hands shake. "I had no idea my wife went to see Susan. She never told me. She lied about when I got home, and I'm sorry to say I went along with it."

"She was giving herself an alibi, Mr. Robbe, not you," said Ramos.

Kristjan had never considered that. "You don't really think Barbara had anything to do with Susan's death."

Sterling turned slightly, one arm dangling over the back of his chair. "You're aware that your wife brought us your laptop. Howtomurderyourwife.com. She thought it seemed pretty clear why you were looking at those websites."

"She's wrong."

"Is she?" asked Sterling. "I suppose it's possible that your wife used your laptop to look at those sites—before she went to see Mrs. Bowman last Wednesday."

"No," said Kristjan. There was no point in letting them believe that. "I was the one who looked at them."

"Why?" asked Ramos.

"Susan gave me the names, asked me to read through them."

"Because?"

"You were right. She was planning to murder her husband."

Ramos and Sterling traded glances.

"Any particular reason?" asked Ramos.

"She hated him. If they divorced, the prenup she'd signed meant Jack would walk away with just about everything. If he died, if she was able to make it look like an accident, she'd not only inherit his company and all his assets but also a million-dollar life insurance policy."

Sterling dropped his pen. "Fascinating," he said, folding his hands on the table, staring hard at Kristjan. "It's kind of odd that she'd want your opinion on something like that. Unless you intended to help."

"That's why we broke up. I couldn't go along with it. I'm telling you the truth, I swear to god. If she were here, in this room, she'd tell you the same thing."

"The problem is," said Ramos, his expression kindly, "she's not here. But let's work with your theory for a moment. You suggested earlier that her husband may have murdered her. But if Mr. Bowman discovered what his wife was plotting, why not simply leave, let her know that he was going to the police with his fears, and then file for divorce? That would have effectively stopped her. You said he had a prenup. He wasn't going to lose much if they divorced, and she couldn't get away with calling Mr. Bowman's death accidental if the police thought she might be involved in a murder plot. Why would Mr. Bowman kill her and put his own life at risk?"

"Because he's a brutal bastard, that's why. I suspect he found out about Susan and me. If so, he would have wanted to make her pay."

"By murdering her?"

"Maybe he didn't intend for her to die, but a few broken bones would have been fine with him."

"But let's consider another possibility," said Sterling. "Let's say you were terrified by what Susan was proposing. We know that you talked to her Wednesday afternoon. We have her phone records. We also have a text message from you telling Susan——"

Kristjan erupted out of his chair. "I know all about that. It's bullshit. I was advising her about the sale of a house."

"Sit down, Mr. Robbe," said Ramos.

"This is ridiculous. You think I murdered Susan?"

Neither cop responded until Kristjan took his seat.

"Now," said Ramos, "let's think about this. You already stated you knew Susan was planning to murder her husband. It's no stretch, based on what you've just told us, to say you were hyperconcerned that Susan might go through with her plans over your objections. Let's say you were terrified that she wouldn't pull it off successfully, and that the resulting investigation would uncover your affair and ultimately implicate you in the murder. Does any of this sound plausible to you, Mr. Robbe?"

"You have no proof of any of that."

Sterling shifted in his chair. "We believe that whoever murdered Susan Bowman did it without premeditation. It was an impulse."

"It was Jack," insisted Kristjan.

"Jack, or someone in her family. Or your wife. Or you, Mr. Robbe."

"I didn't murder her. Neither did my wife."

Ramos was a man full of patience. "Susan sustained a number of severe injuries. You've undoubtedly already heard that her shoulder was fractured. She had multiple contusions. The lacerations on her head and body were mostly from glass fragments. When she fell, she was holding a crystal vase filled with cut flowers. Our preliminary investigation suggested that some of the injuries were inconsistent with a fall down the stairs. We now know that what killed Mrs. Bowman—what propelled her down those stairs—was a severe blow to the side of the head. Head wounds bleed profusely. None of the other injuries she sustained would likely have been fatal. But, as I said, the head injury was the clincher. Her skull was crushed. She bled out fairly quickly." He paused, watched Kristjan for his reaction. "Next to the stairs is a metal and glass table, Mr. Robbe. On the table is a bronze sculpture—a nude woman. It's not large, but it's heavy. It sits on top of a block of weathered wood. A sprue in the foot anchors the bronze to the wood base. It slips in and out quite easily. Are you familiar with the one I'm talking about?"

"Of course I'm familiar with it. I was with her when she bought it."

"Really. Well, that was the murder weapon. It was there for the taking, selected, most likely, in the heat of the moment. We know it was the weapon because we found trace evidence—microscopic amounts of blood, skin, hair—embedded in the bronze. Our murderer had the presence of mind to wash it before putting it back, but, lucky for us, he missed a spot."

Kristjan felt suddenly light-headed.

"We need your cooperation, Mr. Robbe," said Ramos. "If you didn't murder Mrs. Bowman—"

"I didn't," said Kristjan, his fist hitting the table so hard it made the cans of Pepsi jump. He'd forgotten all about his.

"That's good to hear. We'd like to get your fingerprints today. And we'd like to schedule a polygraph test for sometime tomorrow."

"No way," said Kristjan, sliding back from the table. "This is getting way too crazy for me. In fact, I'm not saying another word until I talk to a lawyer."

Sterling grunted. "So much for cooperation." He closed his file folder, picked up both pop cans, and left the room.

"I do understand," said Ramos. "Even if Sterling doesn't. You should talk to a lawyer."

"Thank you."

"Oh, by the way, we were able to pull another piece of evidence off the sculpture. Whoever washed it had to be in the middle of an adrenaline rush. Speeding through something like that can be risky."

"What was the evidence?"

"A fingerprint. About as clear a print as I've ever seen." He mimicked drinking from a soda can, then smiled. "Thanks again for coming in, Mr. Robbe. You and your wife have been a big help today."

30

Shortly after three, Cordelia pulled her Volvo up behind a mound of dirty snow in the Lyme House parking lot and stared down her nose at Jane. "Call her *again*."

"I've already called her three times and left two messages," said Jane, frustrated not just because Cordelia was issuing commands, but also because she was afraid Annie might be in real danger, and this time not from Jack. All the way home from Stillwater, she'd been trying to think through the possibilities.

"Work with me here for just another minute. Let's say Aunt Grace was right and Curt did attack Susan after his dad died. We have to keep in mind that he was much younger then, a teenager. And that he received psychological help and has, one would assume, been fine ever since. He's in med school. That should mean something. Therefore, it doesn't necessarily follow that Annie's in any danger, or that he was the one who pushed Susan down the stairs."

"Therefore. Forthwith," said Cordelia. "Use the original Latin for all I care. *Non compos mentis*. All I can say is, *res ipsa loquitur*."

"I didn't know you spoke Latin."

"*Ignorantia juris neminem excusat*."

"Pardon me?"

"Ignorance of my genius is no excuse."

"What was the second thing you quoted?"

"*Res ipsa loquitur*? It means the thing speaks for itself. And it does. If Curt was capable of murder *then*, he's capable of it now." She added, under her breath, "Maybe that's what happened to Sunny."

"What?"

"All I'm saying is, Sunny had to know he'd tried to off his mom when they were kids. It's possible she guessed what happened and challenged him about it. Humans are instinctively feral when it comes to protecting their own skins."

"Are you saying that he kidnapped Sunny?"

"Kidnapped smidnapped. I'm saying he got rid of her before she could spill what she knew to the police. He murdered once out of rage. The first time's the hard one. I'm not saying that taking his sister out was easy, but to save himself from rotting in prison for the rest of his life, he might have convinced himself it was necessary."

Jane gazed out the window at the ice covering Lake Harriet. "Annie was so sure Jack did it. She said that when he found out Susan was cheating on him, he must have lost it."

"At this point, it's all conjecture. But I'd put my money on Curt. Call the police. Tell them what Aunt Grace, the family dypso, had to say." She glanced at her watch. "Oh, lord."

"What?"

"I was supposed to be at the theater an hour ago."

"Then you better shove off," said Jane, unhooking her seat belt.

"What are you going to do?"

"I haven't decided yet."

228

"Well, if you need me, or my laserlike intelligence, you know where to find me."

Jane spent the next half hour drinking too much coffee and worrying about Annie. Attempting to OD on caffeine wasn't one of her smarter ideas. She sat for a while at her desk, tapping a pencil against the coffee mug, thinking through the entire situation. She finally phoned Nolan.

"I need your advice and your help."

"Annie Archer again?"

"Afraid so." She explained what she'd just learned from Aunt Grace, and then she asked a favor. They discussed it for a few minutes, Jane making her case. He eventually agreed to help, but in return he insisted that she call the Stillwater PD and tell them what she knew. As soon as they said good-bye, she tapped in the number for directory assistance. She eventually reached a homicide detective named Sterling. She related Aunt Grace's story, and he said he appreciated the tip and would follow up on it.

But it wasn't enough. Jane dug out the white pages and looked up Curt's phone number. Thankfully, there was only one Curt Llewelyn in the Twin Cities. From the address, she figured he lived near the university. She picked up the phone to call him, then slid the receiver back into its cradle. By now he probably knew all about her. He'd never answer the phone if her name or "Lyme House" came up on his caller ID. That left only one option.

Pulling on her peacoat, Jane raced out to her car. Her leg felt much stronger. Maybe it was nervous energy, or excess caffeine. Whatever the case, she was glad for the respite from the pain.

As the digital clock in her Mini Cooper hit four, Jane found a parking space near the condo complex. She ran the half block to the front doors, tension building up inside her like steam in a pressure cooker. If Curt refused to answer his door, she'd break it down. But when she entered the lobby and saw the security system, she knew her Sam Spade approach wasn't going to get her anywhere.

Standing next to a wall of mailboxes, she looked through the list of names until she found Llewelyn. Next to it was a code number. She tapped it into the security phone and waited.

Curt answered before the end of the first ring. "Llewelyn."

"I need to speak to Annie." She didn't identify herself. Surprisingly, he didn't ask.

"She's not here. She left a little while ago."

"Do you know where she went?"

"Sorry. Would you like to leave a message?"

"Do you have any idea when she'll be back?"

"By seven."

He didn't sound angry. If anything, he sounded nice, as if he was trying to be helpful. She had no way of knowing if he was telling the truth and no way to get into his unit to find out. Feeling thwarted, she thanked him and hung up. Maybe Annie *had* left. If so, she might be on the way to her house right now. She might even be there.

Bolting for the door, Jane raced back to her car.

Annie rubbed the sleep out of her eyes and turned to look at the clock above the desk. It read five twenty.

"Jesus H——" she said under her breath. Curt was undoubtedly passed out on the living room couch. As far as she was concerned, this was it. There was no way she could go see Jane and be back in time to make dinner with him at seven.

"Dooley, stop that," she said, annoyed that he was scratching at the door. It occurred to her that she'd forgotten to take him outside when she got back from the funeral. "Come on, baby, you're going to wear a hole in the wood."

She was glad she'd changed into her army sweater and jeans before lying down. It would make leaving—for good—that much faster. She flipped the lock back and pulled the door open. The hallway was dark. Dooley made straight for the bathroom door, digging to get in.

"What's with you, baby?" She switched on the overhead light. "Curt?" she called, knocking softly. He liked to drink and soak in the bathtub, said it helped him relax. "You were supposed to wake me, remember?" She knocked harder.

When he didn't respond, she tried the handle and found that it was unlocked. She pushed inside. Dozens of tiny votive candles were lit and scattered around the room. He'd set up a romantic scene, complete with champagne bottle and two champagne flutes. She needed to be somewhere and he was playing games.

"Forget it. I'm leaving." All she could see of him were his feet.

Dooley sniffed along the edge of the tub, whining.

"Good-bye," she shouted. That's when she noticed that the water looked wrong, darker than it should be.

"Curt?" she said a bit more hesitantly this time. She inched closer, saw that his eyes were closed. "Come on, don't play games." He was unnaturally still. She plunged her hand into the water, pulled out his arm, saw the bleeding gash. "Curt, wake up." She shook his shoulders, felt along his neck for a pulse.

"You crazy idiot," she cried.

Bolting from the room, she flipped on the light in the kitchen and lunged for the phone. She hit 911. As soon as she heard a voice on the other end, she started screaming. "He's cut his wrists. We need an ambulance right away."

Ten minutes later the EMTs were wheeling Curt out on a stretcher. "Can I come with you?" she asked.

"It would be better if you drove your own car," called one of the the paramedics as they rushed down the hall toward the elevator.

"Where are you taking him?"

"It's all on the paperwork you signed. HCMC. Just a few blocks away." They disappeared into the elevator.

Annie felt a cold deep in her bones. She raced around the condo, turning on lights, finding her car keys, making sure she had her pocketbook, all the while dithering about Dooley. Should she take him with her or leave him? She wasn't sure how long she'd be at the hospital. Curt was in bad shape. She might want to stay the night. There was no time to think. She'd make sure Dooley was snuggled into her sleeping bag before she left him in her car. His fur was long. He'd be okay.

Annie walked Dooley along the river before returning to the building. Holding him in her arms, she took the elevator down to the basement. They'd no sooner stepped off into the underground lot when he began to growl.

"It's okay, boy. I don't like it down here either."

The parking garage was dank but well lit. It smelled of wet concrete, mud, and stale exhaust. As she passed the cement pillars, mentally counting them to help her find her car, Dooley struggled to free himself. "Just calm down." The paramedics had frightened him. In his little doggy brain, he must know something was terribly wrong.

She'd parked her Corolla on the far side of column six. As she searched her pocket for her keys, she felt a sudden pain. The next second, she was on the ground. Dooley slid out of her arms. Dark athletic shoes with red shoelaces moved in front of her face. She felt her arms and ankles being tied. Tape was pressed across her mouth and a sack pulled over her face.

"Open the trunk," whispered a gravelly voice.

She felt herself being lifted up, dropped on her side. Something hard dug into her hip.

"Get rid of the mutt."

Dooley gave a terrified yip.

She tried to scream, but all that came out was a groan. She felt a tiny pricking pain in her thigh, heard the sound of the trunk being shut. The engine caught. Her body swayed back and forth as the car backed up. She tried to move her legs and found that she could, but something else was happening. She felt weird. Dizzy. Everything became softened, muted. She began to drift. Red shoelaces. Red . . .

31

Each tick of the clock on Jane's desk propelled a microblast of adrenaline through her body. The only thing she could think of to calm her nerves was a shot—or two—of brandy. At the moment, that was out of the question. When she eliminated caffeine or alcohol from her list of liquid choices, not much was left that appealed to her. Which was why she was sipping from a can of strawberry soda, the nasty junk she kept around for Cordelia. The fact that she was enjoying it worried her more than she would admit.

She'd arrived home by four thirty. One hour, four minutes, and nineteen seconds ago. Mouse greeted her in his usual way, bounding down the stairs from the second floor. He liked to sleep on her bed when she was gone during the day. If someone had rung the doorbell recently, he would have already been downstairs in the living room watching out the window. Since there was no message, no note, and Mouse had been upstairs, she was pretty sure she'd beat Annie back to the house. But if that was the case, where was she?

When the phone rang, Jane snatched it up so fast that Mouse jumped up and barked.

"Hello?"

"Jane?"

"Yes?" She didn't recognize the voice.

"This is Helen James again, remember me? I'm the woman who worked with Mandy Archer at the Bell House Resort back in the midnineties."

"Oh, hi." She tried to work some enthusiasm into her voice.

"You asked me to call if I remembered anything else."

"Sure. Whatever you can tell me is much appreciated."

"Mandy had a sister. She used to talk about her some. I got the impression they were estranged. I used to keep a journal in my younger days, so I dug it out. I was sure I'd written the sister's name down. Do you have a pen? It's Connie Dewing."

Jane pulled a pad out of her desk drawer.

"Don't know if that's a married name or her family name. She lived—or used to live—in a small town in Connecticut called Barkhamsted. That's actually why I made the notation. I thought the name of the town was so unusual."

"It is," said Jane.

"I've always been fascinated by New England. Anyway, like I said, I don't know if she's still living there, but if she is, you might be able to find more information on Mandy. Of course, if all you're interested in is Mandy's child, then I don't think the sister could help you much. But it's worth a try, I suppose. That's all I called to say."

"Thanks so much."

"You're very welcome."

Glad to have something to do, Jane called directory assistance for Barkhamsted, Connecticut. She learned that Connie Dewing was still living in town. She wrote down the number, then tapped it in. Five rings later the voice mail picked up, a woman's voice. "Hi, you've reached the Dewings. Please leave a message and we'll get back to you. Thanks."

At the beep, Jane stated her name, said she was calling from Minneapolis, that she wanted to talk to Connie about her sister, Mandy. She left her phone number and said she hoped to hear from her soon. If Connie and Mandy had been estranged, there was a chance the call wouldn't be returned. And even if it was, Jane wasn't sure what Connie could tell her. Still, it was worth the effort.

By six, Jane's impatience hit the boiling point. She had to do something, go somewhere, make something happen.

"Mouse?" She got up and walked around the desk. He was curled up on the love seat. "I have to go out again."

He looked up at her sleepily, his tail giving a couple of halfhearted thumps.

"I need to make sure Annie's okay. You be a good boy. No long-distance phone calls while I'm gone."

She pulled her coat from the front closet, deciding then and there to go back to Curt's apartment. This time, she intended to identify herself.

Outside, a light mist had begun to form. The temperature had been in the high thirties all day. With excess moisture in the air and no wind, the mist would undoubtedly become more dense as night deepened. Instead of taking the freeway, Jane drove down Lyndale and hung a right directly in front of the Basilica of St. Mary. The marquees along Hennepin's theater district were all lit up. It was a slow slog until she hit Washington Avenue and took another right.

Entering the condo's lobby a few minutes later, she walked up to the security phone and punched in the code numbers for Curt's unit. But this time, after a dozen rings, there was no answer. Turning around, she noticed an old guy in a tan jumpsuit pushing a broom across the granite floor.

"Excuse me," she called, hurrying over to him. "I'm trying to find

237

Curt Llewelyn. He lives in four seventeen. He's in his twenties. Thin, tall. Dark hair tipped blond. It's an emergency." She wasn't sure it was, but it felt like one, so the words just tumbled out. "I don't suppose you know——"

"He the med student?"

"That's him."

"Sorry to be the bearer of evil tidings, lady, but he was hauled out of here about an hour ago. On a stretcher. Don't know what happened, but he looked bad."

"You saw him?"

"Watched the whole thing."

"Did you notice if there was a woman with him? Blond. Pretty."

"Nope, it was just him and the, you know, . . . medics."

"Do you know where they took him?"

"Said HCMC on the side of the van."

"Thanks," said Jane, already on her way to the door.

Hennepin County Medical Center was on the east end of downtown Minneapolis. She found a parking spot in the emergency lot, locked her car, and ran inside. She checked out the waiting room but didn't recognize anyone. Approaching a woman seated behind a glass wall, she said, "I was told Curt Llewelyn was brought in a little while ago."

The woman turned to her computer screen, tapped a few keys on the keyboard. "Are you a relative?"

Once again, she was about to flunk the ethical person test. "His aunt."

"Your name?"

"Jane . . . Johnson."

"Take a seat in the waiting room. I'll have a doctor come out and talk to you."

She found an empty chair and sat down. The room felt claustrophobic, jammed with the maimed and the bleeding. It was a Monday night. She wondered what it was like on the weekends. She picked up a magazine but was too wired to concentrate. Forty-five minutes later, a middle-aged woman wearing blue scrubs and a white lab coat came out from the back and called Jane's name.

She raised her hand and stood.

The woman introduced herself as Dr. Stremel.

"Can you tell me how he's doing?" asked Jane.

"He's stable. We're transfusing him. I understand you're his aunt."

"That's right."

"Were you the one who called 911?"

"No, that was his girlfriend, Annie Archer." It was a guess. Jane said the words with a conviction she didn't feel. "I'm surprised she isn't here."

"Mr. Llewelyn was brought in alone. But someone, I assume it was the girlfriend, made the call and probably saved his life."

"*Probably?*"

"The cuts in his wrists are deep. He's lost a lot of blood."

A suicide attempt. It was the last thing Jane expected to hear.

"I wonder if you could provide us with the names and phone numbers of his parents? We need to contact them."

"Both parents are dead."

"Are you the next of kin?"

"He's going to be okay, right?"

"I hope so. We should know in a few hours."

"His stepfather's name is Jack Bowman. He lives in Stillwater. I don't have the phone number with me."

She nodded. "I'm sorry, but I can't let you see your nephew just yet. Are you planning to stay?"

"I'm not sure what happened to Annie. I'm a little worried. I think I may try to find her."

"Give the stepfather's name to the nurse at the admitting desk before you go."

"I will," said Jane. "Thanks."

After finding a lucky parking spot on Washington, directly across from the condo, Jane walked to the end of the block and waited for the light to turn green. The fog had grown so thick she couldn't see for half a block and couldn't risk crossing against the light. Once back at the security phone, she found the manager's phone code and punched in the numbers. A woman's voice answered.

"My name's Lawless. I just came from the HCMC. A friend, Curt Llewelyn, was taken there by ambulance—"

"Oh, of course, Ms. Lawless. I was so sorry to hear about that. How's he doing?"

"He's holding his own."

"Was it a heart problem?"

"No, his heart is fine. I wonder . . . do you know the woman he was living with? Annie Archer?"

"I saw him with someone. I didn't know the woman had moved in with him."

"Can you let me into his apartment?"

"Well—" She hesitated. "Is this an emergency?"

"Nobody can find Annie. She's not at the hospital and she's not answering her cell. I need to check the apartment to see if she's there. Actually, I don't need to go inside myself. You could do it."

"Are you in the downstairs lobby?"

"That's right."

"I'll check it out. Wait for me. I'll be down in a few minutes."

Jane paced in front of the elevators. It didn't take long for the doors to open and a woman to walk off. She looked to be in her late fifties and introduced herself as Clare Varner. "Sorry. The apartment was empty."

240

Jane could tell by the grave look on her face that she'd found evidence of the suicide attempt. She had the good grace not to mention it. She studied Jane for a couple of seconds and then said, "You're really worried about this person, aren't you."

"I'm afraid I am."

"Do you know what kind of car she drives?"

"A white Toyota Corolla."

"We could check out the garage, see if it's there."

"You're a lifesaver."

On the way down in the elevator, Clare explained that they had more parking spaces than were strictly necessary to accommodate the tenants. "That way, they can invite a friend to park inside during the winter months, if they're willing to come down with their key to let them in."

In the chilly garage, Jane scanned the rows of cars and quickly spied the rusted back bumper of Annie's Corolla. Heading toward it, she said, "There it is."

"What hospital is Curt at?" asked Clare.

"HCMC."

"Maybe she walked over."

"It's possible, I suppose. You know, my mind is so muddled I can't remember what kind of car Curt drives."

Clare nodded to a red BMW. "I think that's it."

If both of their cars were still parked in the garage, what did that mean?

Jane moved slowly around the Corolla, giving it a thorough examination. She wasn't sure what she was looking for but figured she'd know when she saw it. She felt the hood to see if it was warm. It wasn't. A faint growl drew her attention to the next car over. A black Buick Lucerne. Bending down, she peered under the bumper. "Oh, my god," she said, crouching all the way down.

Two small, scared eyes stared back at her.

She struggled to remember the name of Annie's dog. "Dooley? Is that who you are?"

He growled again, then began to whine.

"Come here, boy," she said, reaching for him, letting him sniff her hands. "I know who you are, baby. You're a good boy. Such a good boy." He retreated farther under the car. "Come on, Dooley. Come to me. I won't hurt you."

He gave another growl, this one louder. Suddenly, he bounded out and jumped into her arms. Jane was so startled, she fell backward, but managed to hang on to him.

"He's scared to death," said Clare.

"It's okay, Dooley, I've got you now." She sat on the cold concrete and stroked him, scratching under his chin. He was shivering.

"Why would anyone leave a dog alone in a parking garage?" asked the manager.

"I don't think she did," said Jane, feeling a terrible pressure in the air around her. Annie would never leave Dooley alone in a place like this.

Not willingly.

32

With Annie's little dog sitting next to her, Jane waited impatiently on a wood bench in the lobby. She'd already tried calling Nolan twice. In this instance, the third time was the charm. She filled him in on what had gone down, said that as they spoke, the police were watching the same tape she and the manager had looked at a few minutes ago.

"It showed everything," she said, the scene running through her mind with a cold, almost chilling clarity. "Two guys in black clothes and rubber masks hid behind a van. One guy Tasered her. The other jumped out and duct-taped her arms and legs, slapped a piece of tape over her mouth, a bag over her head, and then they both dumped her into the back of a silver Hyundai Sonata. The license plates had been removed. Before they slammed the hood, one guy pulled a syringe and gave her something."

"Probably to knock her out, keep her quiet."

"I hope that's all it was."

"Sounds semiprofessional," said Nolan.

"Why semi?"

"They didn't take out the security cameras. You say the MPD is looking at it now?"

"With the manager."

"Let me get this straight. You think Curt arranged it?"

"Either Curt or Jack. Makes me wonder if the same thing didn't happen to Sunny."

"For similar reasons."

"Exactly. Maybe they're even being held together at the same location." But something about that scenario didn't quite feel right. "I'm almost done here. I need to stick around to talk to the police, but then . . . honestly, I don't know what to do."

"Sometimes you just have to wait for a break," said Nolan. "Keep me updated."

"Let's hope there is an update." The desperation in her voice was hard to mask. At least Nolan hadn't felt it necessary to give her another lecture on becoming emotionally involved. He could tell that she was well past the point where a warning like that had any meaning at all.

The following morning, Jane stood on her back porch and watched Mouse and Dooley play in the snow. Cordelia had arrived just after eleven—"with the chirp of the first early birdies"—carrying a sack of fresh bagels, cream cheese, and strawberry jam. Jane started the coffee brewing and let the dogs out the back door.

She had spent the night on the couch, occasionally dozing but mostly thinking and worrying. She didn't fall sound asleep until sometime after four. Thankfully, Mouse had taken right away to Dooley. The little dog seemed more tenuous and confused as the evening wore on, and began whining when Jane curled up on the couch. She let him cuddle next to her. He didn't take up much space, and he was a piece of Annie she could hold on to.

"You look pretty punk," said Cordelia, stepping out onto the porch and handing Jane a mug of coffee.

"I need to take a shower."

"Go ahead. I'll let the dogs in."

As awake as Jane had been for most of the night, she felt groggy now. She went upstairs and returned a while later feeling cleaner, wearing fresh jeans and a ski sweater, but not all that much clearer mentally.

When they sat down at the kitchen table, everything that had happened since Jane had said good-bye to Cordelia yesterday afternoon came rushing out. Cordelia listened, chewing with the greatest avidity during the most dramatic revelations.

"I called the hospital a couple of times during the night," said Jane, picking at her bagel. "Curt's better. The EMTs got there in time. I've been thinking. Maybe I should run down to HCMC this morning."

"To grill him about what happened last night?"

She threw up her hands. "I can't exactly do that, now can I. I mean, what kind of ghoul rushes into a suicidal person's room, guns blazing, demanding information?"

"I might," said Cordelia, licking jam off her fingers.

"No, you wouldn't. And I can't either. As much as I want to talk to him—because if nothing else, it would mean I'd be doing *something*—I can't. He already hates me. He'd never open up about what I really wanted to know."

A ringing phone interrupted their conversation. Jane got up to answer it.

"It's me," came Nolan's deep voice. "I've got some news."

Jane locked eyes with Cordelia. "What?"

"First, the cops found the silver Sonata down by the Mississippi, not far from Curt's condo. Turns out it was stolen yesterday afternoon. The trunk was empty."

Jane ran a hand through her hair. "What now?"

"We'll have to wait and see. They're doing a canvas to find out if anybody saw anything."

"And then?"

"They'll talk to Curt and Jack. I don't know anybody who works for the Stillwater PD, but I've still got ins with the MPD. If something breaks, I'll let you know."

"Thanks," said Jane. "Anything else?"

"You know that favor you asked me to take care of yesterday?" he said, sounding more upbeat. "Good instincts, Jane. She's there. Just arrived."

Jane felt a rush of hope. "Will your guy prevent her from leaving if she tries to take off before we can get there?"

"That's the plan. Call me later."

Jane gave Cordelia a triumphant smile. "We caught a break. It's Sunny. She's turned up."

"Where?"

"At the cemetery. I asked Nolan to stake it out after Susan's funeral. I had a feeling that if Sunny was ever going to surface, it would be there."

"Hot damn."

"You've got to take the lead with this. You know her. I don't."

Cordelia raised her chin. "Of course I'll take the lead. In another life, I probably led the Charge of the Light Brigade, or the Battle of the Little Bighorn."

"Cordelia, they were both disasters."

She tut-tutted as she put on her buffalo plaid coat, covering up the jeweled pink hoodie she was wearing. "Lay on, Macduff, and damn'd be him that first cries, 'Hold, enough!'"

"Why are you doing this? Making these awful comparisons? Those were Macbeth's last words—before Macduff slaughtered him."

"Just shut up and move."

33

Annie opened her eyes inside a small knotty-pine-walled room with a deeply slanted ceiling. The smell of coffee drifted in through a partially open door. As her mind struggled up through the fog of memory, pieces of what had happened began to emerge. Curt's suicide attempt. The painful attack in the parking garage. Dooley slipping out of her arms. She must have been drugged after she was dumped inside the trunk. The last thing she recalled was feeling dizzy, floating away.

The sack covering her head had been removed, as had the tape from her mouth. Her arms and feet were still bound, and a blanket had been tossed over her. She drifted in and out for the next few minutes until she heard footsteps, wood floors creaking under a heavy weight.

"Good morning, sleepyhead," said Jack, opening the door all the way. He sat down on the bed next to her, an amused look on his face. "I'm sure you've got lots of questions. We'll get to them. But first, are you hungry?"

She couldn't fathom his easy manner. "I . . . I need to use the bathroom."

He pulled a small red-handled Swiss Army knife out of his pocket, drew back the blanket, and cut her free.

She wondered if she had the strength to fight him. She knew a few moves, but her legs nearly buckled when she stood. Maybe later, after she felt stronger—and if she got lucky—she could catch him off guard. But when she glanced at the door, her hopes dissolved. A man stood in the hallway holding a pistol. He was wearing athletic shoes with red shoelaces.

"Claud will show you the way," said Jack. Turning to the man, he added, "When she's done, bring her down to the kitchen."

Annie's hopes dipped even lower when she saw that there was no window in the bathroom. She searched through every drawer, every cupboard, looking for a weapon, but unless she intended to smother Jack and Claud with towels, there was nothing she could use to defend herself. She stepped back out into the hall a few minutes later.

Claud motioned with the gun. "Down the stairs."

She saw now that she was in a two-story A-frame. It smelled new, the scent of fresh-sawed wood still lingering in the air. A wall of windows faced a frozen lake dotted with ice-fishing houses. Taking her time on the stairway, she surveyed the interior, looking for doors, windows, anything that might provide a way of escape. She judged by the light in the cold jade sky that it was around midday. Whatever they'd given her to knock her out had left her with a pounding headache.

A sofa covered in a northwoodsy-looking fabric sat in front of a huge stone fireplace. Logs sputtered and crackled on the grate. The scene was inviting, peaceful, almost serene, which in a strange way only made her more nervous.

At the bottom of the stairs, Claud ordered her to the kitchen. The entire downstairs was open, with the exception of a door in the back that must lead somewhere. Maybe it was an office, or a bedroom. As with Jack's home in Stillwater, everything looked—even smelled—expensive.

Wearing jeans, hiking boots, and a plaid flannel shirt, Jack stood at the stove, flipping pancakes. "Hope you're hungry."

"I'm not."

"Don't be like that. Have a seat."

"I'd rather stand."

"Sit down, Annie." He nodded to Claud, who shoved her onto a stool next to the center island. "Hey, asshole. Don't manhandle her."

Claud grunted.

"How's it going in the icehouse?"

"Fine."

"Let me know when you're done."

He ducked out a side door.

"That's some gun," said Annie, motioning to the sawed-off shotgun on the kitchen counter. "Twenty gauge?"

"Twelve."

"Who sawed it off?"

"I did. You sound like you know something about weapons."

She knew enough. In an adrenaline-fueled moment, she might risk dodging a handgun, but this kind of weapon was another matter entirely.

Johnny picked it up. With the stock pressed against his hip, holding the pistol grip in his right hand, he turned the heat off under the griddle.

"You know," said Annie, crossing her arms, "all this cheerfulness from a man holding a shotgun sends a rather mixed message."

He laughed. "I suppose it does."

"You're in a good mood."

"Not really."

"Why'd you grab me like that?"

"Because . . . we need to talk."

"We could have talked at your office. Or a coffeeshop."

"This is better. More private."

"What happened to my dog?"

"Dog?" He looked puzzled. "No idea."

"Do you really need the gun?"

He studied her. "Yeah, I think I do." He slid a pitcher of orange juice toward her. "Have some."

"No thanks."

"You were the kid who could never get enough orange juice."

"No walks down memory lane, okay?"

He pulled out a stool opposite her, sat down. "What am I going to do with you?"

"I thought we had a deal."

"It's no good."

"Why? I gave you my word. You come up with the money and I leave town and don't come back."

"But the question is, what's your word worth?"

"More than yours." She regretted it the second she'd said it. She was fighting for her life; she couldn't risk being snotty. "I'm sorry."

"No, you're right. From your perspective, my word isn't worth much."

"Did I ask for too much money?"

"Not really."

"Then what?"

"It's pretty simple. I don't trust you. If you do go to the cops, my life is over. You're the one who came to town making threats. You put yourself in this position, not me."

"You owe me, Johnny. Think about what you did to me. What you did to my mother."

"I had nothing to do with your mother's death. If you don't want to believe that, fine." He got up, moved back to the sink, and leaned against it. "How can I talk to you when you don't believe a word I say?"

"Try the truth."

"I told you the truth."

He was never going to let her out of here alive. To hell with caution. "Then why do I feel like there's a huge piece missing? *Why?*" she shouted at him.

"I loved your mom. She was the one true love of my life."

"Yeah, right. You wrote her from prison, worked your way into her life. She was just a diversion and then a place to stay after you got out."

He set the shogun back on the counter. "Oh, hell, I might as well tell you."

"Tell me what?"

"Blame your mom if you want to know why we never told you."

Annie's stomach tightened.

"She couldn't stand for you to think she'd lied to you. But this is way overdue. I married your mom for the first time when you were three years old. I'm not sure it was a legal marriage, which was why we got married again after I got out of the hole. I was using a false name back then. Kenny Andrews. Ring any bells?"

Annie sucked in a sharp breath. "You—"

"Yeah, that was me." He laughed at her shock.

"But . . . you don't look anything like him."

"Jesus, Annie. When I left you were five years old. What do you really remember about me?"

"That you were . . . gentle."

That made him laugh even harder.

"You're my father?"

"Nah. Can't pin that one on me. See, I'd never been around a kid before. Dogs and cats, but never a little kid. It was all kind of surreal. The thing is, your mom made sure there weren't any really clear pictures of me around after I went to prison. She told me that. And besides, I was pretty skinny back then, had a beard and long hair. When I got out of the joint, I looked different. Heavier. My hair had even turned a little darker. Your mom held her breath when I came to the apartment that first day. She thought you might recognize me."

Her gaze roamed the kitchen. "This is insane. You're making it up just to hurt me."

"Think that if you want, but I'm Kenny."

In less time than it took to make a pot of coffee, her safe, happy childhood had been blown to bits. "But . . . I thought you were my real father. I called you Daddy. You *told* me you were my dad."

"Yeah, I may have. Your mom didn't seem to mind. See, I had a drug problem back then. Mandy only married me after she was sure I was clean. But I started using and dealing so we'd have a little extra money. I worked on charter fishing boats for a time in Rehoboth Beach, remember that? Never made much of a living. When I was arrested, your mom was so furious that she told me she'd never speak to me again, that I was out of her life forever. That's why she lied to you—said I was dead. It was easier than telling a little kid the real story. But then, through a friend of a friend, I found out where she was living. Started writing to her. She didn't write back at first, but after a while I did hear from her. As the years went by, we started writing more regular. Then talking on the phone. We were both still in love. When I got out, I came back."

The best part of her life was dissolving as surely as if he'd thrown acid on it. And yet, even though the truth was ugly, it was also astonishing. She couldn't look away. "I don't get it," she said. "You called yourself my father then, but when you got out of prison, you made a big deal out of not being my father. You wanted to be my friend."

"Yeah, well. It kind of hurt, you know, when I had to leave you and your mom. At first I liked all the daddy stuff. When I'd get home from work, you'd run to the door and jump into my arms. But I was never

252

any good at it. And after spending eight years inside, the emotion wasn't there anymore. You can't make something out of nothing."

"So all this crap about being my friend. You never felt anything for me?"

"Hell, we had a great time together. Remember the dope we used to smoke out by Milford Lake?"

"Wild and crazy, Johnny. Positioning yourself as my friend got you off the hook. You didn't have to worry about the example you set—or rules. I'm sure Sunny loves the same thing about you that I did. But it's empty, Johnny. *You're* empty."

"I have had it with you," he said, slamming his fist against the counter.

"I've had it with you, too. Admit you murdered my mother. If you're going to send me to my grave, give me that much."

He acted as if he'd been slapped. "Don't push me, little girl."

"Tell me!" She didn't care how much it hurt.

"You want every dirty little detail? Fine. Your mom knew about all the guys you were doing."

"*Doing?* You make it sound like it was my choice."

"It was. Hell, Annie, I didn't tie you up, force you to spread your legs. You had to be having some fun, or why keep coming back for more?"

She couldn't believe he was that cruel—or stupid.

He wiped a hand slowly across his mouth. "Your mom pitched a fit when she found out. Threatened to leave and take you with her. But I had two trump cards: her love for me and meth. You probably don't remember the way it was, but shortly after she figured out what was going on, she virtually chased you out. In a funny way, it proved to me how much she really did love me. She chose me over you."

She was beginning to see it now. "You're wrong."

"I'm *not* wrong."

"She hated you for what you made me do."

253

"Oh, boo hoo. Okay, so maybe I did go a little too far with the favors I asked. I suppose you didn't always have such a great time. But you were young. I knew you'd get over it. But your mom, I had to take care of her. She wasn't dealing so well. Maybe it was the meth, or maybe it was something else. I never knew."

"No," said Annie, looking up, feeling a shiver of clarity. "It wasn't like that."

"It was. For once in your goddamn life, accept what I tell you."

"My mother would never choose you over me. If you think that, you didn't know her at all. Sure, she chased me out. But she did it for *me,* to separate us, not because she loved you, and not because of the meth. She was trying to protect me, Johnny. The only way she could. She blamed herself for letting you manipulate me, right there in front of her, in her own home. She probably never forgave herself for that. That's why she kept taking those drugs you offered her. To dull the pain. And maybe, in the end, it was a way to punish herself for letting the love she felt for you blind her to the kind of man you really are."

"I was there. It wasn't like that. You were just a kid. You don't remember it right."

Nothing he said or did could ever shake the sense that she'd finally hit bedrock. If her life ended the next second, she'd die knowing she'd gotten what she'd come for. She had her mom back.

He picked up the shotgun, pointed it at her. "You're so full of your own righteousness. You think I'm a terrible human being. Well, I'm not. I've made mistakes, sure, but . . . look at all the good I've done. I give back to the world. What have you ever given anyone except pussy?"

This time, the words didn't hurt. "You're a loser, Johnny. You murdered my mother and you murdered Susan."

"You only hear what you want to hear."

"What did you do to Sunny?"

"Sunny? Jesus. Nothing."

Standing up, she said, "I don't believe you."

"I did nothing but love her. It was different with her than with you. She's nice. Sometimes she's even sweet. I like that in a woman. You were always so stubborn and so damn pushy. How could anybody love that?" He raised the shotgun, pointed it at her stomach. "It would be so easy to pull the trigger."

"Do it. We both know that's how it's going to end."

His eyes drifted toward the front windows.

Annie turned to look. Out on the ice, Claud had just come out of one of the fishing shacks. She stared at the tiny houses, a sense of dread creeping toward her from the icy depths of the lake.

34

Jane ran down the graveled path to Susan Bowman's grave. The sun had burned away the fog, revealing a perfect February day. With temperatures in the high forties and no threat of freezing hands and feet, it was as good a day as any to visit a graveyard. "Remember, you need to take the lead," she called back to Cordelia, who puffed to keep up.

"Worry not, Janey," she said, edging closer.

They rounded a curve. Up ahead, Sunny, dressed in her motorcycle jacket and jeans, was leaning against a gravestone. "Take it slow, okay?" Jane whispered. "We don't want to spook her."

Jane couldn't hear Sunny but could see her lips move. She looked deep in thought, so deep that she didn't notice their approach until it was too late.

"Sunny?" called Cordelia. "What were you thinking? You gave us such a fright. Where *were* you?"

Jane grimaced. It wasn't what she had in mind at all.

Sunny turned to stare. "Who—"

Cordelia lifted her plaid hunter's cap to reveal her black and red tresses.

"Cordelia?"

She drew the hat wide and bowed. "The very same."

"What are you doing here?"

"Looking for you. Oh, hey, where are my manners? Sunny, this is Jane. Jane, say hello to Sunny."

"Hello, Sunny."

"Splendid," continued Cordelia. "Now that we're all pals . . . Girl, where have you *been*?"

"How did you know I was here?"

"Telepathy," said Cordelia, tapping her forehead.

"Sunny," said Jane. She moved a few steps back to give Sunny more space. "Will you listen to us for a few seconds? It's important. Last week, a woman—her name is Annie—asked me if I could help find her stepfather. Cordelia was actually the one who located him. Annie knew the man as John Archer. You know him as Jack Bowman."

"Curt's girlfriend Annie?"

"That's right."

She looked from face to face, settling at last on Cordelia. "Is that true?"

"Yup, afraid so."

"Jack wouldn't lie to me," she said indignantly. "He'd never even been married before he and my mom hooked up."

"He's not who you think he is," said Jane. She could tell by the determined look in Sunny's eyes that convincing her wasn't going to be easy. "Jack spent time in prison for selling drugs. He was married to Annie's mother for several years. Annie lived with him from the time she was thirteen until she ran away from home when she turned eighteen."

"It all happened once upon a time in a galaxy far, far away," said Cordelia. "In this case, Traverse City, Michigan."

Jane continued, "Jack stole several hundred thousand dollars from his partner—a man named Steve Glennoris—and started a new life here in the Twin Cities. It's possible that he had something to do with Annie's mother's death, although the jury's still out on that one."

"You're both full of it," said Sunny, almost laughing. "Jack's nothing like that. I don't know what your point is—"

"Why did you leave the way you did?" asked Jane. "Jack and your brother have been frantic. You wouldn't do that to them unless you had a good reason."

"Jack wasn't frantic. He knew where I was."

Jane's eyes widened.

"And where was that?" asked Cordelia.

"At Augie Scriven's place."

"Augie? As in Augie from the theater's costume department?"

"Yeah. He's my boyfriend. We met last summer when I was working at the theater. It's kind of a secret. Nobody knows but me and Augie—and Jack."

"That still doesn't tell us why you disappeared," said Jane.

She pulled a pack of cigarettes from her jacket pocket, tapped one out, but didn't light it. "I couldn't face talking to the police."

"Because you thought they would see through it if you tried to lie."

"No. Of course not. What would I lie about?"

Jane felt bad that they were ganging up on her, but this might be their one and only chance to get her to talk to them.

"Annie's missing," said Jane. "She was abducted from the parking garage at Curt's building last night. It was all caught on tape. Two guys in rubber masks Tasered her and dumped her in the trunk of a stolen car. I'm pretty sure Jack was responsible. She came to town to get him to tell her the truth—about her mother's death, about some of the twists and turns in their relationship, and about his past. She was about to go to the police and tell them who Jack really is when she was taken. There's a lot more we could tell you, but time's running out. Annie's in serious danger. You of all people might know where she is."

"This is bullshit," said Sunny, though she sounded less certain than she had before.

Jane kept pushing. "You left to protect him, right? You couldn't face the police, knowing you'd have to lie. Or . . . was it your brother you were trying to protect?"

Her eyes flashed. "Why would I need to protect Curt?"

"We know he attacked your mom after your dad died," said Cordelia. "He's dangerous."

This time Sunny did laugh. "That's just stupid."

"Is it?"

"Curt had nothing to do with my mother's death. Neither did Jack."

"You sound awfully confident."

"I am."

Jane was confident, too. Jack had to be the one behind Annie's kidnapping. As for the murder of Susan Bowman, she was less certain about that but decided to press Sunny where she was the weakest. "It was Jack, wasn't it? When the police hear about his secret life back in Michigan, that will tip the balance against him. He'll be arrested for your mother's murder."

"No," said Sunny, her expression defiant. "That will never happen."

"If he's hurt Annie, I promise *I'll* tell the police what I know. He's not going to get a free pass this time."

"He didn't kill my mother."

"He *did,* Sunny. You know it and I know it. Why won't you admit the truth?"

"You don't have the vaguest idea what happened that day. Neither of you do."

"Do you?"

260

"Yes."

"You mean what Jack told you," said Jane.

"No. I was there."

"You . . . were?" said Cordelia, her eyebrows soaring. "You actually saw him push your mom down the stairs?"

"It wasn't like that."

"What was it like?" demanded Jane. Annie's life was in danger and all she was getting were half answers and a lot of attitude. "He was angry at your mom, right? She was cheating on him."

"Yeah, but that's not why it happened. My dear, sweet mother was going to murder Jack. I heard her talking to her lover on the phone that afternoon. I came home from school early because I had a sore throat. She didn't even know I was there. They were arguing. He didn't want her to go through with it, but she wouldn't listen. *She* was plotting murder, not Jack."

"So you told him about it," said Jane. "He had to stop her before she went through with it. It all comes down to the same thing."

"No!" she screamed.

"Stop protecting him. He's going to prison. When I tell the police what I know—"

"You are so wrong."

"Sunny—"

"He didn't do it. I did."

Jane stared at her, blank faced.

"I had to protect him, don't you get it? What if Mom slipped something into his food? Or messed with his car? Or a dozen other things I couldn't think of or prevent. She promised me I'd totally misunderstood the phone conversation, but I didn't believe her."

"You . . . talked to her about it?" asked Cordelia, her eyes the size of saucers.

"Yeah. She was in the kitchen arranging some of her stupid, dickhead flowers. I confronted her. She just blew me off. But I knew what

261

I'd heard. I followed her, told her I wasn't going to let her get away with it. She said I was just a silly, melodramatic kid. That if I said anything to Jack, I'd get myself in a whole lot of trouble. That's when I picked up the bronze sculpture. I wanted to hurt her. I didn't realize she was close to the stairs until she fell. The whole thing was unreal. I saw her fall, but it was like . . . slow motion. I called her name, but she didn't move. God, I was so sick. I threw up in the bathroom. I panicked and left. But . . . you've got to believe me. I didn't mean to kill her. I just wanted to hurt her, to get her to see that I was serious."

Cordelia walked over and put her arms around Sunny, letting her cry against her shoulder.

"I was terrified," she said, choking back her sobs. "I couldn't tell anybody what really happened. Not even Augie. And I didn't want Jack or Curt to have to lie for me. I was so alone. All I've done for the last few days is puke my guts out. It nearly killed me to stay away from the funeral. That's why I came today. I had to tell her how sorry I was, that I never meant——" She broke down again. "Do you think she knows——"

"I do," said Cordelia.

Jane waited for the sobs to subside. "Sunny? Will you help us find Annie?" She'd cautioned Cordelia in the car not to tell Sunny about her brother's suicide attempt. If she found out, she'd want to go to him right away. Curt was, at least for the moment, not in any danger. Annie was.

Sunny sniffed a few times, wiped the arm of her jacket across her nose. "If Jack did take her, he won't hurt her. Maybe he just wanted to talk."

"Where would he take her if he wanted some privacy?"

Sunny sank down on the edge of a gravestone. "Probably the cabin."

"What cabin?" asked Cordelia.

"It's a new A-frame he built last summer on Little Otter Tail Lake."

"How far away?" asked Jane.

"I don't know. About an hour. Maybe a little more."

"Do you know how to find it?"

"Yeah."

Jane glanced at Cordelia. "It's worth a shot. I say we give it a try. You willing to be our guide?" asked Jane, switching her attention back to Sunny.

"Aren't you going to turn me in to the police?"

"Let's find Annie first."

35

Sunny had badly overstated her ability to find Jack's new cabin. It turned out she'd been there only twice. The first time had been on the back of Jack's Harley; the second time her boyfriend had driven them.

They'd been on the road almost three hours when they finally reached the small town of Malden, on the north end of Little Otter Tail Lake. From the backseat, Sunny directed Cordelia to turn right at the only gas station in town. She'd taken off her seat belt in order to face the side window. "There it is. Blue Water Drive. Turn left where the field ends. We're almost there."

A few minutes later, they pulled off the gravel road and hid the car behind a thick stand of red pine about a hundred yards from the A-frame. It was going on four in the afternoon.

"Let me check things out first," said Jane, pulling on her leather gloves. "If Annie's in the cabin, we'll have to call the police."

"She won't be," said Sunny.

Jane turned to look at her. "Does Jack ever let friends use the cabin?"

"No way." Her tone was sullen.

"You're sure you don't need my help?" asked Cordelia, turning up the heat. It was far colder here than it had been in the cities.

"No. Just sit tight." She glanced at Sunny as she got out. Sunny refused to meet her eyes. Not a good sign.

Jane crept slowly through a mixture of pines and birch, her boot-clad feet sinking deep into the snow. It was rough going, the sun slanting in through the trees and occasionally blinding her. When she reached the edge of the woods, she stopped to get her bearings.

The cabin sat on a rise nestled into the trees. Next to the cabin was a detached two-car garage, a Lexus in the drive. The A-frame had a fairly standard roof peak but an extrawide pitch. It wasn't the small A-frame she was used to finding in rural areas. Shed dormers jutted off the second story. On the side that faced the road, a massive stone chimney rose into the air. A multilevel deck spread out in front of the lake and a smaller deck had been built onto the back, about twenty feet from the garage.

Jane kept low and charged across the road. Rushing up a snowy slope to one of the mullioned windows, she crouched and waited to see if anyone would come out to ask what the hell she was doing. When everything remained quiet, she inched her head ever so slowly upward until she could see into the cabin.

Annie was lying on the living room couch, less than ten feet away. Her hands and feet were bound with duct tape and her eyes were closed. Behind the couch, Jack stood talking to a man with a hemp-colored crew cut and wearing a belted camouflage coverall. It was typical hunter's clothing. The semiautomatic jammed into his waistband wasn't. All her instincts and emotions told her to stay put, that something bad was about to go down, but her better judgment argued that she needed to get help. This wasn't a situation she could handle on her own.

Backing away, Jane slid down the rise and sprinted across the road, back to the safety of the woods. She took out her cell and tapped in 911, swearing under her breath when she saw that it wasn't connecting. No bars appeared in the corner of the screen.

She emerged from the trees a little while later and slipped into the warmth of Cordelia's Volvo. "She's there."

"Awesome," muttered Sunny. "Just awesome."

"Was Jack there?" asked Cordelia.

"Yes. He's got Annie all trussed up with duct tape. The guy Jack's with has a semiautomatic stuffed into his belt, and there's a sawed-off twelve-gauge in the dining room. I tried calling 911 on my cell, but I can't get a signal. Try yours," she said to Cordelia. She turned around and nodded for Sunny to do the same.

"There's no reception up here," mumbled Sunny.

"Are you kidding me?" Jane felt like breaking something. "Okay, here's what we do. You two drive back to town. There's got to be a phone at that gas station. I'll go back to the cabin to make sure nothing happens to Annie."

"How are you going to accomplish that?" asked Cordelia.

"No idea." She was already out the door. Holding it open, she stuck her head back inside and said, "When you get back, just stay in the car. There's no time to argue." She slammed the door and slapped the hood.

With any luck, they'd be gone only a few minutes, and when they returned, the county sheriff would be right behind them.

Making her way back through the woods, Jane wondered how Annie could sleep through what she must know would be the last few hours of her life. While Jane had watched Jack talking to the guy in camouflage, Annie had never moved, never opened her eyes. Maybe Jack had drugged her again. Jane hated to think of what had been in that first syringe.

It took longer this time to reach the edge of the woods. She was tired from trudging through the heavy, wet snow, dodging holes and rocks. Her boots were soaked through. When she reached the road, she ducked behind a tree. The first thing she noticed was that the Lexus was gone. It might be a good sign or a bad one. She had planned to stay in the woods until the cops arrived, but the missing car changed everything. She had to get another look in the cabin.

Running full out up to the same window, she bent low and stayed like that for a good minute. Easing her head upward just enough for her eyes to clear the windowsill, she looked inside. Annie was still on the couch, still had her eyes closed, but nobody else seemed to be around. Jane scanned the interior for any sign of life, but with each passing minute she became more and more convinced that Annie was alone.

She tapped on the window with her fingernails. Annie didn't move. She tapped again, but caution stopped her from making a louder noise. Edging her way to the front deck, she headed up the stairs but stopped when she realized her boots were creaking. In the still air, it almost sounded like a shriek. Before she could decide what to do about it, the sound of distant tires on gravel sent her flying for cover inside a thick clump of junipers.

The Lexus rumbled down the road and came to a stop in the driveway. Jack and his hunter buddy got out, each carrying two six-packs of beer. They made for the small deck at the back of the house.

"I'm gonna stay outside and have a smoke," said the buddy.

"Those things'll kill you," said Jack.

"You want one?"

"Sure."

Jane held her breath and darted to the edge of the cabin. Flattening herself against the wood slats, she edged closer to the back deck. She couldn't see Jack, but the guy wearing the coveralls rested his arms on the railing. He flicked ash into the snow.

"I don't see why we have to wait until dark," he said. "I need to get home. I promised the wife I'd take her bowling tonight."

"Well, now, that was pretty stupid, wasn't it."

He grunted. "Think she's awake in there?"

"Probably."

"You gonna give her another dose before we do it?"

"It'll be easier."

"For us."

"For her, too."

The hunter's arms disappeared. A beer can cracked open.

"Pretty up here," said the hunter. This time, he leaned his back against the rail.

"That's your last one, Claud. Until we're done."

"Yes, Mother."

"Did you take the extra chains and the weights out to the icehouse yet?"

"Nope."

"Do it now."

"Aw, jeez. We got enough stuff out there to sink a battleship."

"We can't be too careful. Put everything in the ice chest and drag it out. Be sure to bring the chest back."

Claud tossed his cigarette into the snow. "Can we order a pizza or something? I'm starving."

In response, Jane heard the back door slam. She pressed herself tighter against the wall as Claud trotted down the steps at the end of the deck and sprinted toward the garage. As soon as he opened the side door and disappeared inside, she ran back to the clump of junipers. She checked her watch, calculated that it had been at least fifteen minutes since Cordelia and Sunny had left for town. With any luck at all, they'd be back soon with help.

Hunkering down, Jane waited until Claud dragged the chest past her down the shoveled walk. Her feet were like blocks of ice, but blocks of ice that stung. Darting to another group of shrubs, she zigzagged her way from tree to tree, back toward the woods.

She was just about to charge across the road when she heard Claud call, "Hey? You there. What the hell are you doing?"

"Moi?" came Cordelia's surprised voice.

"Shit," whispered Jane. She swiveled around and saw that Cordelia was standing by one of the first-floor windows, hands in the air. Why hadn't she stayed in the car?

"Just consider me your local Peeping Tom," she tittered. "Nothing to worry about. And heavens, put that gun away."

"Come down from there."

Jane crept back to the junipers, glad that the landscaping provided so much cover. Peering through the branches, she saw that Cordelia was slipping and sliding her way down from the window.

"I'm just a neighbor," she said, lifting up her red and black plaid hunter's cap. "I was walking by and . . . well, you know how it is. You watch a place being built and you get awfully interested in what it looks like inside."

"What'd you see in there?"

"Just a lot of furniture. Very nice, expensive furniture, I might add. Tasteful. No Swedish modern. I hate Swedish modern, don't you?"

He held the gun with both hands. "I think we better talk to Jack. See what he says to do with you."

"Jack?" She tittered again. "We don't have to tell Jack, do we? He sounds mean."

He drew the slide back and let it snap forward. "Turn around and walk up the deck steps."

"Oh, my. I believe I feel faint."

Jane didn't have time to think. She charged straight for the guy, knocking him into the snow and sending the gun flying.

"What the hell?" he grunted, flipping over, grabbing her by the coat so she couldn't get away. They wrestled in the snow for a few bruising seconds, until he leveraged himself up and pulled Jane's arm behind her back.

Out of the corner of her eye Jane saw Cordelia digging through the snow, looking for the gun.

"There's a bullet in the chamber," she said, spitting out pine needles.

"I know that," said Cordelia, picking up the gun and whirling around. "I used to date a cop."

Claud shoved his hands in the air. "Lady, point that thing at anything other than me."

"You okay?" asked Cordelia, flicking her eyes to Jane.

Jack stepped out on the deck with the shotgun. "Toss the pistol in the snow," he ordered.

Cordelia's back was to him. She locked eyes with Jane.

"Do it," Jane said.

"Pick it up, Claud. Then bring them inside."

They all marched up the steps to the front deck, with Jane leading the parade. The French doors stood wide open.

"Explain?" Jack said to Claud when they'd all come inside.

"I don't know what the hell's going on, just that Paris Hilton and her fat friend got the drop on me."

"Jane's not fat," said Cordelia.

"Cordelia Thorn?" repeated Jack, looking at her for the first time.

"The very same."

"This is absolute bullshit!" he roared. "What the hell do you think you're doing, showing up here like this?"

"Trying to prevent another murder," said Jane.

"It's not such a big problem," said Claud. He moved around in front of them. "We were gonna dump one body down that hole. Two more won't make much more work. Course, we may have to enlarge it a little." He eyed Cordelia, making mental calculations.

"Tie them up," said Jack.

"Have you lost your mind?" demanded Cordelia. She sidestepped Claud and moved directly in front of Jack. "You might be able to get away with killing Jane and Annie, but not me. I'm famous. I am Cordelia M. Thorn. You would be hounded by the police until the day you died. You'd be signing your own death warrant, to quote an over-used and deeply overwrought cliché."

"Shut up," said Jack. "All of you, just shut the fuck up. I need to think." He began to pace.

"The county sheriff will be here any second," said Cordelia.

Jane inched closer to Annie, glad to see that her eyes were open.

"I called them from Malden."

"Shit, shit, shit," cried Claud. "I am outta here."

"You're not going anywhere." Jack pointed the shotgun at him.

"If you call it off, let us go, we'll leave," said Jane. "There's noth-ing to tie you to Annie's kidnapping. As far as I'm concerned, it never happened."

"Jack, man, use your brain," pleaded Claud. "That's bullshit. Let's march them out to the icehouse and get it over with. Five minutes, that's all I need. And then we get the hell out. You know the county sheriff never does anything fast. Hell, the head guy's so stupid he can't find his own dick. And who knows, maybe they never called. Come on, man. Let's just stick with the plan."

One of the French doors opened.

Everyone wheeled toward it.

Sunny walked in.

"Oh, Jesus," said Jack, nearly buckling at the sight of her. "Honey, what are you doing here?"

"I came with Cordelia and Jane. They told me you kidnapped Annie, that you were going to hurt her. I said you wouldn't. I'm right, aren't I?"

"Sunny, sweetheart, you shouldn't be here."

The sound of sirens drew everyone's attention to the side win-dows. Two police cruisers with lights strobing thundered down the gravel road and skidded to a stop next to the cabin.

"We are so fucked," shrieked Claud.

"I need to talk to you," said Sunny, her eyes pleading with Jack. "Alone."

"Honey, not now." He rushed from window to window to get a better look at what the cops were up to.

"It can't wait," said Sunny. "It's important."

"Four of them," said Jack.

"I'm gone," shouted Claud. He rushed to the French doors, yanked one back, and ran outside, leaping over the deck rail.

Jack pointed the shotgun at Cordelia, jacked a shell into the chamber. "Close the door and lock it."

"I will not."

"Do it!" he screamed. His face flushed red.

She backed up and did what he asked.

"Now, go over to the window by the fireplace and open it. Tell them I've got four hostages in here. They make a move on the cabin and you're all dead. Tell them!"

Cordelia relayed the message in her most stentorian voice.

"What are you going to do?" asked Jane.

Jack ran a hand across his mouth, rubbed the back of his neck. "I don't know."

"You've *got* to talk to me," said Sunny, moving toward him.

"No. Stay there." His eyes darted, focused for a second on each person. Sweat dotted his upper lip.

From outside came a man's voice amplified by a bullhorn. "Let the people go, Mr. Bowman. We've got the place surrounded. There's no way out."

Jack looked over at Jane. "Cut Annie free." He tossed her a pocket knife.

"Why?"

"Just do it."

Jane moved over to the couch. In a matter of seconds, the tape around Annie's hands and feet was severed.

Jack ordered Cordelia to give the police another ultimatum. "Tell them I'm leaving. I'm getting in my car and driving off. Nobody is going to stop me because I'm coming out with a hostage. They try anything—anything at all—and her death will be on their hands."

"Get over here," he directed Annie. "We're going to take a little ride together."

"Take me," said Jane, straightening up to face him. "You've done enough damage to her."

He wet his lips with the tip of his tongue. "Christ, why should I give a shit. Get over here."

Annie grabbed her arm, but Jane shook it off. She walked toward him. He hooked his arm around her neck and yanked her back against him, pressed the barrel of the gun to her head.

Cordelia shouted his message out the window.

"Jack, this is insane," said Sunny. "This isn't you."

"You don't have a clue who I am."

"That's not true. Listen to me, okay? The cops aren't going to rush the place, not with four hostages inside. Come on. Give me one freakin' minute. That's all I ask."

Jane felt the arm around her neck loosen. A second later, Jack shoved her away. "Go sit down. All of you, sit down and keep your mouths shut."

Outside, another cop's voice came over the bullhorn. "Mr. Bowman. This is Clyde Ewalt. You know me. You know I'm a fair man. Let me come in and talk to you. I know we can work this out."

"Tell him no," said Jack, motioning Cordelia back to the window.

"He says no," shouted Cordelia.

"Only a minute," Jack said to Sunny, sitting down at the island in the kitchen. He kept the gun pressed to his hip, his hand on the trigger.

Jane sat next to Annie. "You okay?" she whispered, carefully monitoring Sunny and Jack's conversation.

"I'm . . . numb."

Jane pulled her close. "It's almost over," she whispered. "We'll get out of this."

"I'm glad you came," Annie whispered back, "although I wish you hadn't. This is my battle, not yours."

Jane looked up, hearing Sunny and Jack begin to argue. They kept their voices so low that she couldn't make out what they were saying, just that it was intense. Several minutes went by. Then several more. Sunny was crying now. Jack's face had lost some of its color.

"I can't lose both of you," cried Sunny.

The cops were on the bullhorn again. "Mr. Bowman. Ewalt here. Can we get you anything? Something to eat? I understand you don't have a landline. We'd like to bring you a two-way radio so we can talk to you. What do you say?"

Jack got up up from the stool. His eyes roamed the room, coming to rest on Annie. Placing the shotgun on the granite countertop, he said, "Tell the cops that they can come in."

"Me?" said Cordelia.

"Yes, you."

Sunny leaned against him, as if she was too unsteady to stand without help.

Jack kissed her, whispered something in her ear.

Cordelia rushed over to the window and delivered the message.

"Unlock the French doors," said Jack.

When the two officers walked in, guns drawn, he held his hands in the air. "I did it. I brought Annie here against her will. I'm also responsible for my wife's death."

Jane and Cordelia fired each other shocked looks.

"You'll want to contact the Stillwater PD," continued Jack, his voice a monotone. "They've been working the homicide investigation. I'll give you—or them—a complete statement."

Jack had just admitted to a murder he hadn't committed. The only logical reason he'd do that was to protect Sunny. He was offering the

275

police himself instead of her. Everything Jane knew about him argued against him making that kind of a move, and yet she'd witnessed him say the words.

"You have a right to a lawyer," said the older of the two deputies, cuffing him and then maneuvering him through the room to the front doors.

"No lawyers," said Jack, lowering his eyes. "I just want to get this over with."

36

Jane and Annie stood in the dark foyer of Jane's house as Mouse and Dooley scrambled down the stairs. The police interrogation was over; so was the long drive home. Annie crouched all the way down and let Dooley jump into her arms.

"I thought I'd never see you again," she said, ruffling his curly black fur, kissing his ears. Glancing up at Jane, she added, "I don't know how to thank you." Her voice caught.

"I'm just glad I found him."

The dogs raced off into the living room, circled the couch, then tore off through the dining room, their enthusiasm, their normality, almost too much to bear.

"I think they're kindred spirits," said Jane. She reached down for Annie's hands, drew her up next to her. With Sunny along for the ride, they hadn't talked much on the way back in the car. Jane had so many questions. She moved to turn on the overhead light.

"No, leave it off," said Annie. She took off her coat, sat down on the stairs.

"How's your headache?" asked Jane.

"Better."

She sat down next to her. "Were you scared?"

"Yeah, at first. But then, I don't know. I stopped caring."

Annie seemed to grow pensive

"You want to talk about it?"

"Yeah, I do."

The dogs charged past again, Mouse with a tennis ball in his mouth, Dooley stopping long enough to spin around a couple of times before resuming the race.

Jane had already decided that she wouldn't tell Annie about Jack's rare moment of altruism. She had no proof that Sunny had murdered her mother. Just the conversation in the graveyard.

Jane sat next to Annie, looking down at her hands, as Annie began to talk. It wasn't a long story, although it had its share of twists and turns. "Bedrock" was what Annie called what she'd learned, what had been missing from her life for way too long. It might be a cliché, but the truth, she insisted, had freed her from a haunted past. Jane nodded as she listened, all the while feeling Annie move closer—but never quite close enough. Body language was subtext, the perfect agony of nearness and distance. Jane understood that it was a dance they had to play, a necessary step.

When Annie was all talked out, she turned to Jane. "You saved my life."

"I think, in a way, you saved mine, too."

"That sounds complicated. I can't do complicated anymore to-night."

The dogs had stopped playing and were now asleep at their feet.

"Seems like a shame to wake them," said Annie.

"They've probably been snoozing all afternoon."

"We should let them out."

"I'll do it," said Jane. But she didn't move. "If you want, you can go upstairs. You'll find clean towels in the bathroom. The bed in the guest room is all made up."

"I don't want to sleep in the guest room." Her hand strayed to the wisps of hair at the back of Jane's neck.

"You don't? The couch in the living room?"

"Not there either."

"Where, then?"

"On the roof under the stars."

Jane smiled. "I'll join you."

"You won't mind the cold?"

"If I'm with you, it won't be cold."

It was a difficult choice. Cordelia tossed her coat and car keys on a table by the door and dragged herself, with superhuman effort, into the kitchen. She was exhausted. Enervated. At times like this she needed either a bracing can of strawberry or black cherry soda, or a stiff chocolate martini. She didn't have the makings for the martini, so that left the soda. She selected one, popped the top, and went into the living room, where she flopped on the hideous orange IKEA couch. Melville, her most acrobatic cat, was hanging from the chandelier in the dining room. She had no idea why he did this. Perhaps it was one of his preferred methods of exercise.

Blanche, the matriarch of her cat colony, hopped up on her stomach, curled her elegant tail underneath her, and sat down.

"Yeah, one of those days," said Cordelia, stuffing a pillow behind her head.

It was just after nine, not remotely late, but she could hardly keep her eyes open. She'd driven more than five hours today. Too much, when most of the ride had been in silence. Jane and Annie sat in the backseat on the way home. Annie had fallen asleep with her head against Jane's shoulder. Sunny hunched morosely in the front seat, resolutely refusing to be engaged in any sort of conversation.

Before they entered the sheriff's department, Sunny had pulled Cordelia and Jane aside and asked if they planned to tell the cops what she'd told them.

"Jane said she wasn't sure," said Cordelia, tapping Blanche on the nose. "But I was. I mean, why not let Jack take the fall. Eventually, Jane gave in and let me make the call. That's when moi had the presence of mind to jump in and ask what she and Jack had talked about back at the cabin." She took a thoughtful sip of pop. "Sunny immediately began to rage about Annie. She insisted that the kidnapping was all her fault, that she'd come to town with some sort of sick revenge fantasy. Jane tried to calm her down but didn't have much luck.

"But, I mean, *heavens,*" said Cordelia, "when you think of all the criminal acts Jack might be on the hook for, I can see why he did it. Why not fall on his sword for Sunny? He's going to jail for the rest of his life anyway." She counted off the offenses on her fingers. "Kidnapping. Kidnapping with intent to commit murder." As an aside, she added, "The guy he hired to help him was singing like a lark even before he was escorted into the interrogation room. And when you take into consideration Annie's information about who Jack Bowman really is, that means he'll be investigated back in Michigan for the two hundred thousand he stole from his partner, and even the possible death of Annie's mother. And from what Jack told Sunny, one of the reasons he left Michigan was that the cops were about to arrest him for dealing drugs. Sunny was, of course, devastated and looking to blame someone other than Jack."

Blanche hopped up on the back of the couch.

Melville fell off the chandelier and landed on the dining room table between the silver candlesticks.

"Am I boring you two?" asked Cordelia.

Lucifer took the opportunity to slink into the room and jump to the pillow behind Cordelia's head. He batted at her hair.

"Stop that." She pushed his paw away. "Now that I have everyone's attention, I shall continue. When we told Sunny about her brother's suicide attempt, she was appalled. She made us drop her off at the hospital so she could see him. She said her boyfriend would pick her up later." Eying Blanche, she added, "Not that *you* care."

Lucifer batted at her hair again.

"I thought you were hiding out in the bathtub," said Cordelia. "Maybe you should go back there."

All the cats generally showed up for the evening drinking-of-the-pop-or-martini ritual. Normally, Melanie was part of the ceremony. But she wouldn't be back until tomorrow night. Still, as long as Cordelia kept sipping, she had a captive cat audience, and that was better than no audience at all.

"Jane took Annie back to her house. Don't you just wonder about *that?*"

Cordelia had finished her strawberry soda and was about to crush the can in her fist—to amaze the credulous felines—when she heard a soft knock on the door.

"I'm not going to answer it," she muttered. But then it occurred to her that it might be Octavia, back for round two.

Stomping over to the door, she flung it back.

"Hello, Cordelia." Radley Cunningham removed his fedora.

"Deeya," cried Hattie, rushing at Cordelia's knees.

Cordelia was so gobsmacked she nearly fell over backward.

"I know this is a controlled-access building," said Radley apologetically. His accent was pure upper-crust British. "Perhaps we should have rung up, but a nice young couple allowed us to ride up in the lift with them. Apparently, they didn't take us for terrorists."

Cordelia barely heard his words. She hugged Hattie to her with all the pain and joy there was in the world. "I can't believe it," she said, crying and laughing at the same time. She touched Hattie's hair, amazed to think she could have forgotten how soft those blond curls were. Her face looked older. She was taller, bigger, less toddlerlike, but her eyes were exactly the same. Mischief and intelligence fairly beamed. Cordelia picked her up, carried her inside. She even smelled the same. Bubble gum and Kids' Crest Cavity Protection. Sweet, sweet, and more sweet.

"Lucifer!" cried Hattie. "Blanche! Melville!"

Cordelia was stunned. "She can say her *l*'s now?"

"Has been for a good six months," said Radley. "May I come in, too?"

"Oh, of course," said Cordelia. She set Hattie down so that she could greet the cat colony. "How? Why . . ." she stammered, turning to Radley.

"May I sit?" he asked. He looked as tweedy as he sounded. He unbuttoned his heavy topcoat and took a chair in the living room. "She's exhausted. Our flight was late leaving New York. Hattie, come here, please. Let's remove your coat."

"No, let me do it," said Cordelia. Now that the first shock had worn off, the real shock set in. Hattie was back. But for how long? "Hatts, come here."

"Hatts," repeated Hattie, laughing her way over to the couch. "That's funny."

"I always called you Hatts." She was devastated to think Hattie had forgotten even a moment of their time together. She removed the bright pink coat. Underneath, Hattie was dressed in black jeans and a black sweater. Looking over at Radley, she said, "I'd heard my sister had called a moratorium on her black and pink period." Hattie was either a pink-loving princess with biker tendencies, or a Goth with a sense of humor. Either way, her potential to be an odd, fascinating adult was, under the right tutelage, vast.

"We don't always listen to your sister's edicts," said Radley with a pained smile.

Cordelia hugged her again, breathing in her scent as if it were the breath of life.

Hattie ran off to play with the cats, calling, "I missed you guys."

"Are you and my sister—"

"We've started divorce proceedings. It's for the best. Please understand that I love Octavia very much, but she's not the woman I thought I was marrying. I realized that the moment I first saw her with Hattie. But I was selfish. I wanted Hattie to come live with us. It wasn't your sister's idea, it was mine."

"I assumed."

Radley leaned forward, planted his elbows on his knees, and let his fedora dangle between them. "I've come to make amends. Hattie was almost inconsolable when she first came to us. She missed you so terribly. Missed Yucifer and Gainey."

"Lucifer and Janey," whispered Cordelia.

"But children are adaptive creatures. Hattie still isn't close to her mother; perhaps she never will be. I believe Octavia loves her, but at the moment, Hattie is, shall we say, an inconvenience. On the upside, Hattie and I have bonded. I love her beyond measure, as she loves me."

Cordelia's smile dimmed. "Meaning?"

"Not what you think." He dropped his hat on an end table next to him. "I agreed to give your sister a quick divorce—on one condition. It was a deal breaker, may I add. If she didn't agree, I said I'd fight the divorce until she was an old woman. She has money, but so do I. And I'm not timid about using it to get what I want. I told her that Hattie belonged with you. That to get her divorce, she had to grant you full legal and physical custody."

Cordelia's mouth dropped open. "Did she agree?"

"Yes. Much too quickly." He looked up as Hattie motored toward them with a gray puppet in her hands.

"Look, it's Arnold. You still have him."

"Of course we have him," said Cordelia. "I kept everything in your bedroom just the way it was when you left."

Hattie climbed up on her lap and planted a kiss on her cheek.

"If you look around your room a little more," said Cordelia, brushing Hattie's hair away from her eyes, "you might find a few surprises."

"Really?" Excitement bloomed in her China blue eyes. Handing Arnold to Cordelia, she flew off.

Radley smiled a bit ruefully. "She's very happy here. I thought she might be a little reticent. A year and a half is a long time in a child's life."

"She's never been reticent about anything. She's a true Thorn."

"Yes, well put." He leaned back in the chair, crossed his legs. "You see, my career as a film producer takes me all over the world. It's no life for a child. You can give her a stable home, something I can't. As hard as it is for me to give her up, I want what's best for her."

Tears welled in Cordelia's eyes. "Octavia's the one who should be sorry. She's losing a good man."

He cleared his throat. "Before you heap too much praise on my head, I do want something in return. I can't lose Hattie altogether. I need time with her as she's growing up, need to be an important part of her life. What I'm hoping is that you'll allow Hattie to spend her summers with me. That way I can take her with me when I travel. And, during the Christmas holidays, I would like very much to come to Minnesota to spend them with her—and with you and your loved ones. I'm really very charming and easy to be around. I clean up after myself and am surprisingly handy. I'll find my own accommodations and won't interfere with your plans. Beyond that, she's yours. I trust," he added, "that you will allow me to weigh in on important matters in her life. But the final decision will always belong to you. And of course, you're welcome in my home whenever you'd like to come, which I hope is often." He held out his hand. "Do we have a deal?"

It took Cordelia a moment to process everything he'd said. In life, the cards were usually stacked against happy endings. But this time, she was staring one square in the face. Standing up, she said, "Arise."

Looking uncertain, Radley got up, then remained suitably still for her crushing hug.

Cordelia felt a tug on her slacks.

"I wish you and Radley would be my mommy and daddy," said Hattie. She'd already put on her new pink and black feathered hat, the one Cordelia had ordered specially made for her last Christmas. She looked very Ziegfeld Follies–ish.

Radley hoisted her into his arms. "That's just what we'll be, Poppit." He kissed her cheek.

Cordelia kissed her other cheek. "Group hug," she called, squeezing them in her arms and closing her eyes, an unspoken prayer of thanks on her lips.

37

With a Bruce Springsteen song playing on the jukebox in the corner, Kristjan entered the Magic Grill the next morning. He glanced down the narrow row of booths until he found Barbara. He walked toward her, feeling a swarm of angry bees take up residence in his stomach.

"I'm glad you called," she said as he eased onto the bench opposite her.

"I needed to make sure you'd heard about Jack Bowman."

"Sergeant Ramos called me first thing. But," she added, glancing over at the long counter, touching the back of her immaculately combed hair, "I'm still glad you called."

"From the very first," said Kristjan, "I always said Jack was responsible."

"I should have believed you."

"I was a bit surprised when I heard you went to talk to Susan the afternoon she died."

"I was so angry. I had to give her a piece of my mind, tell her what

I thought of her. And I did. I was horrible. I screamed and ranted and raved. I did everything but foam at the mouth." She looked up at him with her large brown eyes. "I couldn't lose you."

"Barbara—"

"No. I get it now. You were already lost. A long time ago."

"I want to come home. I miss the kids."

"Yeah, they miss you, too."

Reaching his hand across the table, he said, "And I miss you."

"You don't have to say that. You can come home. We don't have the money for you to stay in a motel."

"No, I don't mean like that. I want to try again. Do you think you could ever forgive me for . . . you know?"

A waitress appeared to take their order.

"Just coffee," said Barbara.

Kristjan hadn't eaten anything since yesterday afternoon. "What pies do you have today?"

"For breakfast?" said the waitress, a disapproving frown on her face.

"I'm Norwegian. It's our breakfast of champions."

"Okay, then." She took a deep breath. "Apple, cherry, boysenberry, peach, blueberry, pecan, strawberry rhubarb, pumpkin, lemon meringue, French silk, coconut cream, and banana cream."

"Boysenberry," said Kristjan. "Warm it up. And I'd like a scoop of ice cream. And coffee, black."

She jotted it down. "That it?"

"That's it," said Kristjan.

The song switched to another Springsteen number.

"This diner is all Springsteen, all the time," said Barbara, not hiding her dislike.

"I know. That's why I suggested it. I like this place, like the atmosphere. So? What do you think? I know I've hurt you. Maybe it was a midlife crisis. Or maybe it was just plain stupidity. If you want to go to couples counseling, I'm totally on board with that. Barbara, please. Can't we try again?"

"I don't know what to say."

"Just say that you love me as much as I love you. I've had some time to think these last few days. I want us to work through our problems. I know we can if we try."

"I'm not so sure."

"You're still angry with me."

"Of course I'm angry. And hurt. Don't I have a right to be?"

"But . . . for all we've meant to each other, can't you give me another chance?"

He didn't get why she kept putting him off. She'd fought so fiercely for him, he didn't understand the reticence.

"The truth is," she said, moving back as the waitress set coffee cups down and then filled them. "I think I . . . I might be in love with someone else. I didn't go looking for it, it just happened."

"I don't believe you," he said. It came out as a gasp. "Who is he?"

"Someone I met at work. A doctor. His name is John Malcolm. You've never met him."

Her words twisted inside him. "How could you do that to me—to us?"

"*Me?* What about you? I never would have been open to someone else if you hadn't been so cold, so critical of everything I do. I've never been enough for you, Kristjan. Never worn the right clothes or been your idea of the perfect wife. Working my ass off and trying to be a good mother keeps me pretty busy, but you don't value any of that."

"That's not true."

"John loves me for who I am."

"I could kill him," said Kristjan. He didn't mean it, it just slipped out.

"That's exactly how I felt about Susan."

The waitress set the pie à la mode in front of Kristjan. "Kind of a frosty day out there."

"Excuse us," said Barbara. "We're in the middle of a marital crisis."

"Well, then, you'll need more coffee." She topped off their cups.

Barbara's gaze drifted back toward the counter. "It's a terrible thing when someone cheats on you."

"Have you slept with him?"

"Did you sleep with Susan? Was she better than me in bed? Do you want to know if John is better than you?"

He had the urge to throw the pie plate across the room, put his fist through a wall, do something—anything—to relieve the pressure inside him.

"Hurts, doesn't it."

"Yes, it hurts."

"You feel betrayed. Desperation just rolls over you. You could drown in it. It's agony, a scar you'll never get rid of. It's your own fault. You're unlovable. You're fatally flawed. If you weren't such a disappointment, you could have kept your man—or your woman. In the end, all you want to do is reach out and hurt the other person. Hurt him back the way he hurt you." She took a sip of coffee. "Does that about cover it?"

He glowered.

"Let me ask you a question. When was the last time you viewed love as selfless? You know what I mean? Putting the other person's needs and wants ahead of yours."

His answer was a scowl.

"How come it's always about us, what we want, what we need? Doesn't 'for better or worse' mean anything anymore?"

Kristjan watched the ice cream melt on his pie. He couldn't seem to look at her. Her gaze was too penetrating, as if she could see through each layer of his deception down to his soul, which she found deeply wanting.

"There is no John."

He looked up. "What?"

"I just needed you to know what it feels like. All this 'oh, baby, baby, take me back. I made a mistake, but you'll forgive me, right? It's not that big a deal.' "

"I never said that."

"Sure you did. You just weren't listening."

He fell silent.

"Like I said, I agree you should come home. But it's never going to be the same. Trust is a hard thing to resurrect when it's been shattered. I'm not sure I'll ever trust you again."

"But I can change."

"I wouldn't bet on it. With our financial situation the way it is, I'd say we're going to be roommates for quite some time. You can sleep in the study."

"What do we tell the kids?"

"We'll think of something."

"I'll win your trust back. I don't care if it takes forever."

Her face was calm, almost motionless. "Let's go home," she said, tapping a napkin over her mouth.

"Yeah. Home." He reached for her hand, but she was already on her way out of the booth.

Without a word or a parting glance, she walked out alone, leaving him to ponder what had just happened.

38

Shortly after eleven on Wednesday morning, Annie spoke to a re-ceptionist at HCMC to find out Curt's room number. She was di-rected to the elevators.

Up on three west, she passed the nursing station, walking briskly down a long corridor, wondering if she was making a mistake. She'd talked to Jane about it over breakfast but hadn't really formed a con-clusion. It might be best simply to disappear from his life. But that, she suspected, was taking the easy way out. For all Curt had come to mean to her, he deserved better.

Annie dreaded talking to him because, by now, he knew everything—and worse, he'd learned it all last night from Sunny, who had her own ax to grind. It would only add to Curt's overall low impression of women, that they were all liars and manipulators. If that's what she was, then she'd better own up to it. Except her rea-sons for staying with Curt, while initially pragmatic and strategic, had morphed into something far more personal.

Standing for a few seconds in front of room 3709, she tried to think of what she should say first. But in the end, she just walked in.

Curt was sitting on the edge of the bed, looking up at the TV set. He was wearing jeans and a green scrub top, and looked pale and startlingly sober. It was likely the first time she'd seen him entirely sober since they'd met. His wrists were bound in white gauze. He stiffened when he saw her.

"Who let you in?"

"I came to say good-bye."

"Right. The rat leaves the sinking ship." He returned his attention to the TV.

She stood at the foot of the bed, squeezing the bed rail. She wanted to touch him but knew it would only make this harder. "How are you feeling?"

"Fantastic."

"Why did you do it? You promised me you'd get help."

"Why the hell do you care? You're leaving."

"I have to leave, Curt. You knew I wasn't planning to stick around. I never lied about that."

"But you lied about everything else."

"Not everything."

He got up, turned his back to her, and moved to the windows, staring down at the street. "Why didn't you tell me you were Jack's kid?"

"I'm not. He was my stepfather."

"But why keep it from me?"

"It didn't really have anything to do with you and me."

"Like hell."

She stepped up to the window, stood next to him, but didn't look at him. "What happens now? Will you go back to your condo?"

"Can't. I'm on a seventy-two-hour hold. I'll be transferred up to the mental health unit later today."

"And then what?"

"I'm already on some drugs, something to help with alcohol withdrawal, and Paxil. It's an antidepressant. I start psychotherapy tomorrow."

"How long will you have to stay in the hospital?"

"A week? Maybe more. Depends."

"The world will look different to you once the antidepressant starts to work. I knew a guy in Denver who'd been depressed for years. His doctor put him on Zoloft and after a few weeks, he felt a lot better. He said he had energy again, that he wanted to get up in the morning."

"Super."

"Maybe you'll want to go back to medical school."

"Maybe I'll want to run for president. Or become a unicorn."

"Just stop, okay? Can't we at least be civil?"

He sat down on the only chair in the room, began wringing his hands. "I don't want you to go. I want you to stay in town, move in with me permanently. Would that be so awful?"

"Curt, I can't. You know I can't."

"Because you don't love me."

"Even if I did, I can't stay. I have to get away from here. It's just like Michigan. Everything reminds me of Jack."

"Just for a couple of weeks? Just until I get out, until I'm back on my feet."

"I have no money, no job."

"I'll give you money. I've got plenty in the bank. We'd be fine. We could travel. I've always wanted to go to Europe. More than anything, we'd be together. I feel so alone, Annie. I've felt this way . . . forever. I can't stand it anymore. It's too much. Too hard. I'll get better, you even said that yourself. I'll take the drugs and do everything the doctors tell me. I'll stop drinking. I'll get healthy. I'll take up yoga. I'll build up my abs and swallow enough Viagra to make me the biggest stud in the world. I'll do anything. *Anything.* Just don't leave." He gave a low, animal moan, pulled his legs up to his chest. "*Please.*"

If anyone understood loneliness, she did. But she couldn't give up her life for his. She wasn't selfless enough to make that kind of trade. "I can't. It won't work."

"It will. You're penniless. I'm not. We're both . . . like, adrift. We can be each other's moorings."

She shook her head.

"If you don't have any money, where did you stay last night? The condo, right? You've still got the key. Keep it."

"I picked up my things before I came over here. I left the key on the kitchen counter."

He looked up at her. She could see the wheels turning inside his mind.

"Where did you sleep last night, Annie?"

"What's it matter?"

"You stayed with that woman. Oh, Jesus—" He leaned his head back and squeezed his eyes shut.

"Curt, don't do this."

"You slept with her. I'm right, aren't I? Tell me."

"It's none of your business."

"You did. You came from her bed to this hospital room. You disgust me."

She moved back to the foot of the bed. Finding the strength somewhere inside her, she said, "I want to thank you. You took me in when I didn't have a place to stay. You were kind to me. I'm sorry if I hurt you."

"Get out," he said, a savage look in his eyes.

"I left my cell phone number on the counter with your key. I hope . . . I really hope you'll call me one day soon, that you'll let me know how you're doing. I can't be with you, but I wish you only the best."

"Please," he said, bursting into tears, "leave."

39

I can't believe it," said Jane. "This all happened last night after we got home?"

"I told you she'd be home by Christmas," said Cordelia. "I was just a couple of months off. Radley's sticking around for a few days to ease the transition. I thought maybe you and Annie would like to come over for dinner tonight."

"It's fine with me. I'll ask her."

"Did you two have an . . . interesting . . . evening?"

"Fascinating," said Jane.

"You're not going to tell me a thing, are you?"

"Nope."

"I'll wheedle the details out of you. Not to change the subject, but do you know what a sweet thing Radley did? Remember that picture book I made for Hattie? The one with all the important people in her life. Me. You. Her deceased but famous father. The cats. Mouse."

"Bette Davis. Katharine Hepburn."

"Yeah, that's the one. Well, it turns out Hattie had it with her when she went to stay with them in that hotel, before they kidnapped her."

"I think 'kidnapped' is a bit strong."

"I don't. Anyway, Radley and Hattie looked at it almost every night. He said he didn't want her to forget me—us. Everyone. They'd talk about the things she loved. Isn't that incredible?"

"Incredibly loving."

"I'll give you all the details tonight. Bring the Christmas gift I made you get for Hattie. It's going to be one kick-ass rock-and-roll celebration."

"I'll be there. And Cordelia, congratulations."

Jane spent the next few minutes on the phone with Judah Johanson, her business partner. They'd just begun a belated discussion about the restaurant in Stillwater when she got a call interrupt. Glancing at the caller ID, she saw the name "Constance Dewing" pop up. Jane was about to blow it off when she remembered the conversation she'd had with Helen James, the woman who had worked with Annie's mother back in Michigan.

"Judah, I'm getting another call. I have to take it. I'll call you back." Clicking over, she said, "Hello?"

"I'm calling for Jane Lawless."

"This is Jane."

"My name's Connie Dewing. You left a message for me on my voice mail. I wasn't planning to return your call, but then my curiosity got the better of me. I'm Mandy Dewing's sister."

Jane dug out a notebook from her bottom desk drawer. "Yes, thanks so much."

"Do you know Mandy personally?"

"No, we've never met. But I know her daughter, Annie."

"Oh, sure. She must be in her late twenties now."

"Thirty-two."

"Really. My sister and I had a falling-out many years ago."

"Must have been serious."

"How is Mandy?"

Jane hadn't considered the possibility that this woman might not know about her sister's death. She hated to be the one to break the news. "Mandy died back in the midnineties."

"Died? How?"

"A heart attack. I'm very sorry."

"What happened to Annie?"

"She's been living in Colorado since she turned eighteen."

"Is she married?"

"No. I can put you in touch with her—"

"I think it's better to let sleeping dogs lie."

Jane didn't understand that kind of sentiment. "When was the last time to you talked to Mandy?"

"Oh, gee. Annie must have been five. Kenny had just been sent to prison."

Jane grabbed a pen, wrote the word "prison" in bold letters in the notebook, and then circled it. Annie had told her the entire story last night.

"Mandy met Kenny when she was a senior in high school, fell madly in love."

"In high school?"

"He was older, in his midtwenties if I recall correctly. They dated for a few months, and then he took off for greener pastures. Everyone in the family expressed the opinion that she was well rid of him. He was a wheeler-dealer type. Always looking to make a big score. And I didn't know it at the time, but my brother told me later that he was a drug addict. He used and sold drugs. In fact, that's why he went to prison."

"Yes, I've heard all about that."

"So you know about the pregnancy, too."

"What pregnancy?"

301

"During the few months Mandy and Kenny dated, Mandy got pregnant. By the time she realized it, Kenny was gone. She gave birth to the child, against our mother's and father's wishes, and as soon as she put some money together, she left home, found a job working at a resort in Rehoboth Beach. That's where she ran into him again."

Jane felt a sick feeling in her stomach. "You're saying Kenny was Annie's biological father?"

"That's correct. Not that Mandy told him. It was just another one of Mandy's little secrets. She loved Kenny, but she didn't trust him. I went to visit them a couple of times after they got married. You have to understand, all of my siblings went on to college except for Mandy. I received my master's in political science from Cornell. My younger sister has a doctorate from Rutgers. My brother made *Harvard Law Review*. It seemed ridiculous to us that Mandy was living in a crummy apartment with a lowlife like Kenny, but I suppose it was her choice. As I said, Annie had just turned five when Kenny was arrested for possession. Cocaine, I believe. And he was selling it, too. That's when we found out he'd been using an alias. His real name was John William Archer."

This was a train wreck Jane had never seen coming. "Annie didn't know Kenny was her father?" asked Jane, just to make sure she understood. "And Kenny didn't know Annie was his child?"

"That's right."

"So when Kenny, alias John Archer, got out of prison—"

"I couldn't tell you about that. My relationship with Mandy blew up when I found out Kenny had been dealing drugs and was headed to prison. The police were the ones who established his true identity. Mandy and I had a terrible fight about it. In fact, the entire family tried to talk some sense into her, but she knew best. She left Rehoboth Beach a few months after the trial. We never knew where she went."

"Nobody ever tried to find her?"

"If she wanted to contact us, she knew where we lived."

It sounded as if Connie was still angry with her sister. As if the entire family was.

"I washed my hands of her," said Connie.

"And of Annie."

"Well, I felt sorry for the little girl, for both of them really, but what could I do? Mandy chose the life she wanted to live. I'm sorry she's gone. Where was she living when she died?"

"You know," said Jane, "I'm not really sure."

"Do you know if she was happy?"

"Yes, I think she was very happy."

"Well. I must say, I doubt that, but if that's what she told you."

"Thanks for calling," said Jane. "Have a nice day."

You miserable bitch.

Jane was standing at the window in her dining room when Annie pulled up outside a few minutes before noon. "Hey, boys," she called. "Annie's back."

Mouse and Dooley trotted out of the kitchen. Dooley gripped a sock in his teeth. Mouse nipped at it, trying to get him to play tug.

When she opened the door, she could see that Annie's eyes were glistening.

"How'd it go?"

"About as well as I expected it would."

Jane folded her protectively in her arms, kissed her eyelids. "I'm sorry."

"Maybe I should have stayed away, just left it at that."

"It was a hard call."

Dooley scratched at Annie's leg.

"Come on," said Jane. "The coffee's still on. I'll make us some sandwiches for lunch." She started for the kitchen, still thinking about what Connie Dewing had told her.

"Jane?"

"Hmm?" She turned her head. "Hey, take off your coat."

"I can't. It's time."

"I thought—" She turned all the way around. "You're leaving today? Now?"

"I have to. If I don't go while I still have the courage, I might never do it."

"That would be fine with me."

Annie's expression softened. "I'll never forget last night. You have a rare gift, you know that? You make people feel like they matter. You helped me get what I came for—even more than I came for. I've got my mother back. And Jack's getting what he deserves. I'm finally free of him. You don't know how great that feels. I don't need to hate him anymore. I don't even need to think about him."

Connie Dewing's words still rang in Jane's ears. Mandy Archer had lied to Annie and to Jack. Jack was Annie's biological father. Neither one of them knew the truth. If Annie found out, after everything she'd been through, what would it do to her? The answer to that question was something Jane didn't want to know.

"What will you do when you get back to Colorado?" she asked, trying to hide the turmoil she felt inside.

"Go back to my job in Steamboat Springs if they'll have me. Live my life. Try to be happy."

"Will I ever see you again?"

"I hope so. There are these modern conveniences called phones and airplanes. I'd like you to be a part of my life . . . for the rest of my life. But the fact is, you can't leave Minnesota and I can't stay."

It was a painful refrain Jane had heard before.

Annie called for Dooley to come. As he trotted out of the living room, her soft, warm hand slipped inside Jane's. "So I guess this is it."

Jane crushed her in her arms, kissed her with every ounce of tenderness she possessed, then reluctantly let her go.

Lifting Dooley into her arms, Annie said, "Thanks. For everything." She leaned in for one last kiss.

Jane held the door open and watched Annie walk out to her car. She struggled to compose herself. Fighting tears, she smiled, waved, called, "Be safe."

In the end, perhaps it was the dream of winning the unwinnable heart. That was Annie. She might eventually settle, move in with someone, even get married, but Jane knew part of her heart would always remain separate.

As Annie drove away, Jane said the words she'd repeated to herself so many times in the last few days but never said out loud.

She whispered, "I could have loved you."

Closing the door, she leaned against it. Her home was back to normal, a quiet, solitary place. The kind she liked best. But she and Annie shared something fundamental. Their hearts were also solitary, a mystery to others, and to themselves.